STAR WARS
THE HIGH REPUBLIC
ADVENTURES

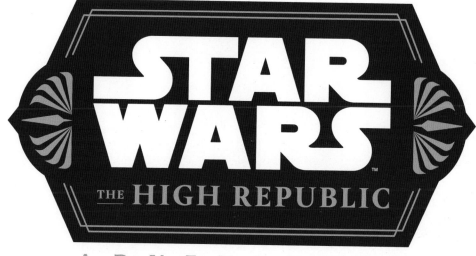

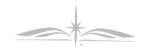

VOLUME TWO

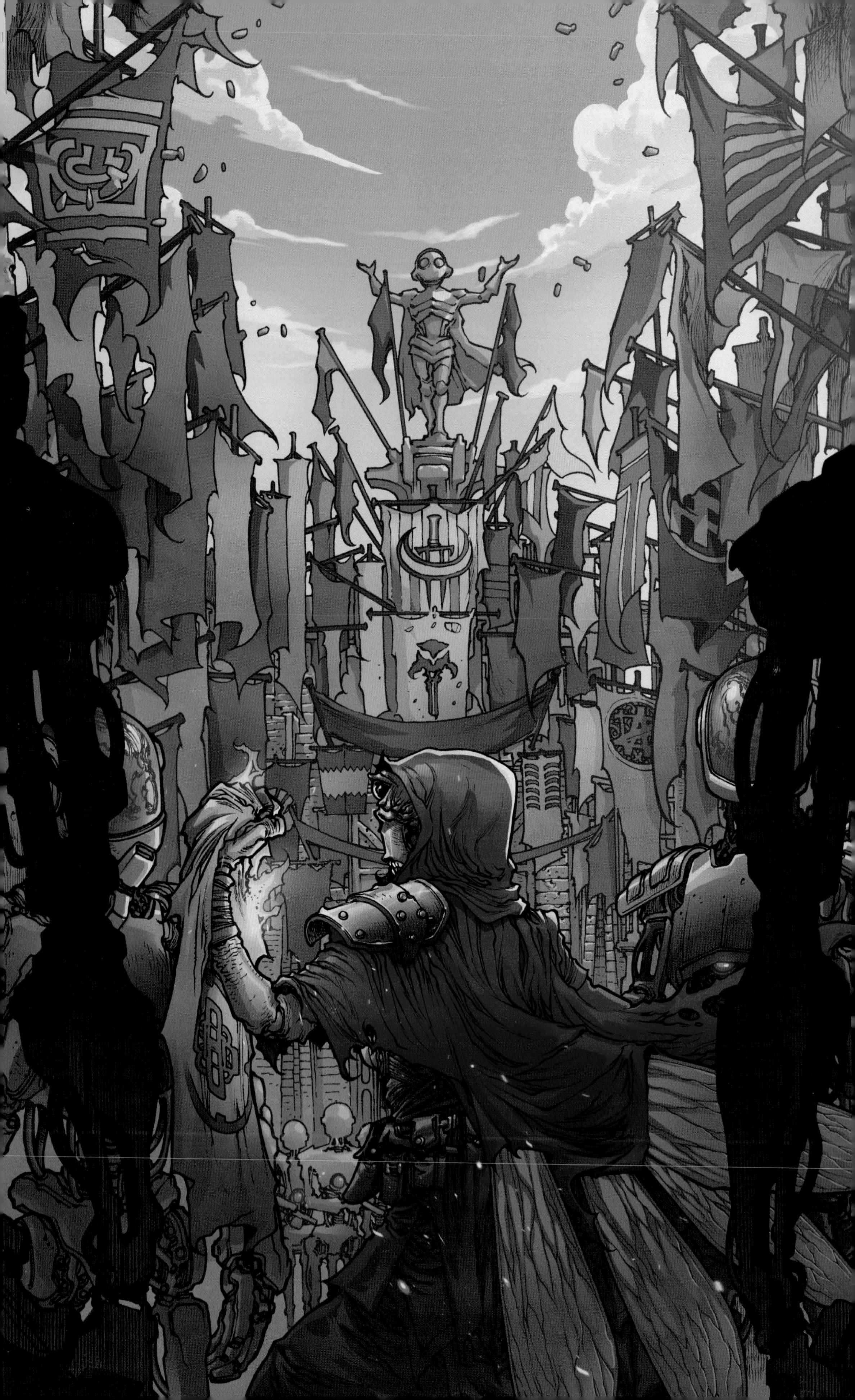

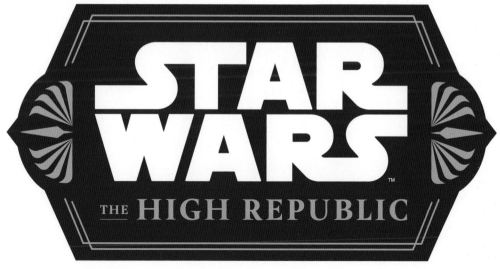

STAR WARS
THE HIGH REPUBLIC
ADVENTURES
VOLUME TWO

WRITTEN BY
DANIEL JOSÉ OLDER

ILLUSTRATED BY
HARVEY TOLIBAO
AND TONI BRUNO

COLORS BY
MICHAEL ATIYEH

LETTERS BY
COMICRAFT'S TYLER SMITH
AND JIMMY BETANCOURT

COVER ART BY
HARVEY TOLIBAO
WITH KEVIN TOLIBAO

Disney Lucasfilm Dark Horse Books

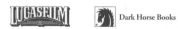

PRESIDENT AND PUBLISHER
MIKE RICHARDSON

EDITOR
MATT DRYER

ASSISTANT EDITOR
SANJAY DHARAWAT

DESIGNER
STEPHEN REICHERT

DIGITAL ART TECHNICIAN
SAMANTHA HUMMER

FOR LUCASFILM

CREATIVE DIRECTOR
MICHAEL SIGLAIN

SENIOR EDITOR
ROBERT SIMPSON

ART DIRECTOR
TROY ALDERS

LUCASFILM STORY GROUP
MATT MARTIN, PABLO HIDALGO, AND EMILY SHKOUKANI

CREATIVE ART MANAGER
PHIL SZOSTAK

Published by Dark Horse Books
A division of Dark Horse Comics LLC.
10956 SE Main Street
Milwaukie, OR 97222

StarWars.com DarkHorse.com
To find a comics shop in your area, visit ComicShopLocator.com

First edition: December 2023
Ebook ISBN 978-1-50673-295-4
Trade paperback ISBN 978-1-50673-293-0

1 3 5 7 9 10 8 6 4 2
Printed in China

MIX
Paper | Supporting responsible forestry
FSC® C016973
FSC www.fsc.org

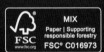

STAR WARS: THE HIGH REPBULIC ADVENTURES, VOLUME 2

STAR WARS
TIMELINE

THE HIGH REPUBLIC

FALL OF THE JEDI

THE PHANTOM MENACE

ATTACK OF THE CLONES

THE CLONE WARS

REVENGE OF THE SITH

REIGN OF THE EMPIRE

THE BAD BATCH

SOLO: A STAR WARS STORY

OBI-WAN KENOBI

AGE OF REBELLION

REBELS

ANDOR

ROGUE ONE: A STAR WARS STORY

A NEW HOPE

THE EMPIRE STRIKES BACK

RETURN OF THE JEDI

THE NEW REPUBLIC

THE BOOK OF BOBA FETT

THE MANDALORIAN

RISE OF THE FIRST ORDER

RESISTANCE

THE FORCE AWAKENS

THE LAST JEDI

THE RISE OF SKYWALKER

STAR WARS
THE HIGH REPUBLIC

QUEST OF THE JEDI

There is conflict in the galaxy. Chaos on the Pilgrim Moon of Jedha has resulted in a devastating battle. In its aftermath, the Jedi have learned of the involvement of the seemingly benevolent group THE PATH OF THE OPEN HAND in violent interplanetary conspiracies.

With communications down, the leader of the Path, THE MOTHER, races back to the planet Dalna to make her ultimate escape.

Little do the Jedi know that the Mother is about to unleash mysterious, nameless creatures with the power to destroy the Order once and for all …

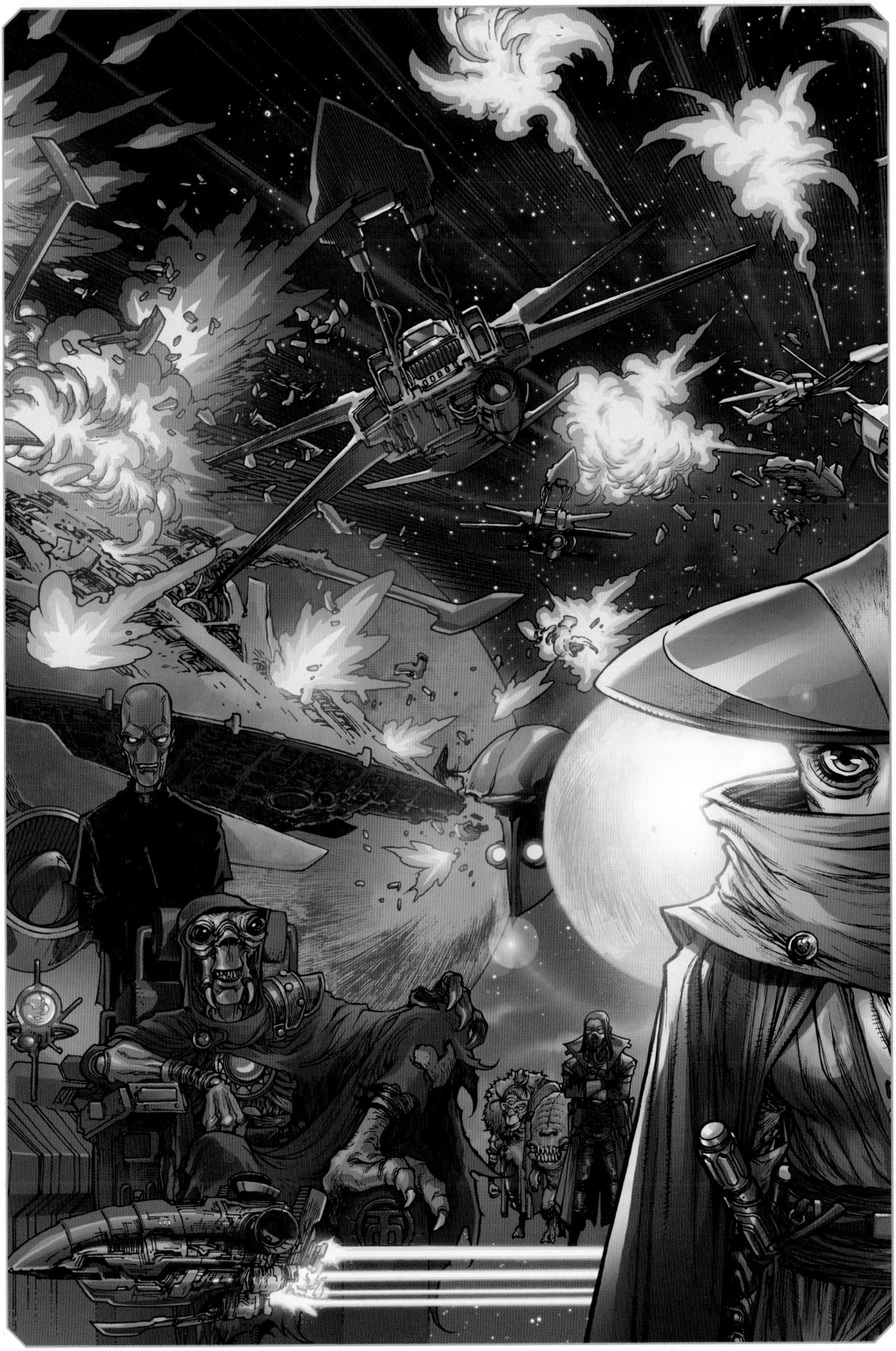

PART 1: FIRE IN THE HOLY HEART, PART 1
COVER ART BY HARVEY TOLIBAO WITH KEVIN TOLIBAO

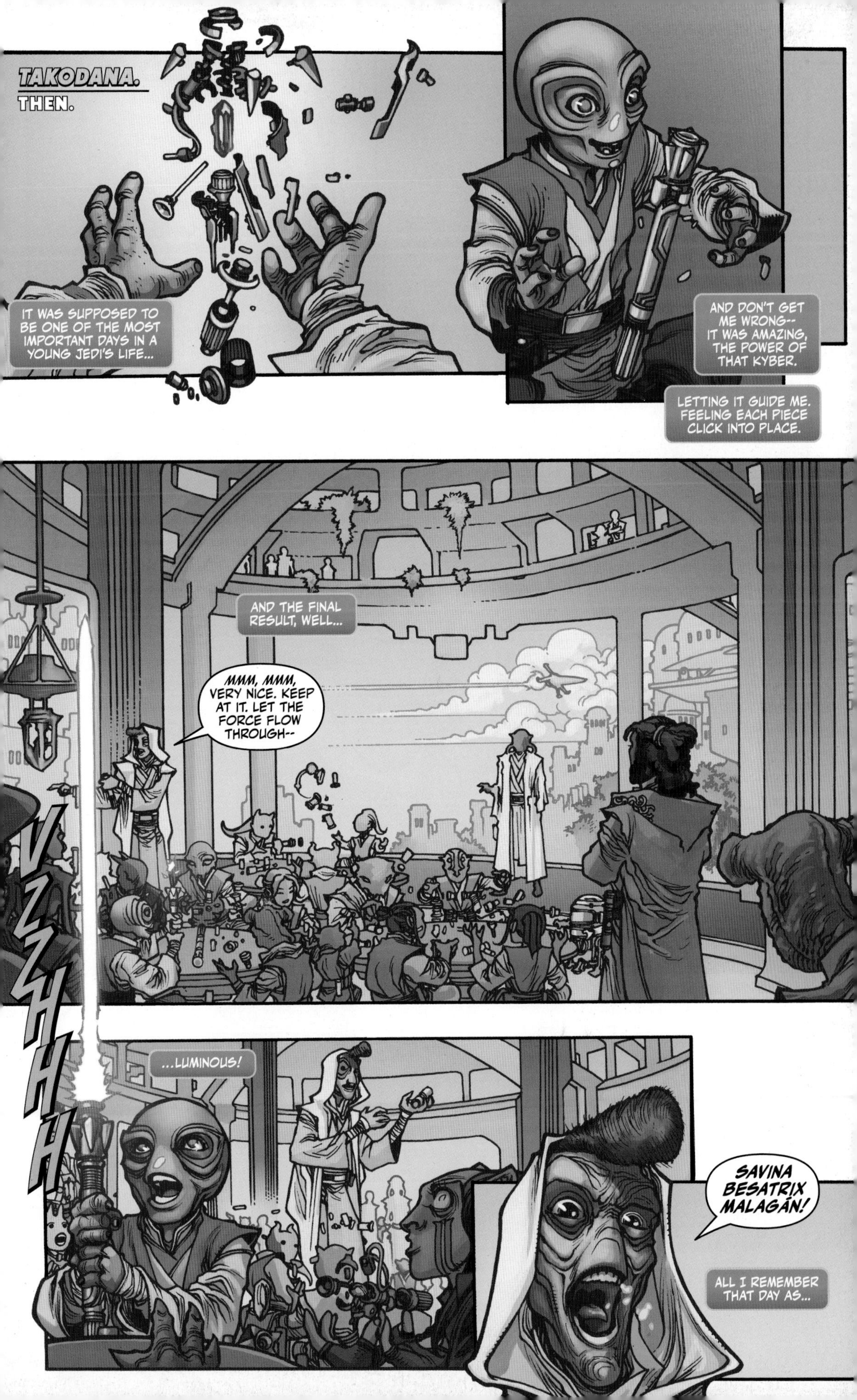
TAKODANA.
THEN.
IT WAS SUPPOSED TO BE ONE OF THE MOST IMPORTANT DAYS IN A YOUNG JEDI'S LIFE...
AND DON'T GET ME WRONG-- IT WAS AMAZING, THE POWER OF THAT KYBER.
LETTING IT GUIDE ME. FEELING EACH PIECE CLICK INTO PLACE.
AND THE FINAL RESULT, WELL...
MMM, MMM, VERY NICE. KEEP AT IT. LET THE FORCE FLOW THROUGH--
VZZZHHHH
...LUMINOUS!
SAVINA BESATRIX MALAGÁN!
ALL I REMEMBER THAT DAY AS...

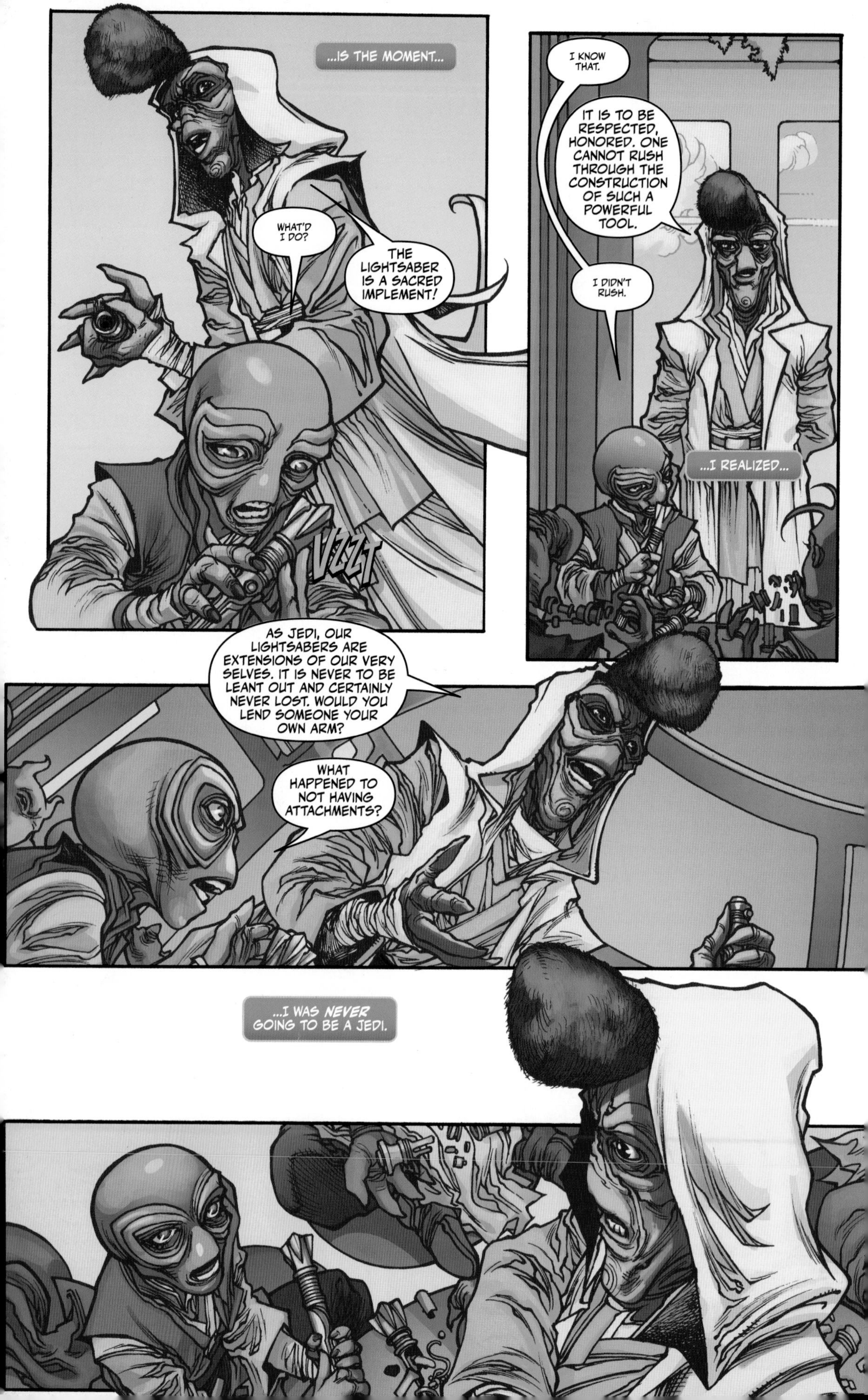
...IS THE MOMENT...
WHAT'D I DO?
THE LIGHTSABER IS A SACRED IMPLEMENT!
VZZT
I KNOW THAT.
IT IS TO BE RESPECTED, HONORED. ONE CANNOT RUSH THROUGH THE CONSTRUCTION OF SUCH A POWERFUL TOOL.
I DIDN'T RUSH.
...I REALIZED...
AS JEDI, OUR LIGHTSABERS ARE EXTENSIONS OF OUR VERY SELVES. IT IS NEVER TO BE LEANT OUT AND CERTAINLY NEVER LOST. WOULD YOU LEND SOMEONE YOUR OWN ARM?
WHAT HAPPENED TO NOT HAVING ATTACHMENTS?
...I WAS *NEVER* GOING TO BE A JEDI.

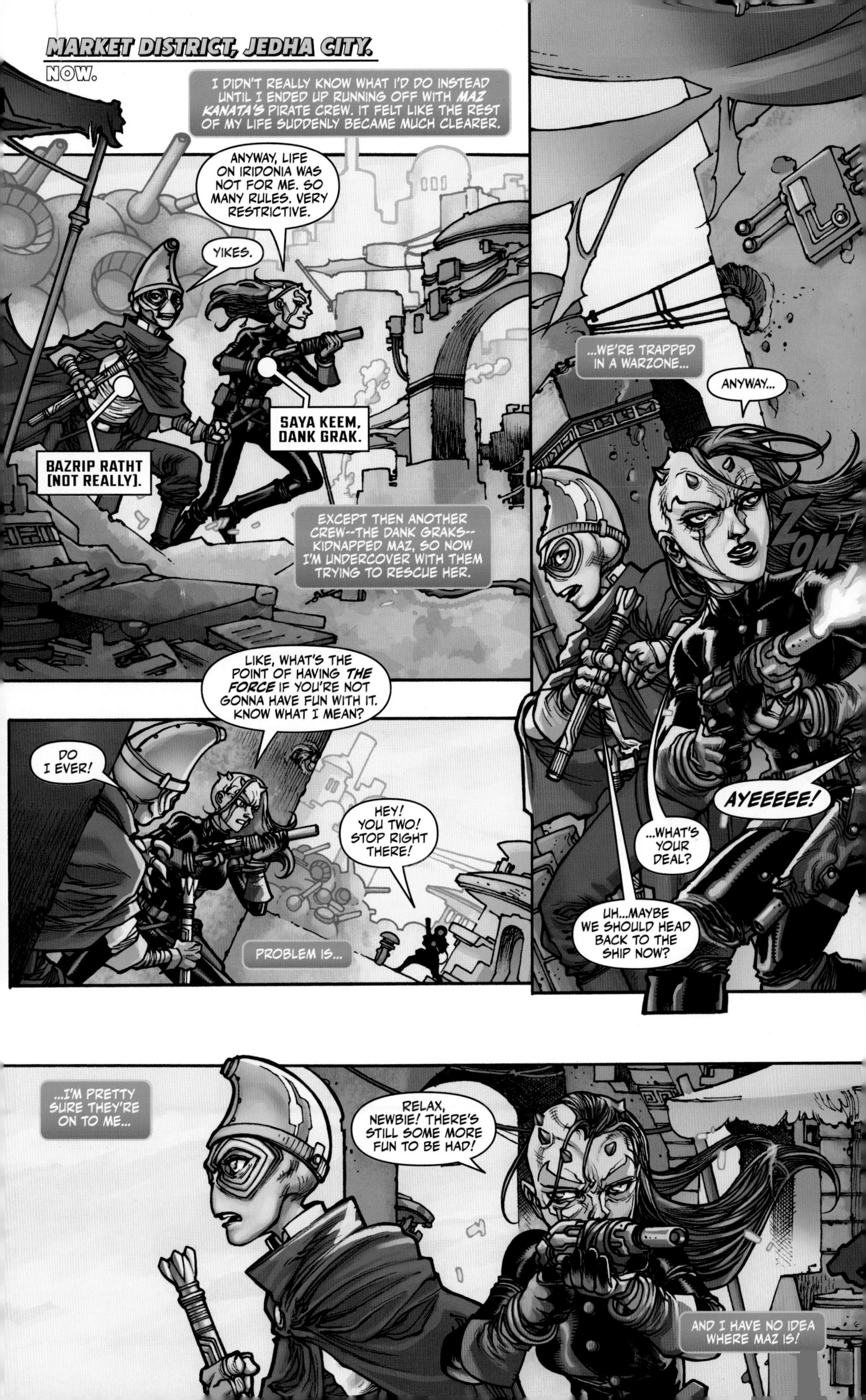

MARKET DISTRICT, JEDHA CITY.
NOW.
I DIDN'T REALLY KNOW WHAT I'D DO INSTEAD UNTIL I ENDED UP RUNNING OFF WITH MAZ KANATA'S PIRATE CREW. IT FELT LIKE THE REST OF MY LIFE SUDDENLY BECAME MUCH CLEARER.
ANYWAY, LIFE ON IRIDONIA WAS NOT FOR ME. SO MANY RULES. VERY RESTRICTIVE.
YIKES.
SAYA KEEM, DANK GRAK.
BAZRIP RATHT [NOT REALLY].
EXCEPT THEN ANOTHER CREW--THE DANK GRAKS--KIDNAPPED MAZ, SO NOW I'M UNDERCOVER WITH THEM TRYING TO RESCUE HER.
LIKE, WHAT'S THE POINT OF HAVING THE FORCE IF YOU'RE NOT GONNA HAVE FUN WITH IT. KNOW WHAT I MEAN?
DO I EVER!
HEY! YOU TWO! STOP RIGHT THERE!
PROBLEM IS...
...WE'RE TRAPPED IN A WARZONE...
ANYWAY...
ZOM
AYEEEEE!
...WHAT'S YOUR DEAL?
UH...MAYBE WE SHOULD HEAD BACK TO THE SHIP NOW?
...I'M PRETTY SURE THEY'RE ON TO ME...
RELAX, NEWBIE! THERE'S STILL SOME MORE FUN TO BE HAD!
AND I HAVE NO IDEA WHERE MAZ IS!

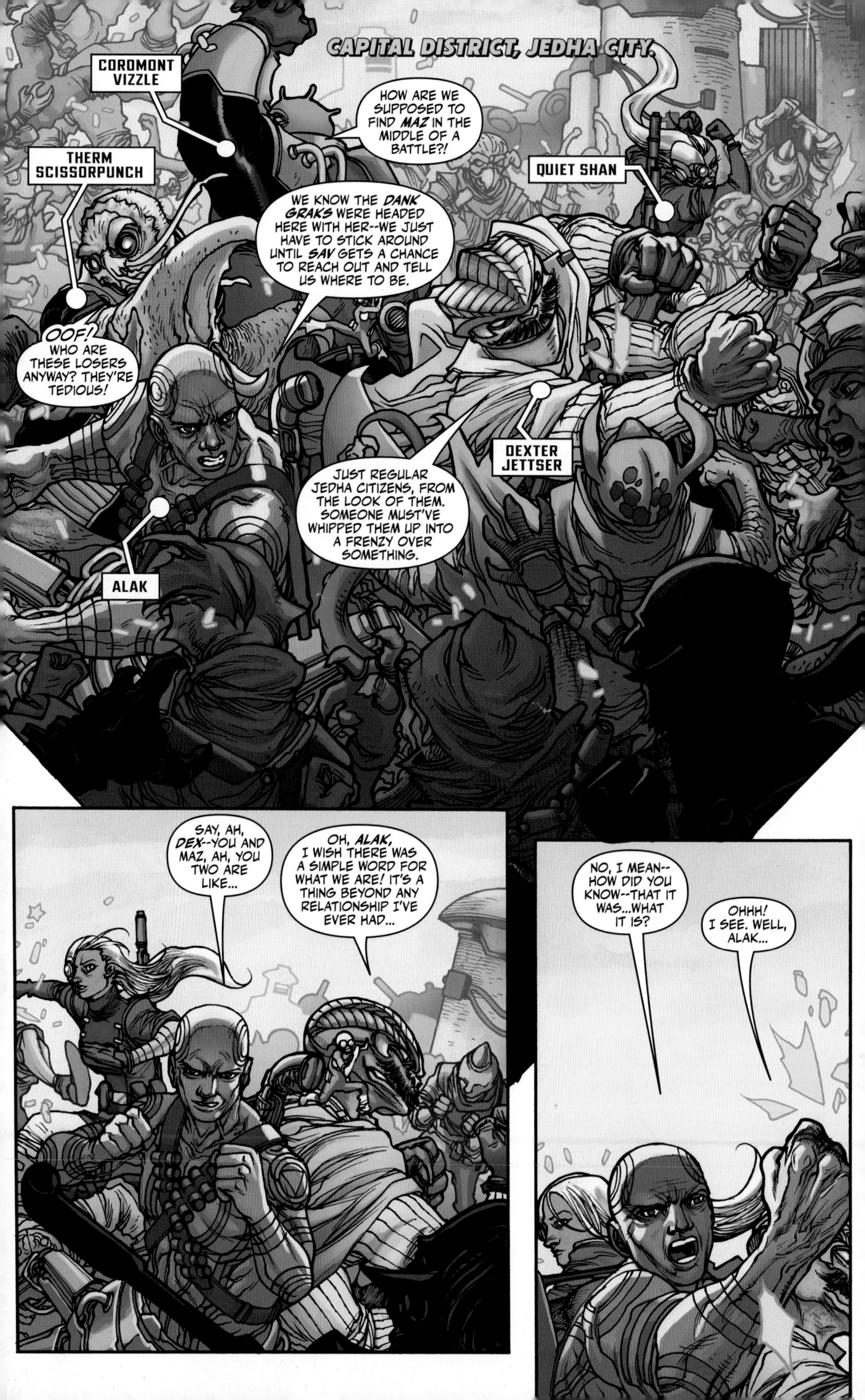
CAPITAL DISTRICT, JEDHA CITY.
COROMONT VIZZLE
THERM SCISSORPUNCH
HOW ARE WE SUPPOSED TO FIND MAZ IN THE MIDDLE OF A BATTLE?!
QUIET SHAN
WE KNOW THE DANK GRAKS WERE HEADED HERE WITH HER--WE JUST HAVE TO STICK AROUND UNTIL SAV GETS A CHANCE TO REACH OUT AND TELL US WHERE TO BE.
OOF! WHO ARE THESE LOSERS ANYWAY? THEY'RE TEDIOUS!
DEXTER JETTSER
JUST REGULAR JEDHA CITIZENS, FROM THE LOOK OF THEM. SOMEONE MUST'VE WHIPPED THEM UP INTO A FRENZY OVER SOMETHING.
ALAK
SAY, AH, DEX--YOU AND MAZ, AH, YOU TWO ARE LIKE...
OH, ALAK, I WISH THERE WAS A SIMPLE WORD FOR WHAT WE ARE! IT'S A THING BEYOND ANY RELATIONSHIP I'VE EVER HAD...
NO, I MEAN--HOW DID YOU KNOW--THAT IT WAS...WHAT IT IS?
OHHH! I SEE. WELL, ALAK...

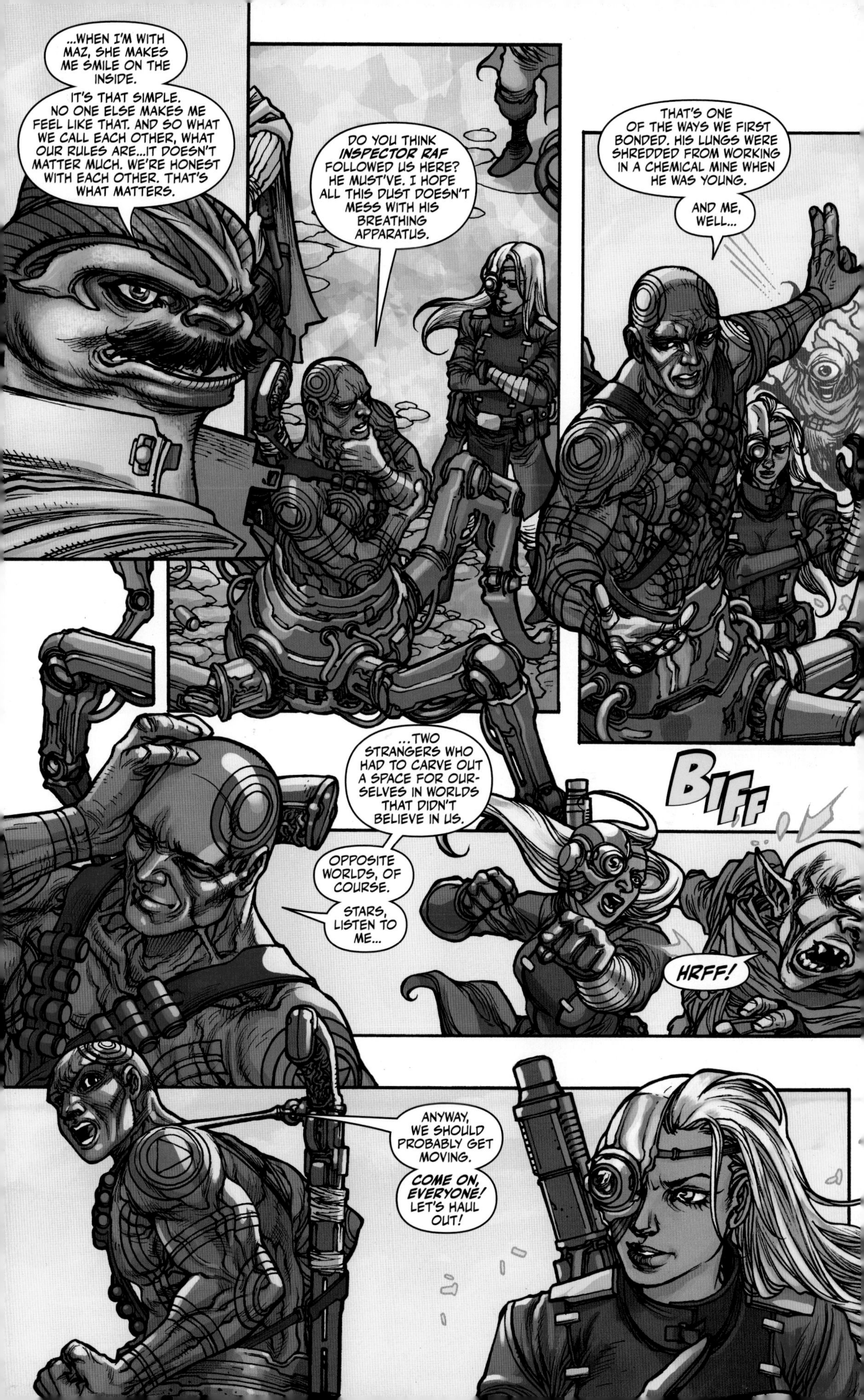

...WHEN I'M WITH MAZ, SHE MAKES ME SMILE ON THE INSIDE.
IT'S THAT SIMPLE. NO ONE ELSE MAKES ME FEEL LIKE THAT. AND SO WHAT WE CALL EACH OTHER, WHAT OUR RULES ARE...IT DOESN'T MATTER MUCH. WE'RE HONEST WITH EACH OTHER. THAT'S WHAT MATTERS.
DO YOU THINK *INSPECTOR RAF* FOLLOWED US HERE? HE MUST'VE. I HOPE ALL THIS DUST DOESN'T MESS WITH HIS BREATHING APPARATUS.
THAT'S ONE OF THE WAYS WE FIRST BONDED. HIS LUNGS WERE SHREDDED FROM WORKING IN A CHEMICAL MINE WHEN HE WAS YOUNG.
AND ME, WELL...
...TWO STRANGERS WHO HAD TO CARVE OUT A SPACE FOR OUR-SELVES IN WORLDS THAT DIDN'T BELIEVE IN US.
OPPOSITE WORLDS, OF COURSE.
STARS, LISTEN TO ME...
BIFF
HRFF!
ANYWAY, WE SHOULD PROBABLY GET MOVING.
COME ON, EVERYONE! LET'S HAUL OUT!

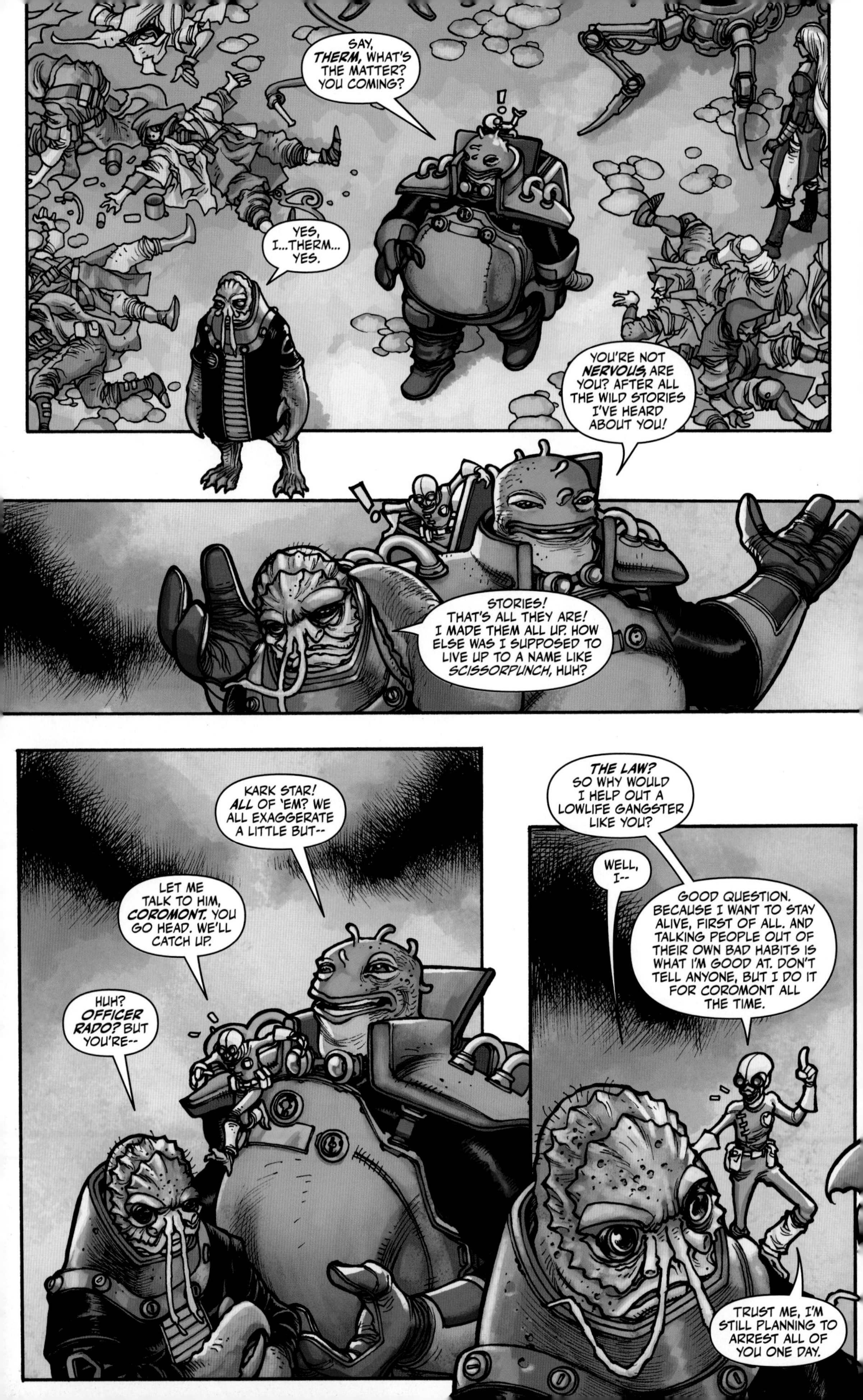
SAY, *THERM,* WHAT'S THE MATTER? YOU COMING?
!
YES, I...THERM... YES.
YOU'RE NOT *NERVOUS,* ARE YOU? AFTER ALL THE WILD STORIES I'VE HEARD ABOUT YOU!
!
STORIES! THAT'S ALL THEY ARE! I MADE THEM ALL UP. HOW ELSE WAS I SUPPOSED TO LIVE UP TO A NAME LIKE *SCISSORPUNCH,* HUH?
KARK STAR! *ALL* OF 'EM? WE ALL EXAGGERATE A LITTLE BUT--
LET ME TALK TO HIM, *COROMONT.* YOU GO HEAD. WE'LL CATCH UP.
HUH? *OFFICER RADO?* BUT YOU'RE--
THE LAW? SO WHY WOULD I HELP OUT A LOWLIFE GANGSTER LIKE YOU?
WELL, I--
GOOD QUESTION. BECAUSE I WANT TO STAY ALIVE, FIRST OF ALL. AND TALKING PEOPLE OUT OF THEIR OWN BAD HABITS IS WHAT I'M GOOD AT. DON'T TELL ANYONE, BUT I DO IT FOR COROMONT ALL THE TIME.
TRUST ME, I'M STILL PLANNING TO ARREST ALL OF YOU ONE DAY.

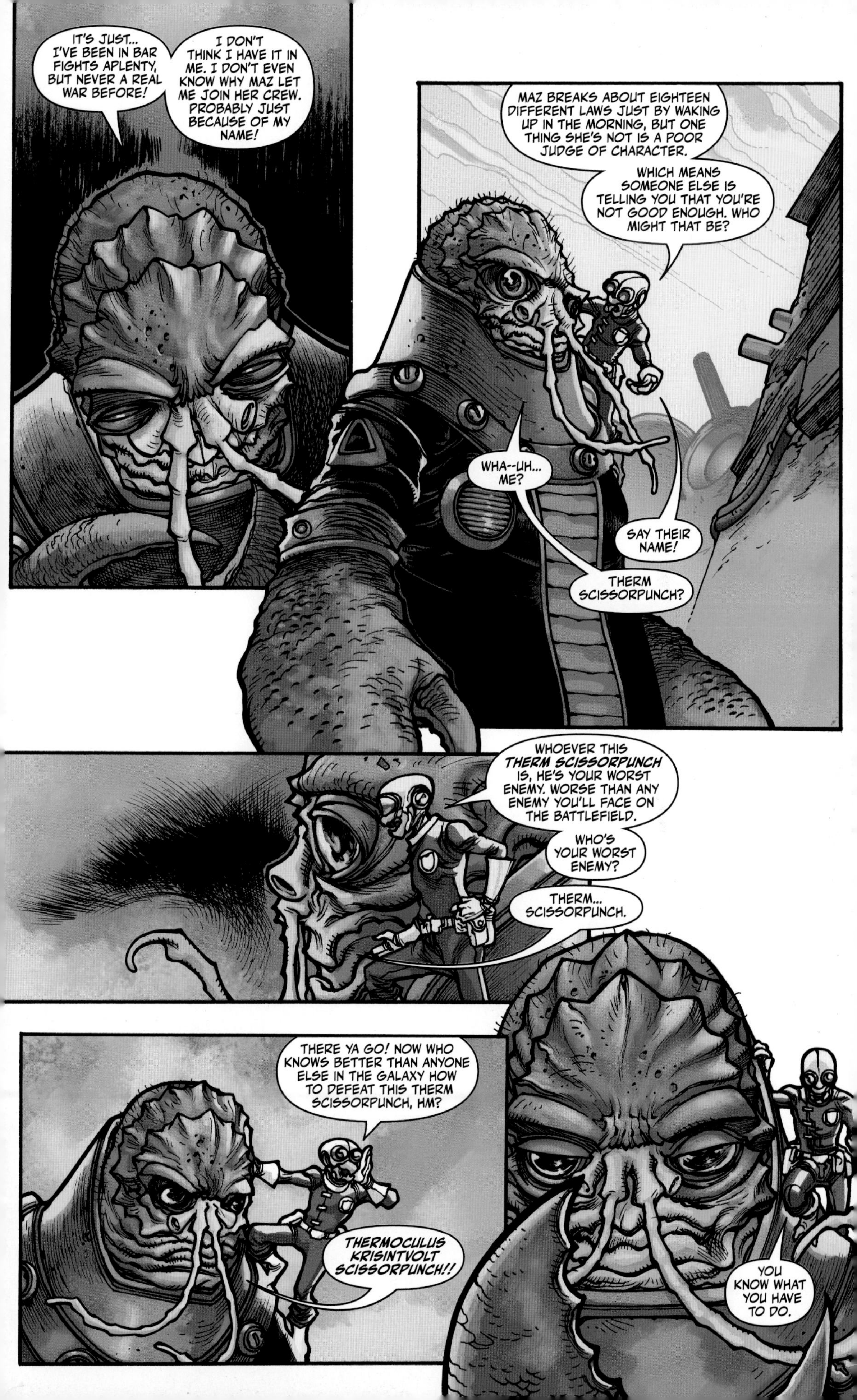
IT'S JUST... I'VE BEEN IN BAR FIGHTS APLENTY, BUT NEVER A REAL WAR BEFORE!
I DON'T THINK I HAVE IT IN ME. I DON'T EVEN KNOW WHY MAZ LET ME JOIN HER CREW. PROBABLY JUST BECAUSE OF MY NAME!
MAZ BREAKS ABOUT EIGHTEEN DIFFERENT LAWS JUST BY WAKING UP IN THE MORNING, BUT ONE THING SHE'S NOT IS A POOR JUDGE OF CHARACTER.
WHICH MEANS SOMEONE ELSE IS TELLING YOU THAT YOU'RE NOT GOOD ENOUGH. WHO MIGHT THAT BE?
WHA--UH... ME?
SAY THEIR NAME!
THERM SCISSORPUNCH?
WHOEVER THIS *THERM SCISSORPUNCH* IS, HE'S YOUR WORST ENEMY. WORSE THAN ANY ENEMY YOU'LL FACE ON THE BATTLEFIELD.
WHO'S YOUR WORST ENEMY?
THERM... SCISSORPUNCH.
THERE YA GO! NOW WHO KNOWS BETTER THAN ANYONE ELSE IN THE GALAXY HOW TO DEFEAT THIS THERM SCISSORPUNCH, HM?
THERMOCULUS KRISINTVOLT SCISSORPUNCH!!
YOU KNOW WHAT YOU HAVE TO DO.

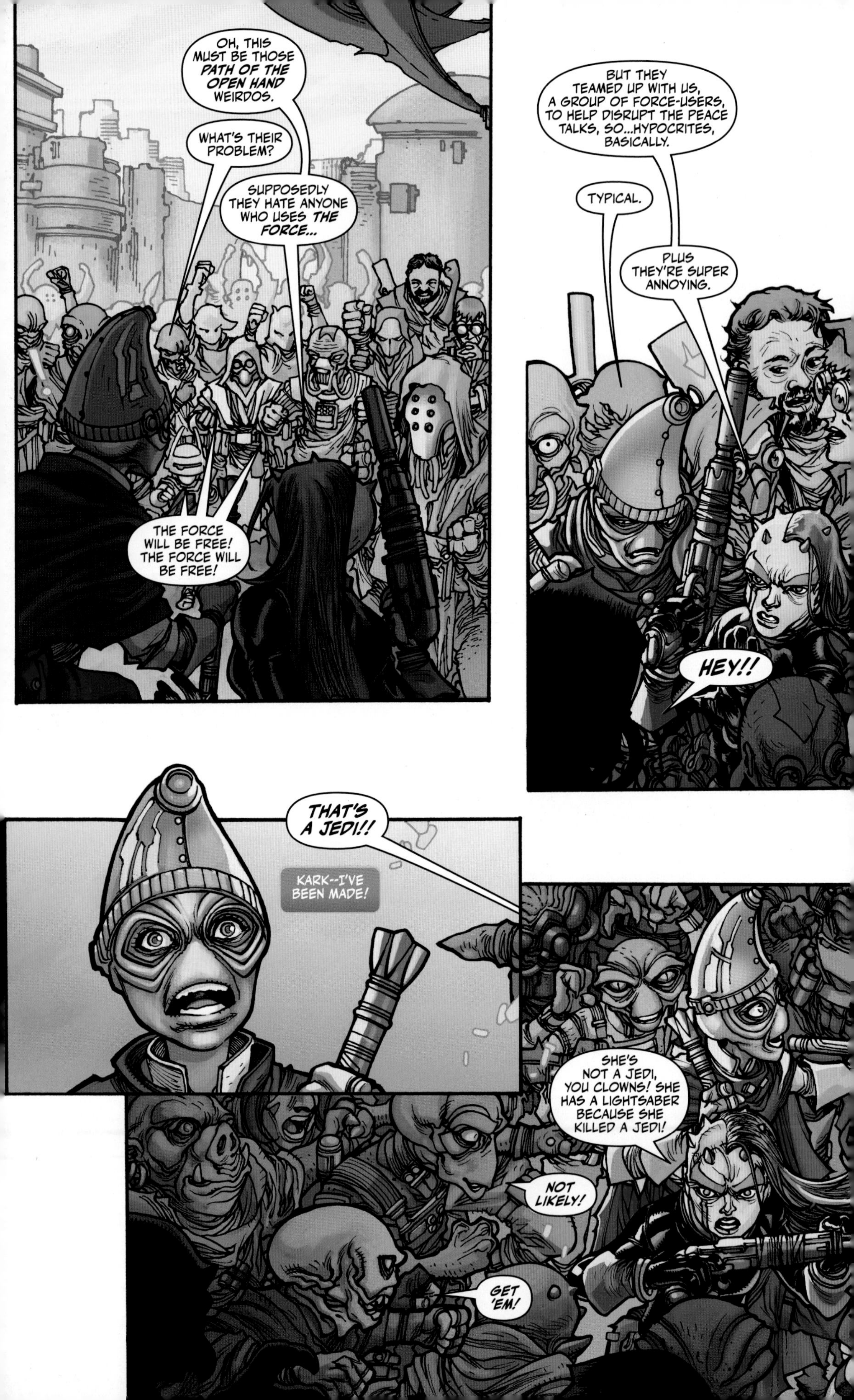
OH, THIS MUST BE THOSE *PATH OF THE OPEN HAND* WEIRDOS.
WHAT'S THEIR PROBLEM?
SUPPOSEDLY THEY HATE ANYONE WHO USES *THE FORCE*...
THE FORCE WILL BE FREE! THE FORCE WILL BE FREE!
BUT THEY TEAMED UP WITH US, A GROUP OF FORCE-USERS, TO HELP DISRUPT THE PEACE TALKS, SO...HYPOCRITES, BASICALLY.
TYPICAL.
PLUS THEY'RE SUPER ANNOYING.
HEY!!
THAT'S A JEDI!!
KARK--I'VE BEEN MADE!
SHE'S NOT A JEDI, YOU CLOWNS! SHE HAS A LIGHTSABER BECAUSE SHE KILLED A JEDI!
NOT LIKELY!
GET 'EM!

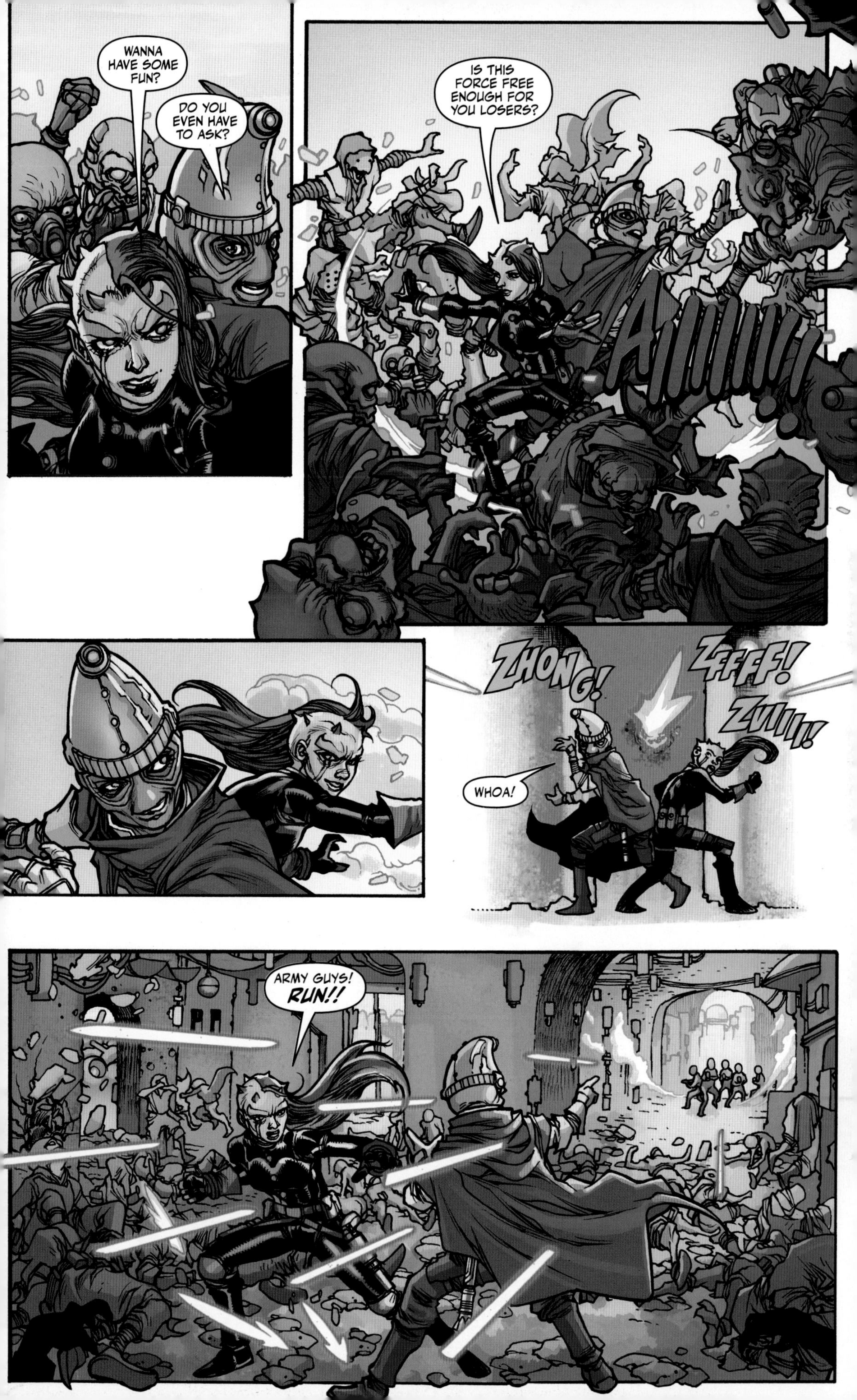
WANNA HAVE SOME FUN?
DO YOU EVEN HAVE TO ASK?
IS THIS FORCE FREE ENOUGH FOR YOU LOSERS?
AIIIIIII!!
ZHONG!
ZFFFF!
ZVIIII!
WHOA!
ARMY GUYS! RUN!!

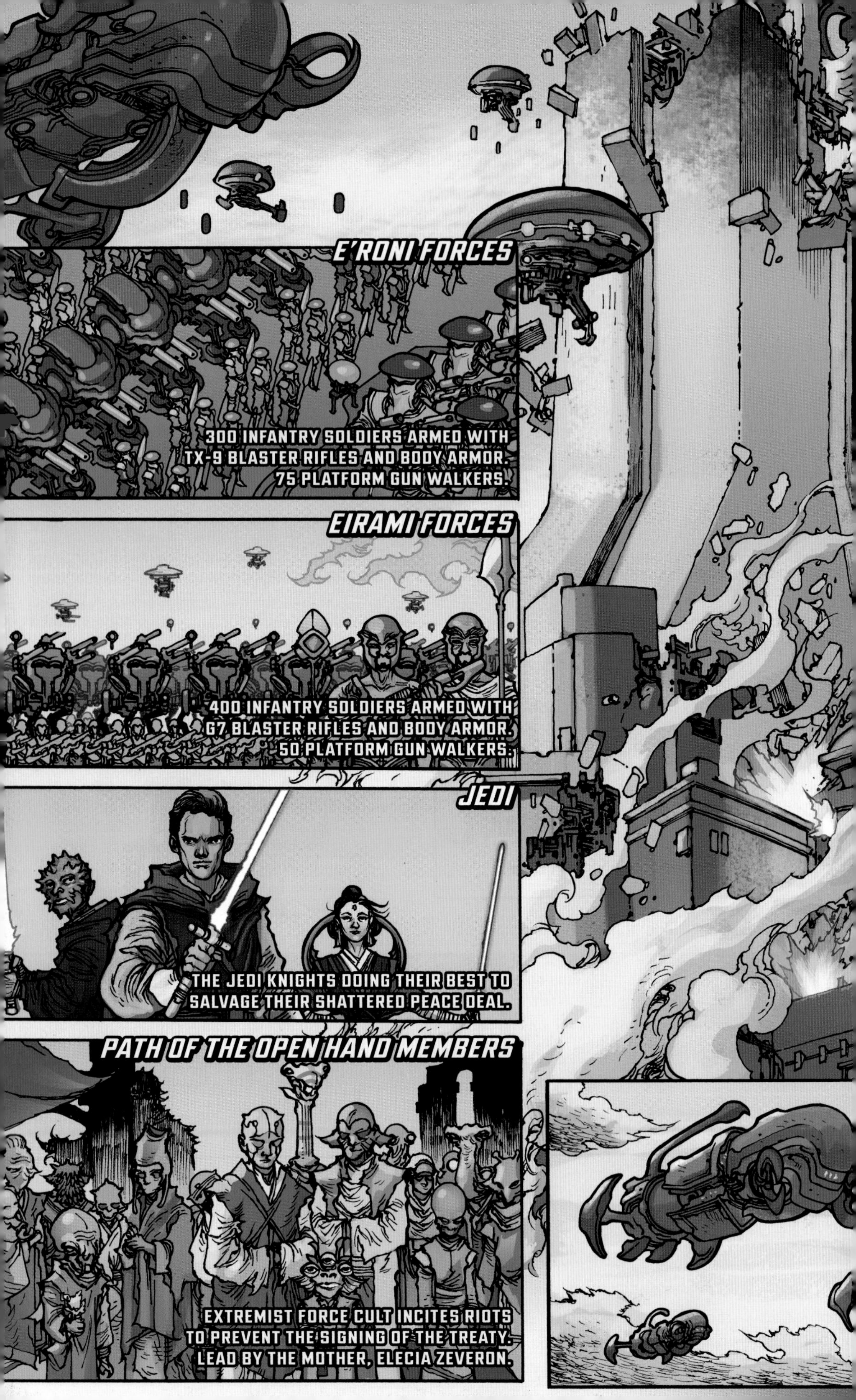

E'RONI FORCES
300 INFANTRY SOLDIERS ARMED WITH TX-9 BLASTER RIFLES AND BODY ARMOR. 75 PLATFORM GUN WALKERS.
EIRAMI FORCES
400 INFANTRY SOLDIERS ARMED WITH G7 BLASTER RIFLES AND BODY ARMOR. 50 PLATFORM GUN WALKERS.
JEDI
THE JEDI KNIGHTS DOING THEIR BEST TO SALVAGE THEIR SHATTERED PEACE DEAL.
PATH OF THE OPEN HAND MEMBERS
EXTREMIST FORCE CULT INCITES RIOTS TO PREVENT THE SIGNING OF THE TREATY. LEAD BY THE MOTHER, ELECIA ZEVERON.

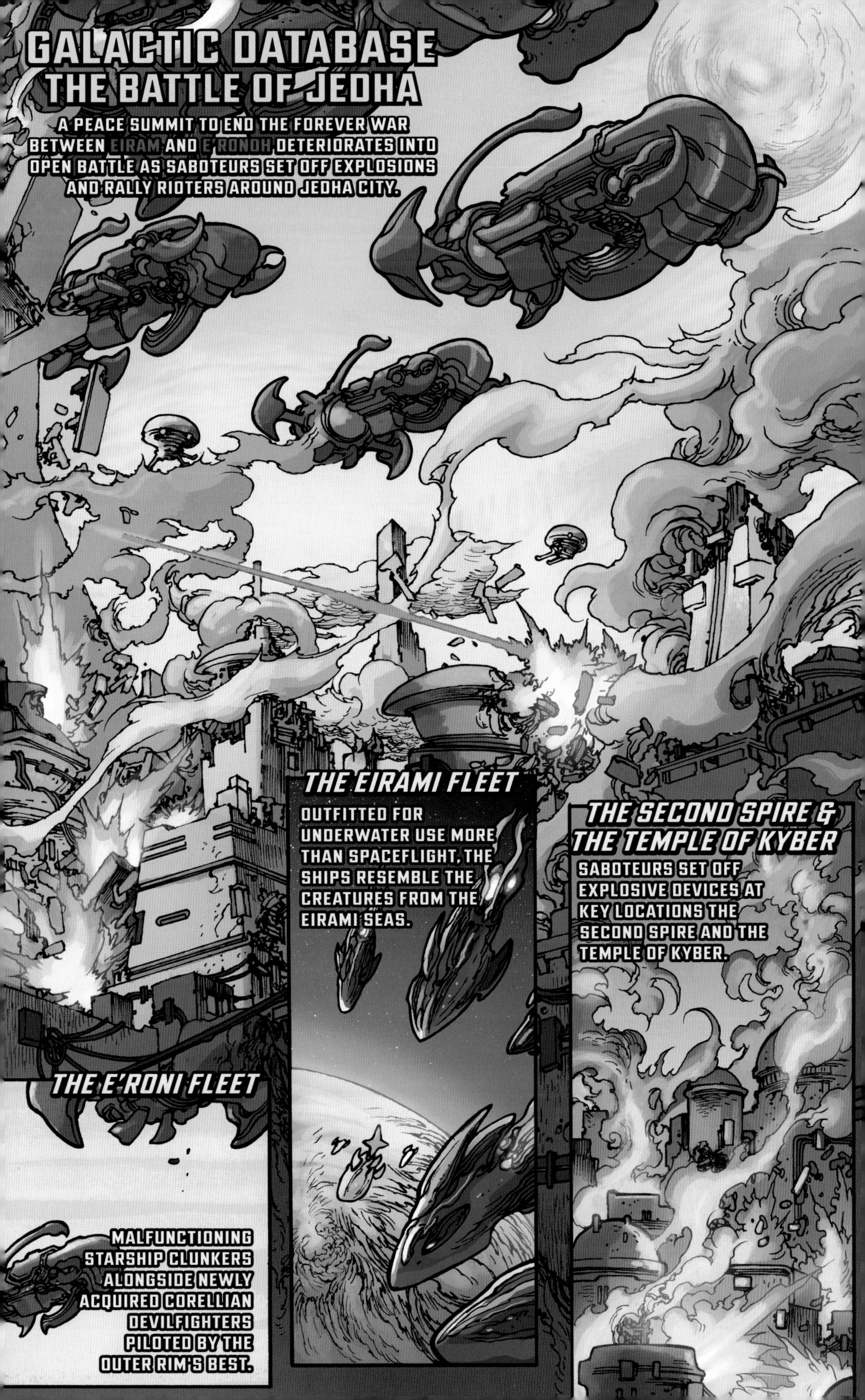
GALACTIC DATABASE
THE BATTLE OF JEDHA
A PEACE SUMMIT TO END THE FOREVER WAR BETWEEN EIRAM AND E'RONOH DETERIORATES INTO OPEN BATTLE AS SABOTEURS SET OFF EXPLOSIONS AND RALLY RIOTERS AROUND JEDHA CITY.
THE EIRAMI FLEET
OUTFITTED FOR UNDERWATER USE MORE THAN SPACEFLIGHT, THE SHIPS RESEMBLE THE CREATURES FROM THE EIRAMI SEAS.
THE SECOND SPIRE & THE TEMPLE OF KYBER
SABOTEURS SET OFF EXPLOSIVE DEVICES AT KEY LOCATIONS THE SECOND SPIRE AND THE TEMPLE OF KYBER.
THE E'RONI FLEET
MALFUNCTIONING STARSHIP CLUNKERS ALONGSIDE NEWLY ACQUIRED CORELLIAN DEVILFIGHTERS PILOTED BY THE OUTER RIM'S BEST.

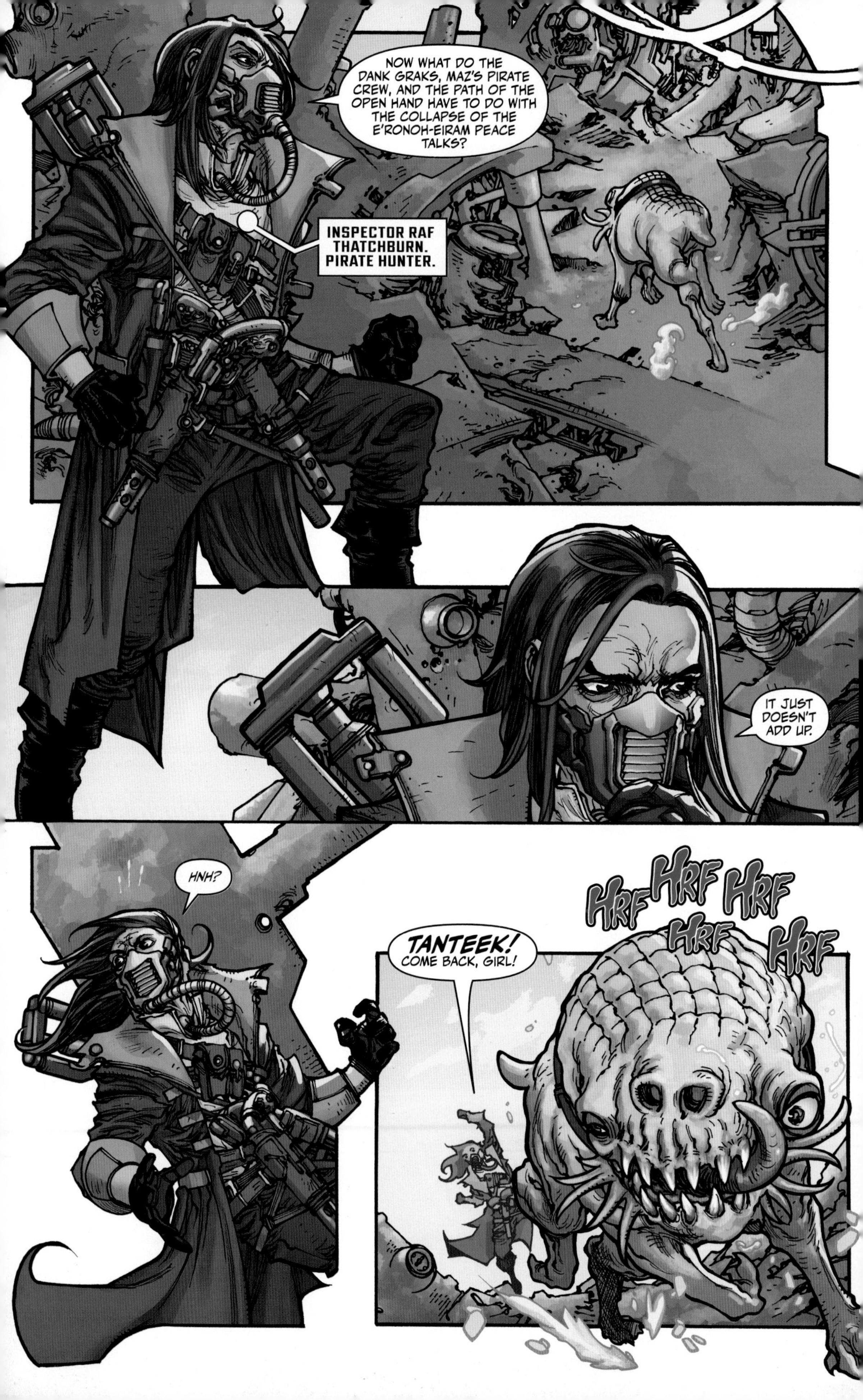
NOW WHAT DO THE DANK GRAKS, MAZ'S PIRATE CREW, AND THE PATH OF THE OPEN HAND HAVE TO DO WITH THE COLLAPSE OF THE E'RONOH-EIRAM PEACE TALKS?
INSPECTOR RAF THATCHBURN. PIRATE HUNTER.
IT JUST DOESN'T ADD UP.
HNH?
HRF HRF HRF HRF HRF
TANTEEK! COME BACK, GIRL!

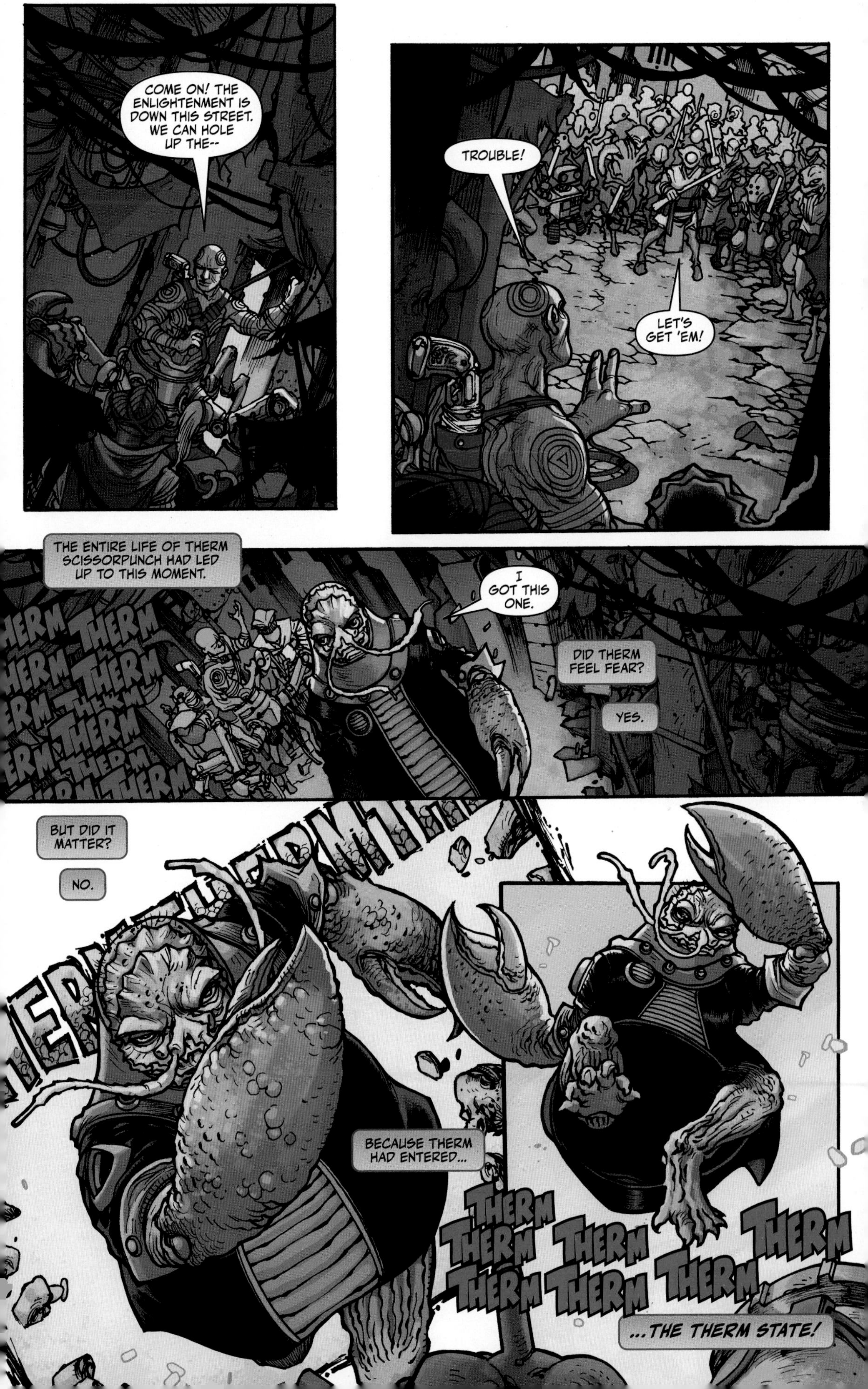
COME ON! THE ENLIGHTENMENT IS DOWN THIS STREET. WE CAN HOLE UP THE--
TROUBLE!
LET'S GET 'EM!
THE ENTIRE LIFE OF THERM SCISSORPUNCH HAD LED UP TO THIS MOMENT.
I GOT THIS ONE.
DID THERM FEEL FEAR?
YES.
THERM THERM THERM THERM THERM THERM THERM THERM THERM THERM
BUT DID IT MATTER?
NO.
BECAUSE THERM HAD ENTERED...
THERM THERM THERM THERM THERM THERM THERM
...THE THERM STATE!

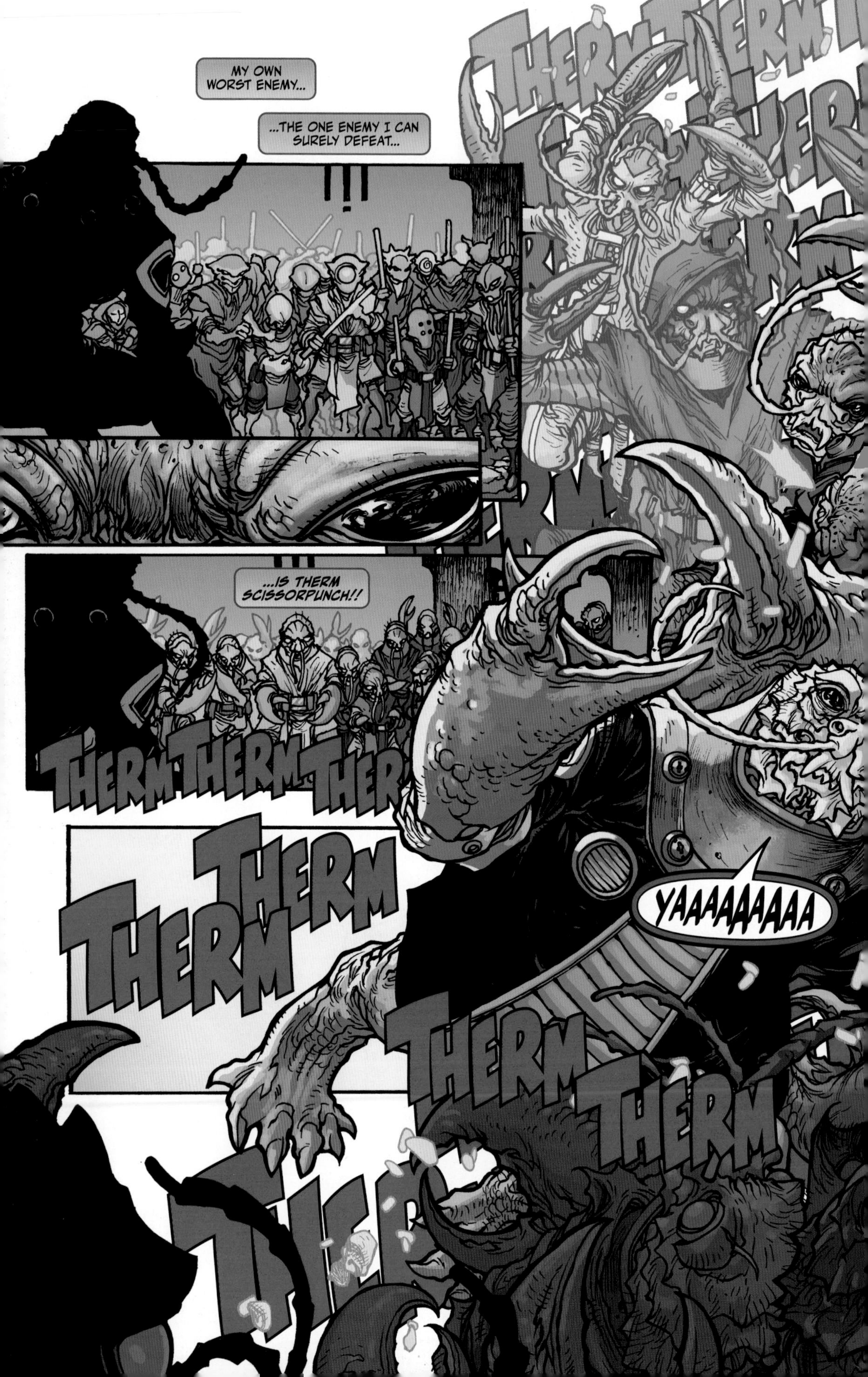

MY OWN WORST ENEMY...
...THE ONE ENEMY I CAN SURELY DEFEAT...
!!!
...IS THERM SCISSORPUNCH!!
THERM THERM THER
THERM THERM
YAAAAAAAAA
THERM THERM

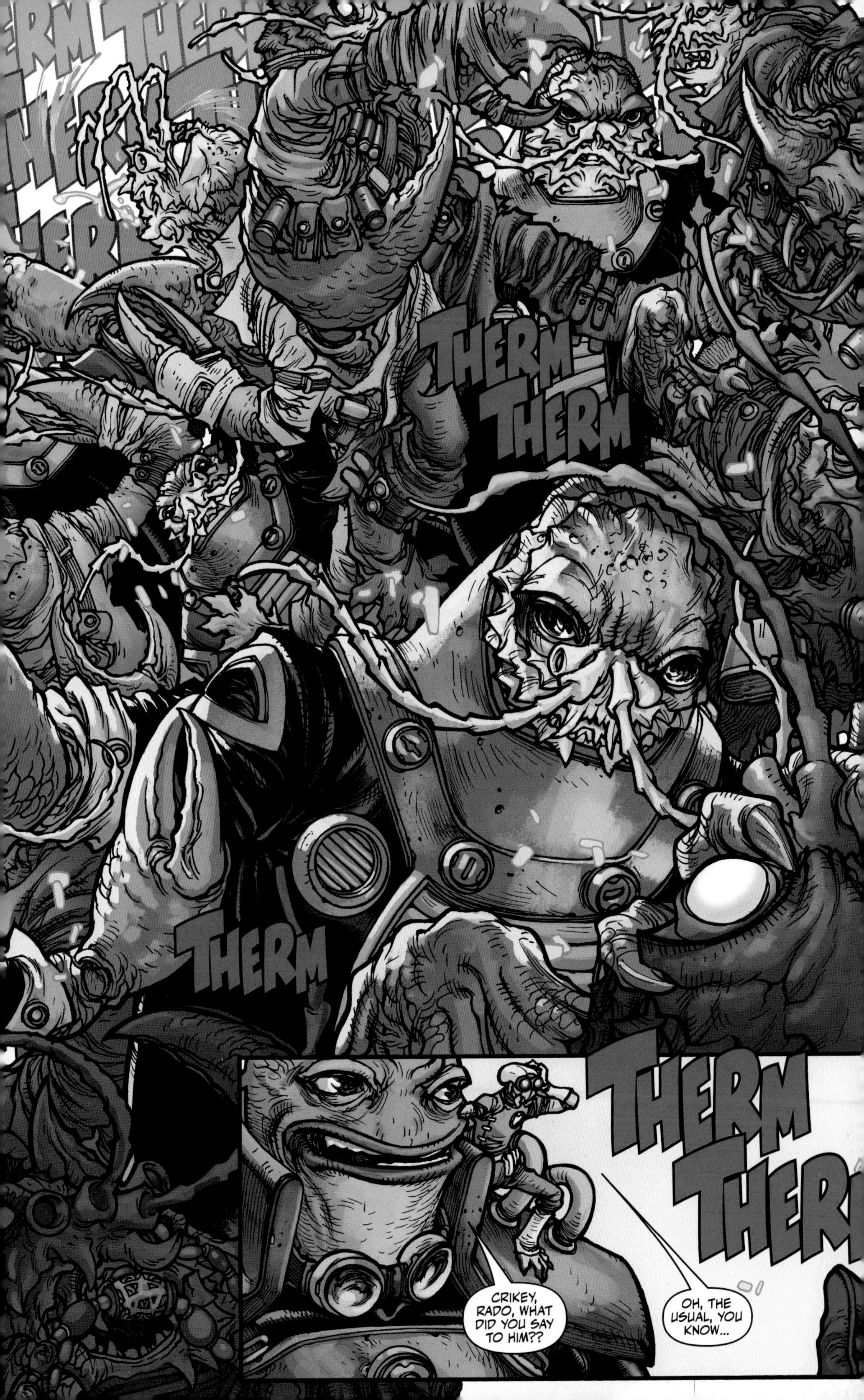
THERM
THERM
THERM
THERM
CRIKEY, RADO, WHAT DID YOU SAY TO HIM??
OH, THE USUAL, YOU KNOW...

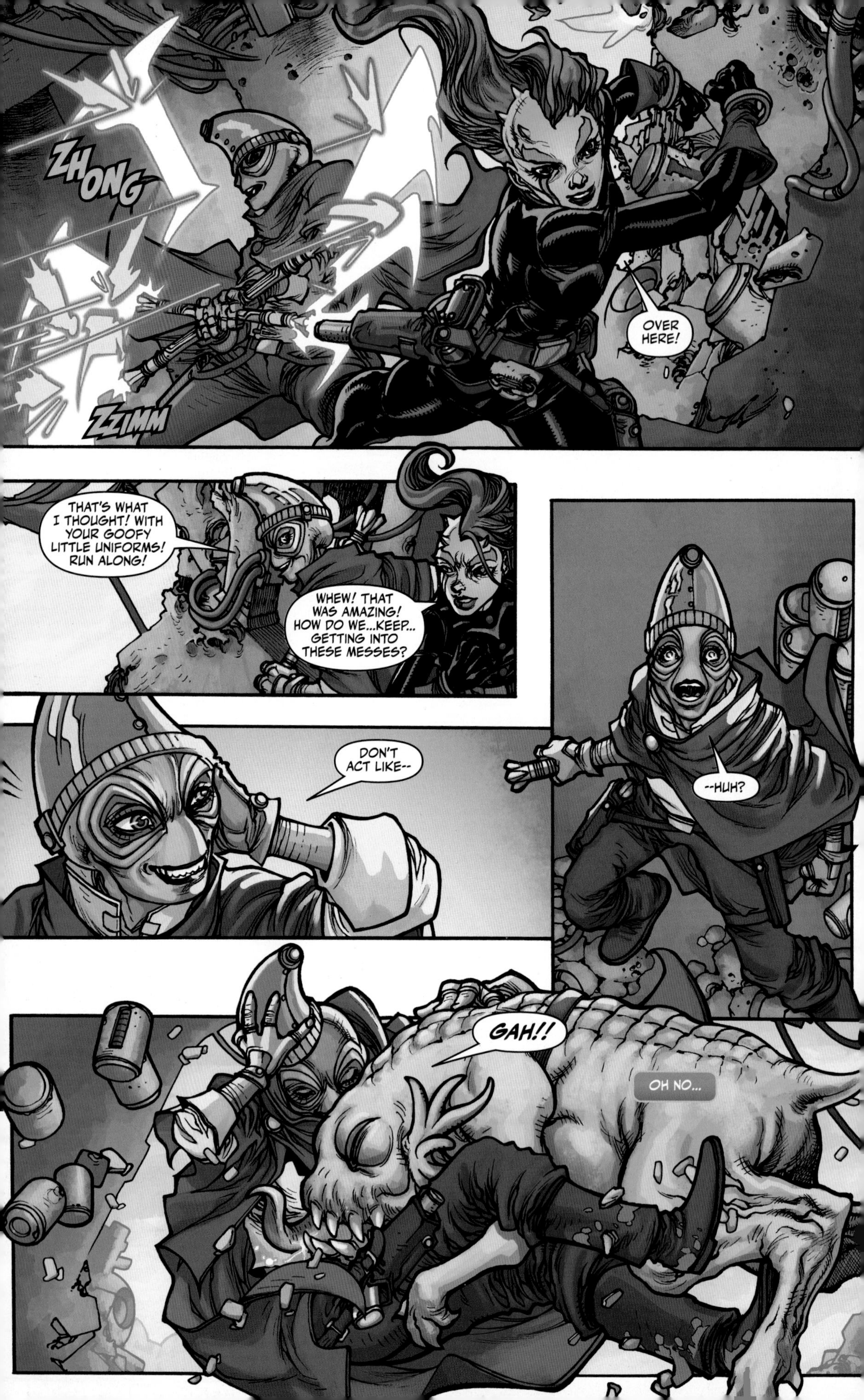
ZHONG
ZZIMM
OVER HERE!
THAT'S WHAT I THOUGHT! WITH YOUR GOOFY LITTLE UNIFORMS! RUN ALONG!
WHEW! THAT WAS AMAZING! HOW DO WE...KEEP... GETTING INTO THESE MESSES?
DON'T ACT LIKE--
--HUH?
GAH!!
OH NO...

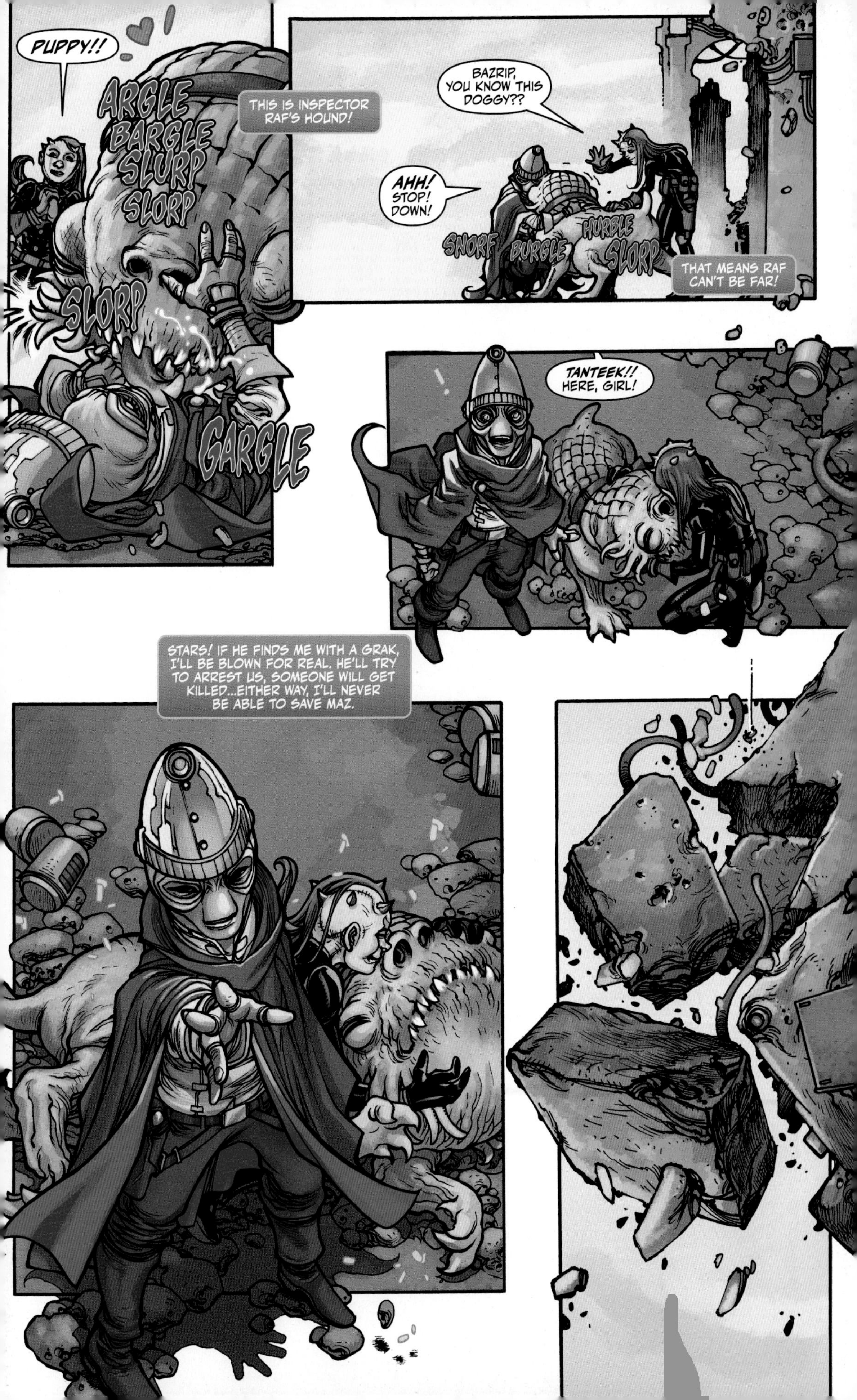

PUPPY!!
ARGLE
BARGLE
SLURP
SLORP
SLORP
GARGLE
THIS IS INSPECTOR RAF'S HOUND!
BAZRIP, YOU KNOW THIS DOGGY??
AHH! STOP! DOWN!
SNORF
BURGLE
HURBLE
SLORP
THAT MEANS RAF CAN'T BE FAR!
TANTEEK!! HERE, GIRL!
STARS! IF HE FINDS ME WITH A GRAK, I'LL BE BLOWN FOR REAL. HE'LL TRY TO ARREST US, SOMEONE WILL GET KILLED...EITHER WAY, I'LL NEVER BE ABLE TO SAVE MAZ.

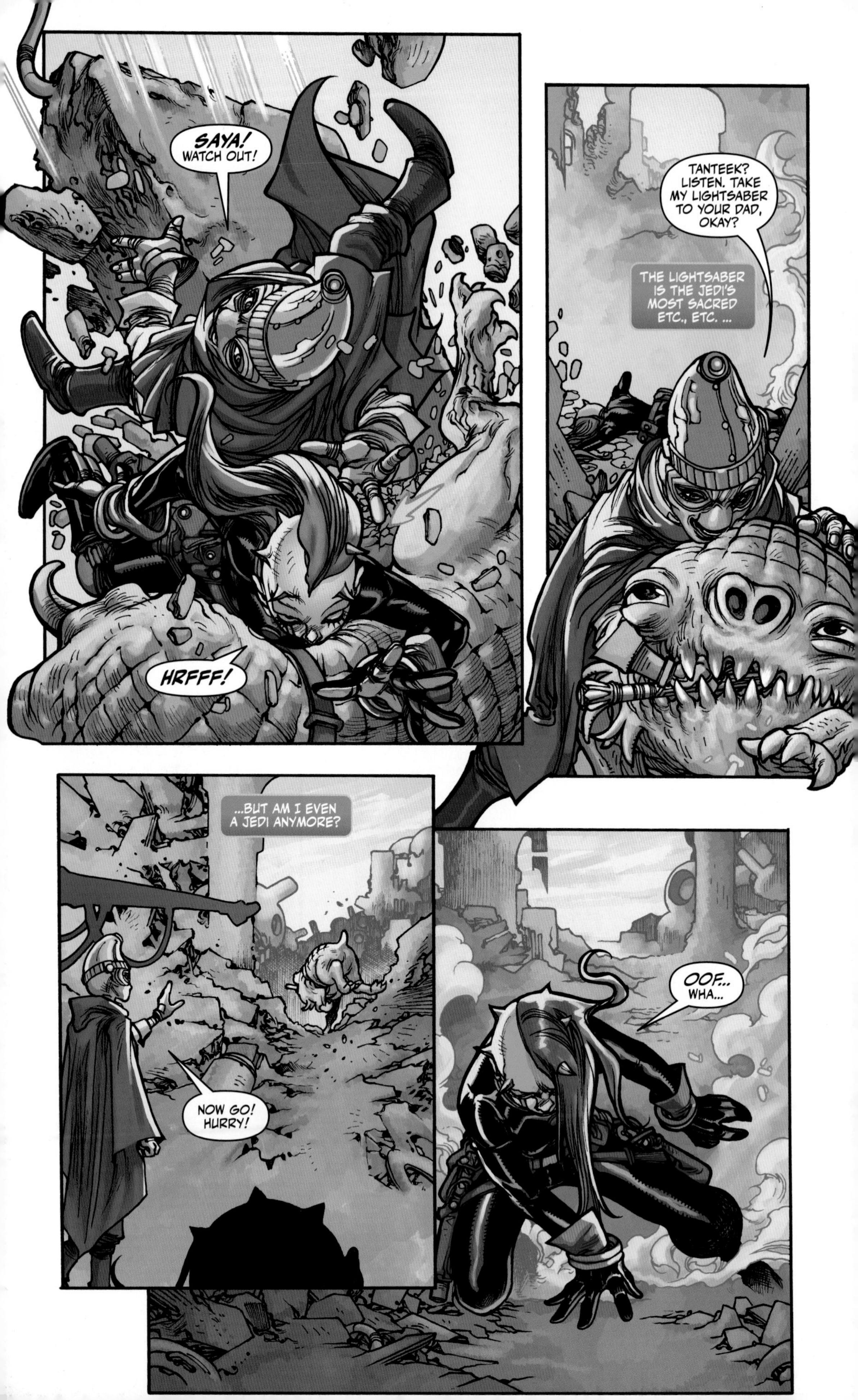
SAYA! WATCH OUT!
HRFFF!
TANTEEK? LISTEN. TAKE MY LIGHTSABER TO YOUR DAD, OKAY?
THE LIGHTSABER IS THE JEDI'S MOST SACRED ETC., ETC. ...
...BUT AM I EVEN A JEDI ANYMORE?
NOW GO! HURRY!
OOF... WHA...

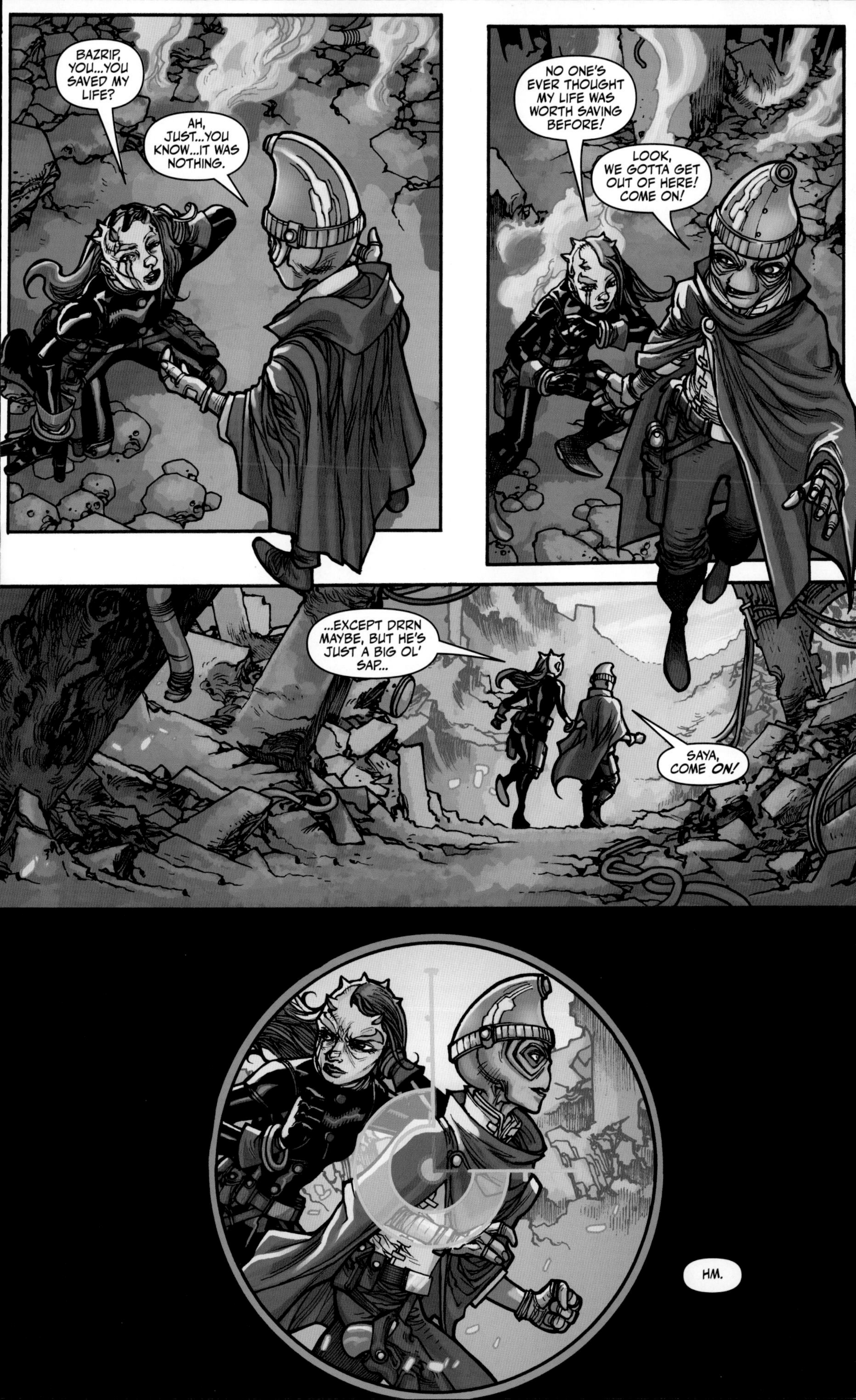
BAZRIP, YOU...YOU SAVED MY LIFE?
AH, JUST...YOU KNOW...IT WAS NOTHING.
NO ONE'S EVER THOUGHT MY LIFE WAS WORTH SAVING BEFORE!
LOOK, WE GOTTA GET OUT OF HERE! COME ON!
...EXCEPT DRRN MAYBE, BUT HE'S JUST A BIG OL' SAP...
SAYA, COME ON!
HM.

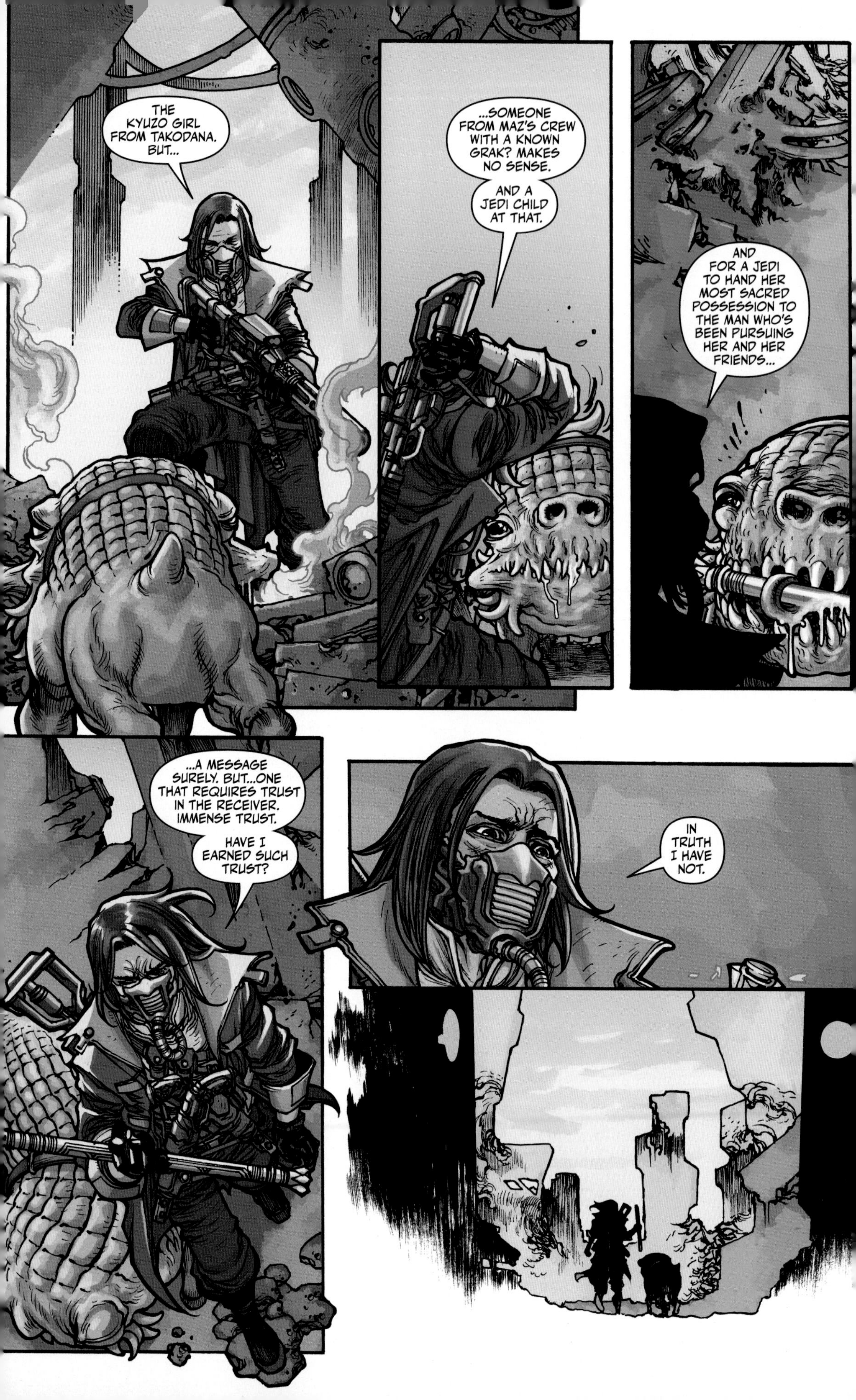
THE KYUZO GIRL FROM TAKODANA. BUT...
...SOMEONE FROM MAZ'S CREW WITH A KNOWN GRAK? MAKES NO SENSE.
AND A JEDI CHILD AT THAT.
AND FOR A JEDI TO HAND HER MOST SACRED POSSESSION TO THE MAN WHO'S BEEN PURSUING HER AND HER FRIENDS...
...A MESSAGE SURELY. BUT...ONE THAT REQUIRES TRUST IN THE RECEIVER. IMMENSE TRUST.
HAVE I EARNED SUCH TRUST?
IN TRUTH I HAVE NOT.

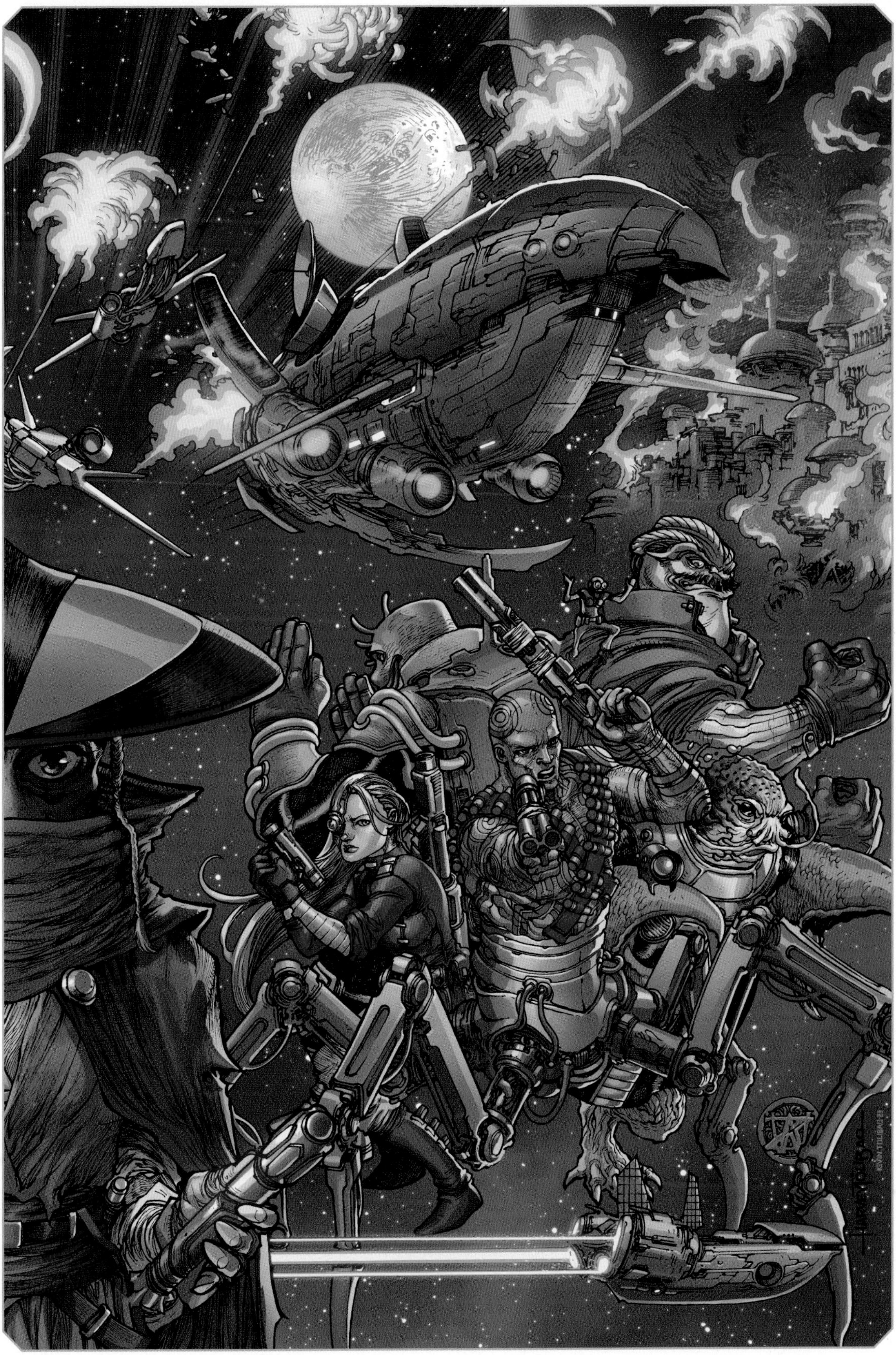

PART 2: FIRE IN THE HOLY HEART, PART 2

COVER ART BY HARVEY TOLIBAO WITH KEVIN TOLIBAO

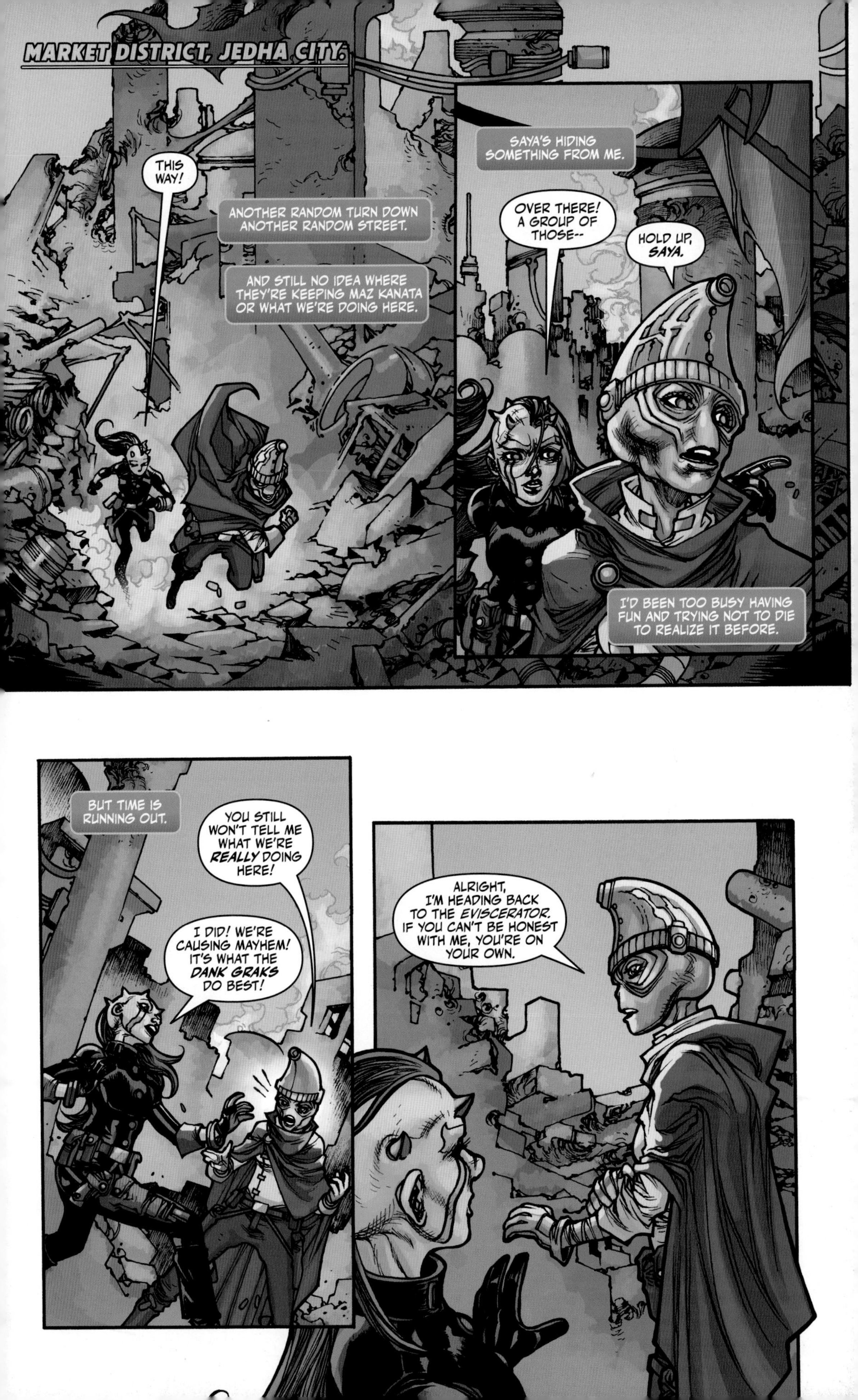

MARKET DISTRICT, JEDHA CITY.
THIS WAY!
ANOTHER RANDOM TURN DOWN ANOTHER RANDOM STREET.
AND STILL NO IDEA WHERE THEY'RE KEEPING MAZ KANATA OR WHAT WE'RE DOING HERE.
SAYA'S HIDING SOMETHING FROM ME.
OVER THERE! A GROUP OF THOSE--
HOLD UP, *SAYA.*
I'D BEEN TOO BUSY HAVING FUN AND TRYING NOT TO DIE TO REALIZE IT BEFORE.
BUT TIME IS RUNNING OUT.
YOU STILL WON'T TELL ME WHAT WE'RE *REALLY* DOING HERE!
I DID! WE'RE CAUSING MAYHEM! IT'S WHAT THE *DANK GRAKS* DO BEST!
ALRIGHT, I'M HEADING BACK TO THE *EVISCERATOR.* IF YOU CAN'T BE HONEST WITH ME, YOU'RE ON YOUR OWN.

NOW WAIT A MINUTE! YOU'RE THE NEWBIE! WHAT MAKES YOU THINK YOU CAN--

GOOD LUCK FINDING A RIDE BACK TO THE *DEVOURER*, SAYA.

FINE FINE FINE! I'LL TELL YOU WHAT YOU WANT TO KNOW! SHEESH.

WHERE ARE YOU KEEPING MAZ KANATA?!

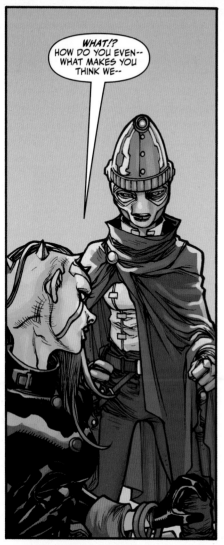

WHAT!? HOW DO YOU EVEN-- WHAT MAKES YOU THINK WE--

SEE YOU OUT IN THE GALAXY, SAYA KEEM.

BAZRIP! *WAIT!!*

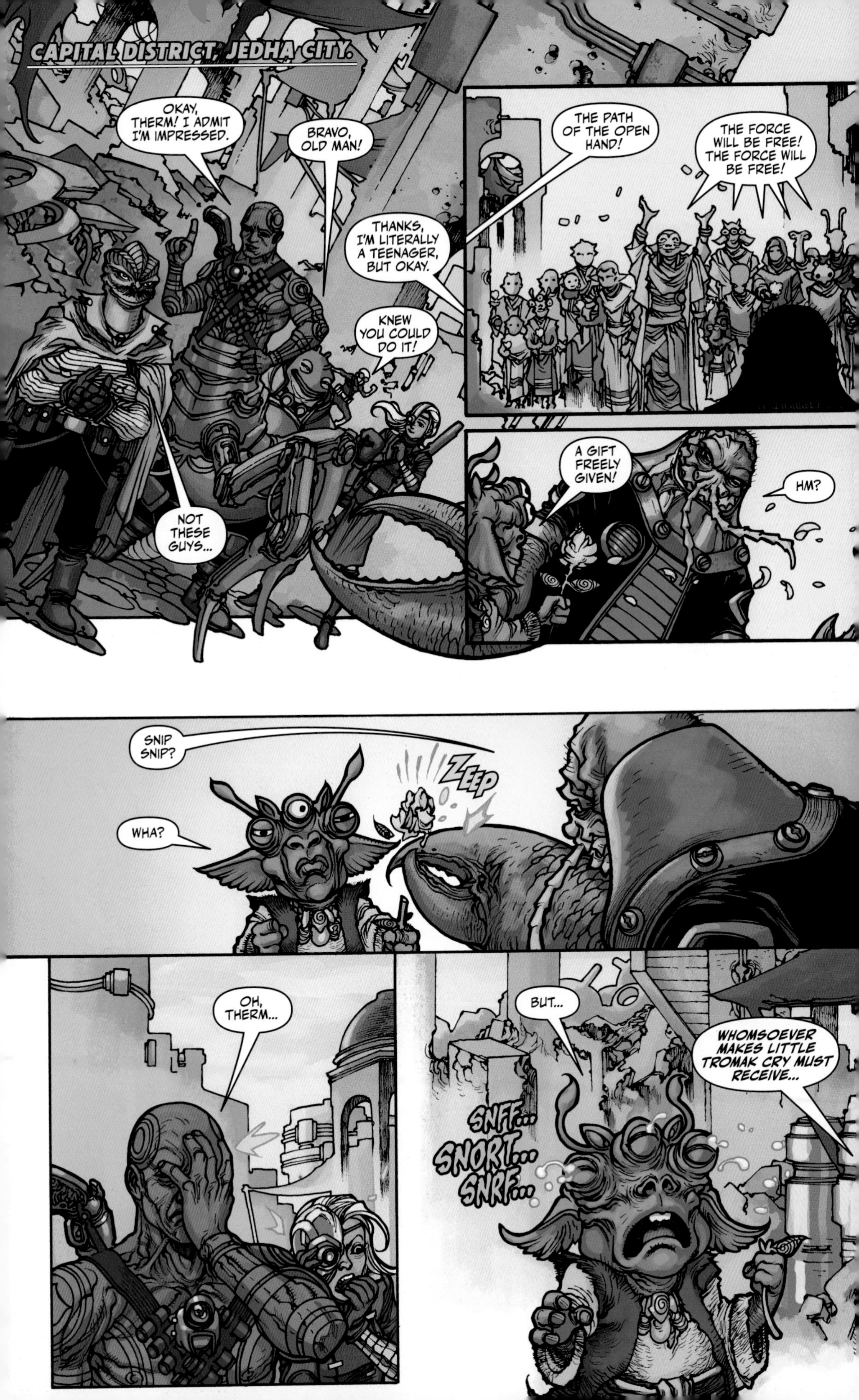
CAPITAL DISTRICT, JEDHA CITY.
OKAY, THERM! I ADMIT I'M IMPRESSED.
BRAVO, OLD MAN!
THANKS, I'M LITERALLY A TEENAGER, BUT OKAY.
KNEW YOU COULD DO IT!
NOT THESE GUYS...
THE PATH OF THE OPEN HAND!
THE FORCE WILL BE FREE! THE FORCE WILL BE FREE!
A GIFT FREELY GIVEN!
HM?
SNIP SNIP?
WHA?
ZEEP
OH, THERM...
BUT...
SNFF... SNORT... SNRF...
WHOMSOEVER MAKES LITTLE TROMAK CRY MUST RECEIVE...

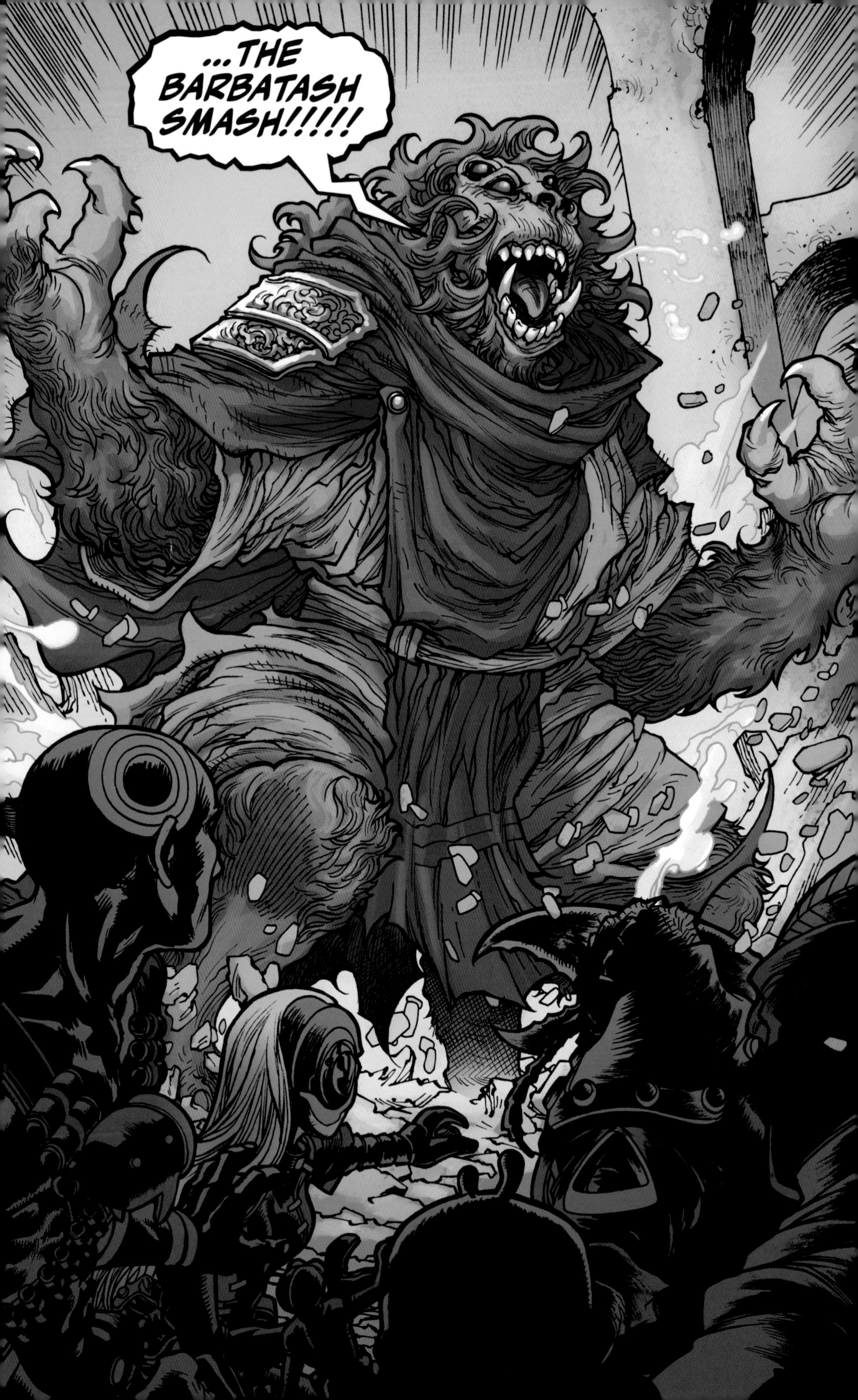
...THE BARBATASH SMASH!!!!!

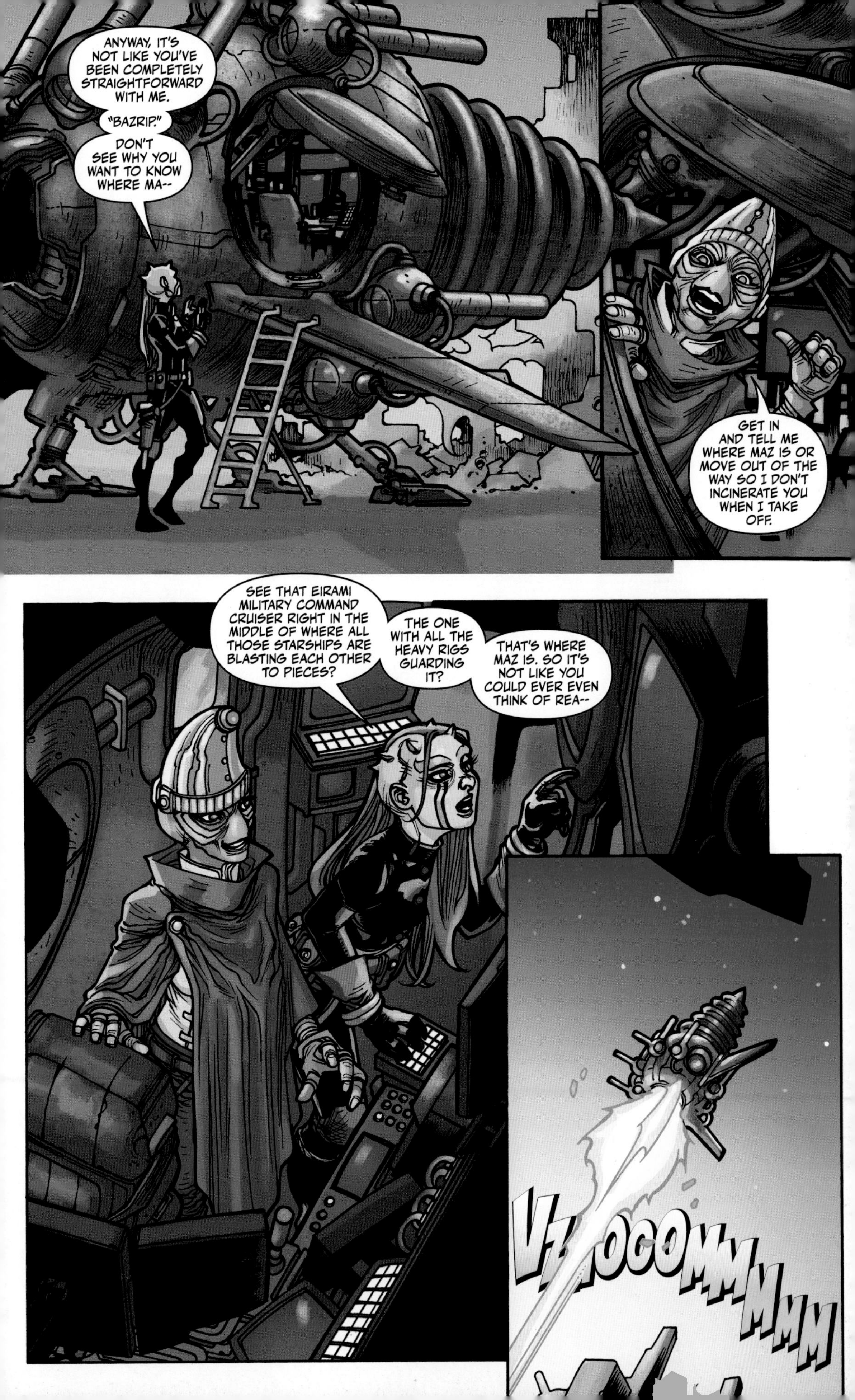
ANYWAY, IT'S NOT LIKE YOU'VE BEEN COMPLETELY STRAIGHTFORWARD WITH ME.
"BAZRIP."
DON'T SEE WHY YOU WANT TO KNOW WHERE MA--
GET IN AND TELL ME WHERE MAZ IS OR MOVE OUT OF THE WAY SO I DON'T INCINERATE YOU WHEN I TAKE OFF.
SEE THAT EIRAMI MILITARY COMMAND CRUISER RIGHT IN THE MIDDLE OF WHERE ALL THOSE STARSHIPS ARE BLASTING EACH OTHER TO PIECES?
THE ONE WITH ALL THE HEAVY RIGS GUARDING IT?
THAT'S WHERE MAZ IS. SO IT'S NOT LIKE YOU COULD EVER EVEN THINK OF REA--
VZHOOOMMMMMM

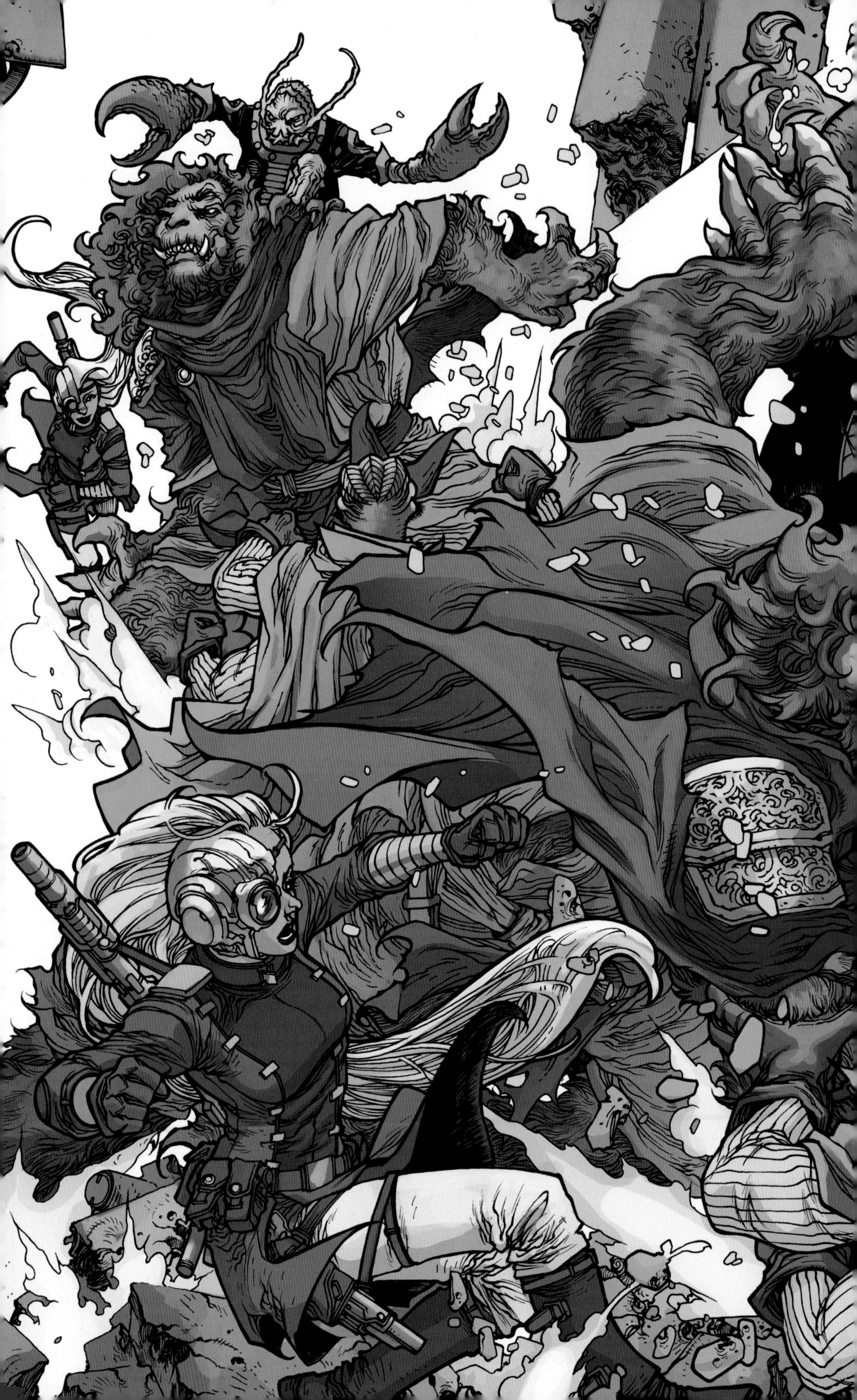

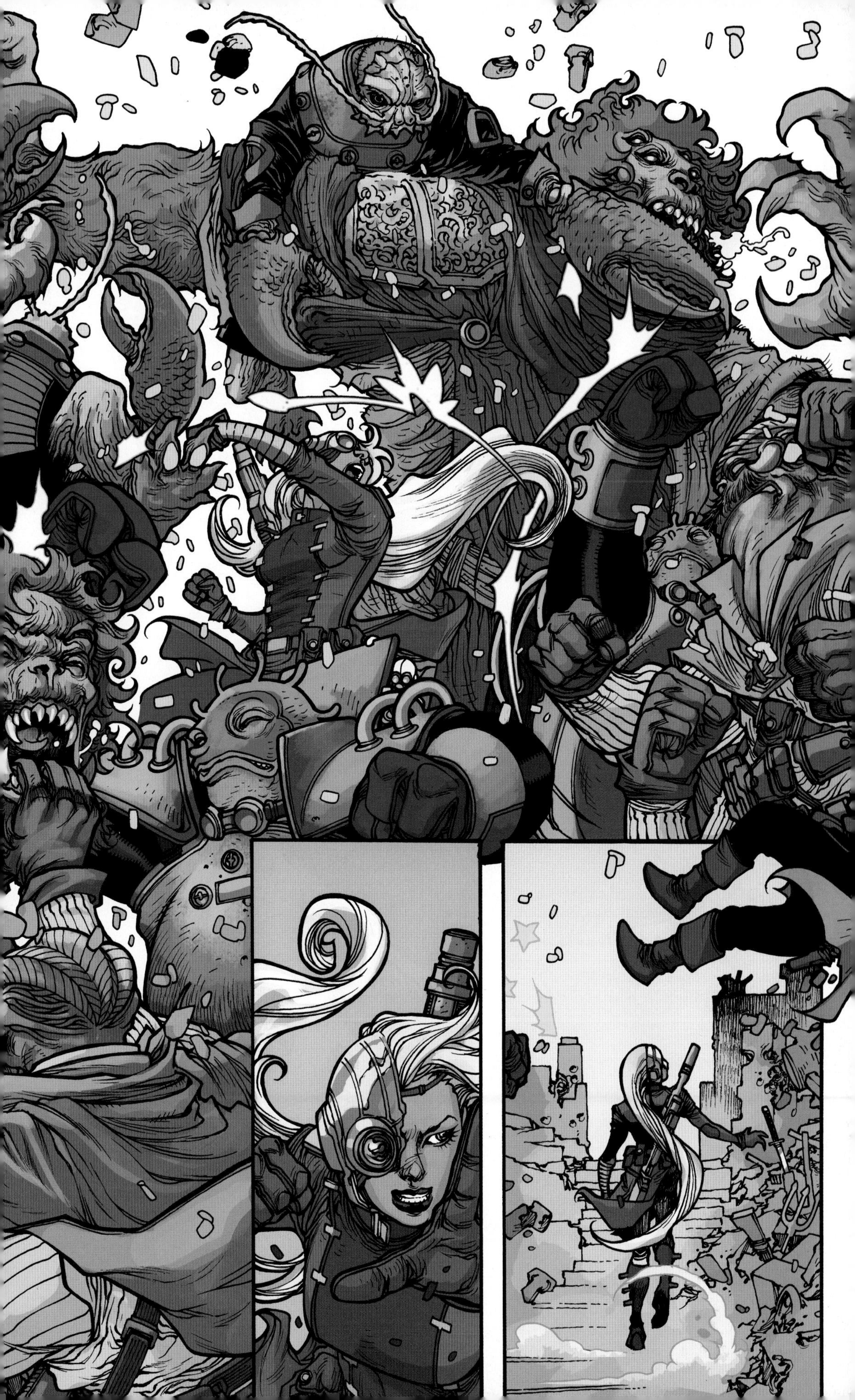

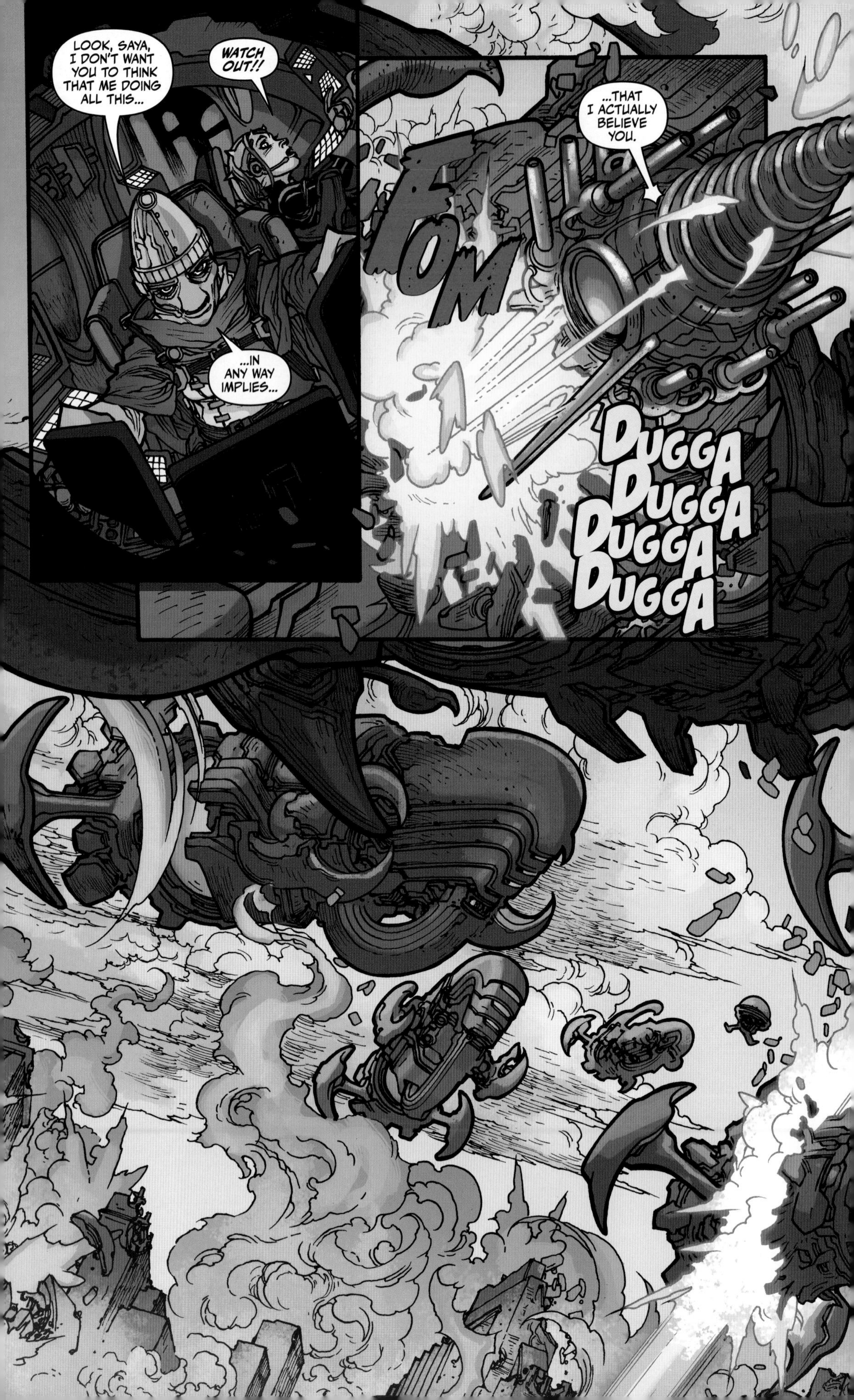
LOOK, SAYA, I DON'T WANT YOU TO THINK THAT ME DOING ALL THIS...
WATCH OUT!!
...IN ANY WAY IMPLIES...
FOM
...THAT I ACTUALLY BELIEVE YOU.
DUGGA DUGGA DUGGA DUGGA

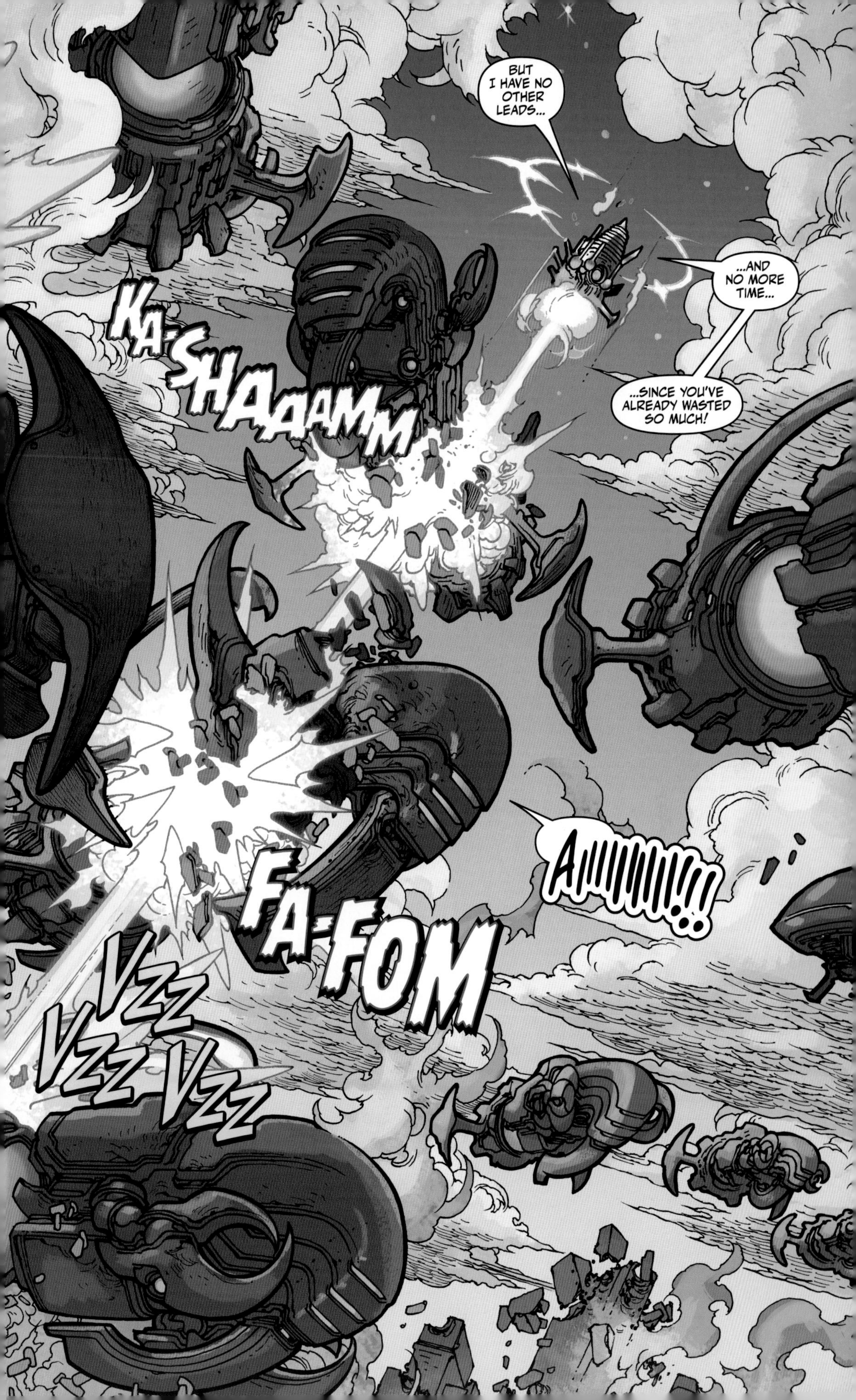
BUT I HAVE NO OTHER LEADS...
...AND NO MORE TIME...
...SINCE YOU'VE ALREADY WASTED SO MUCH!
KA-SHAAAMM
FA-FOM
AIIIIIIIII!!!
VZZ VZZ VZZ

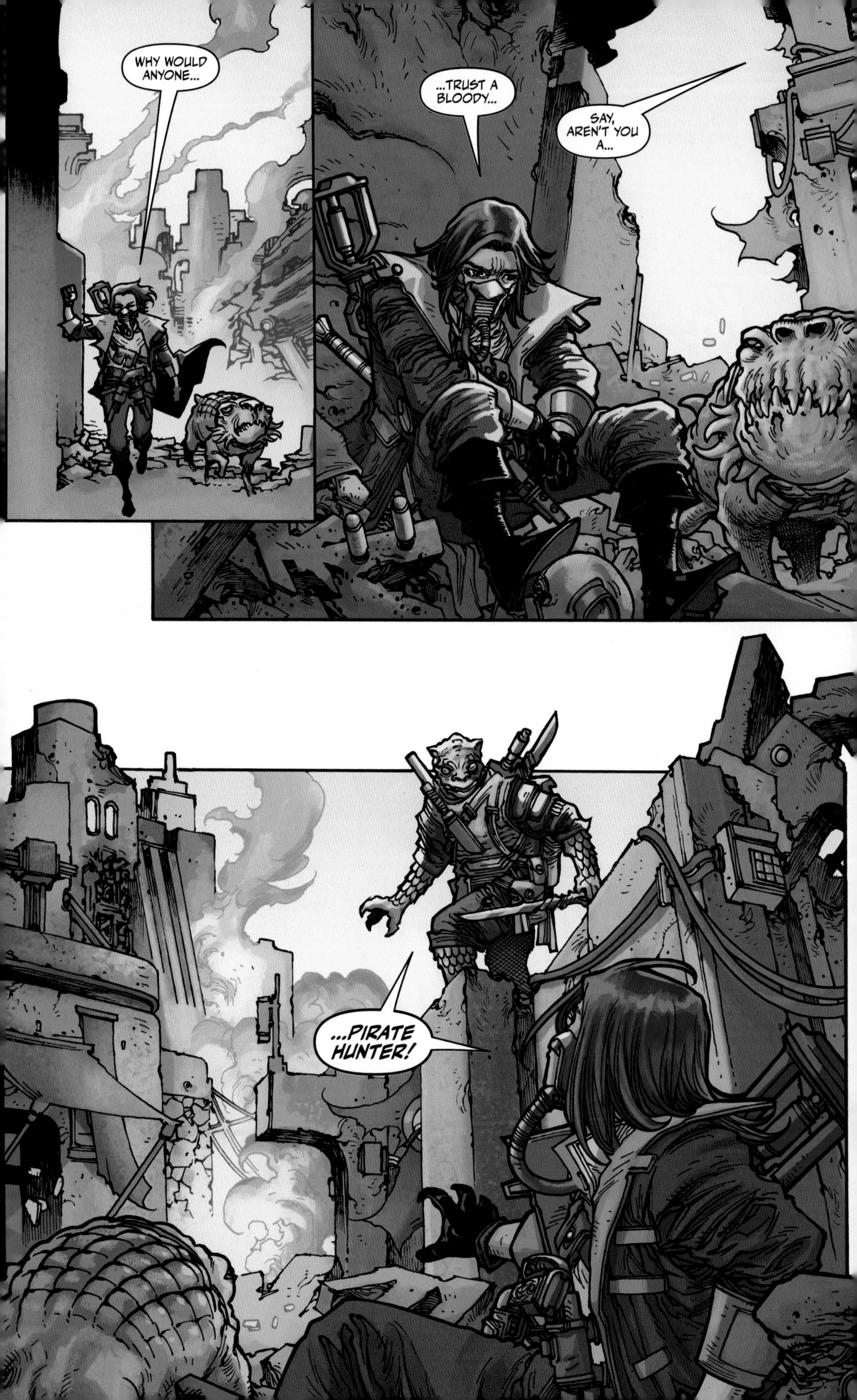
WHY WOULD ANYONE...
...TRUST A BLOODY...
SAY, AREN'T YOU A...
...PIRATE HUNTER!

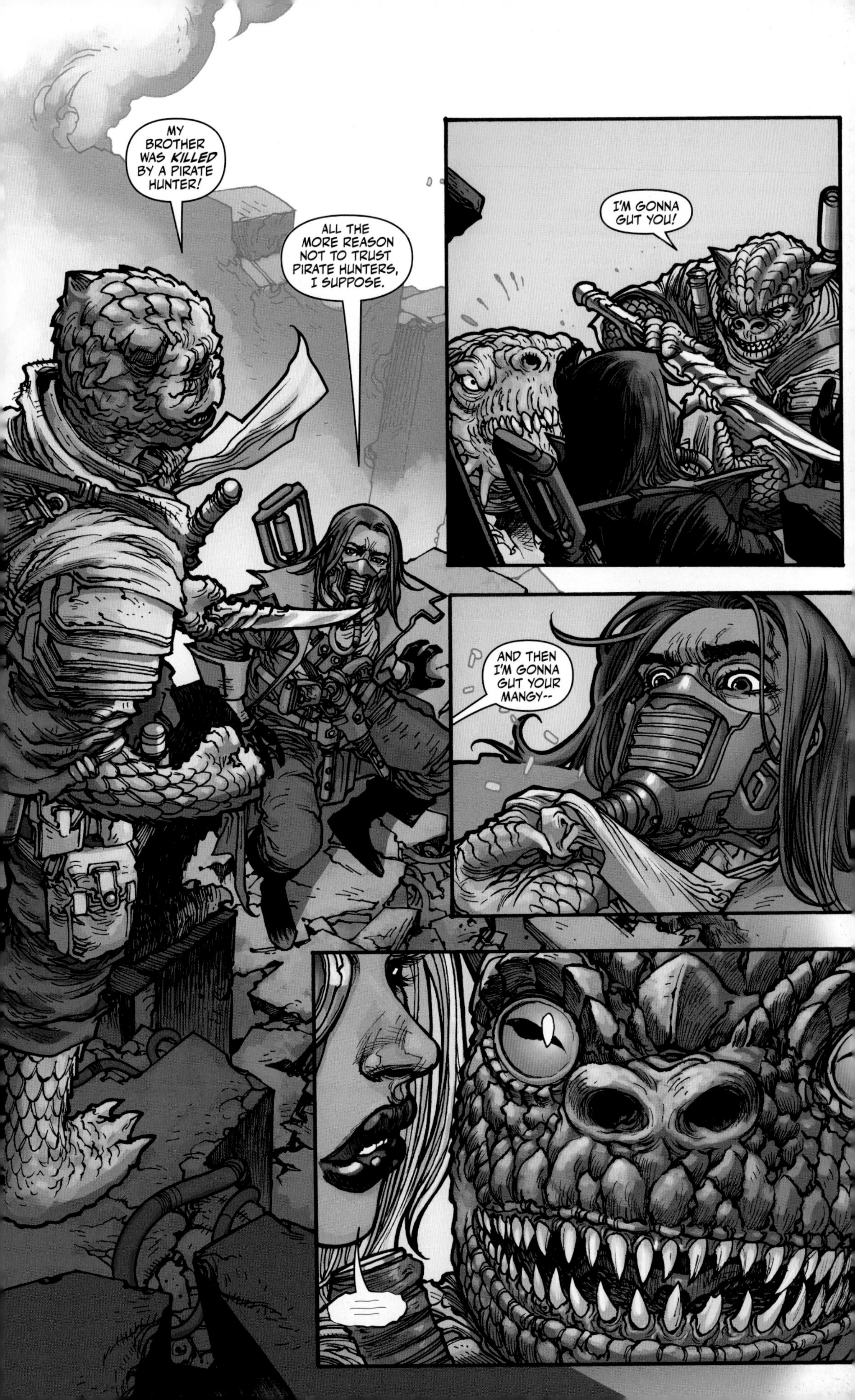
MY BROTHER WAS *KILLED* BY A PIRATE HUNTER!
ALL THE MORE REASON NOT TO TRUST PIRATE HUNTERS, I SUPPOSE.
I'M GONNA GUT YOU!
AND THEN I'M GONNA GUT YOUR MANGY--

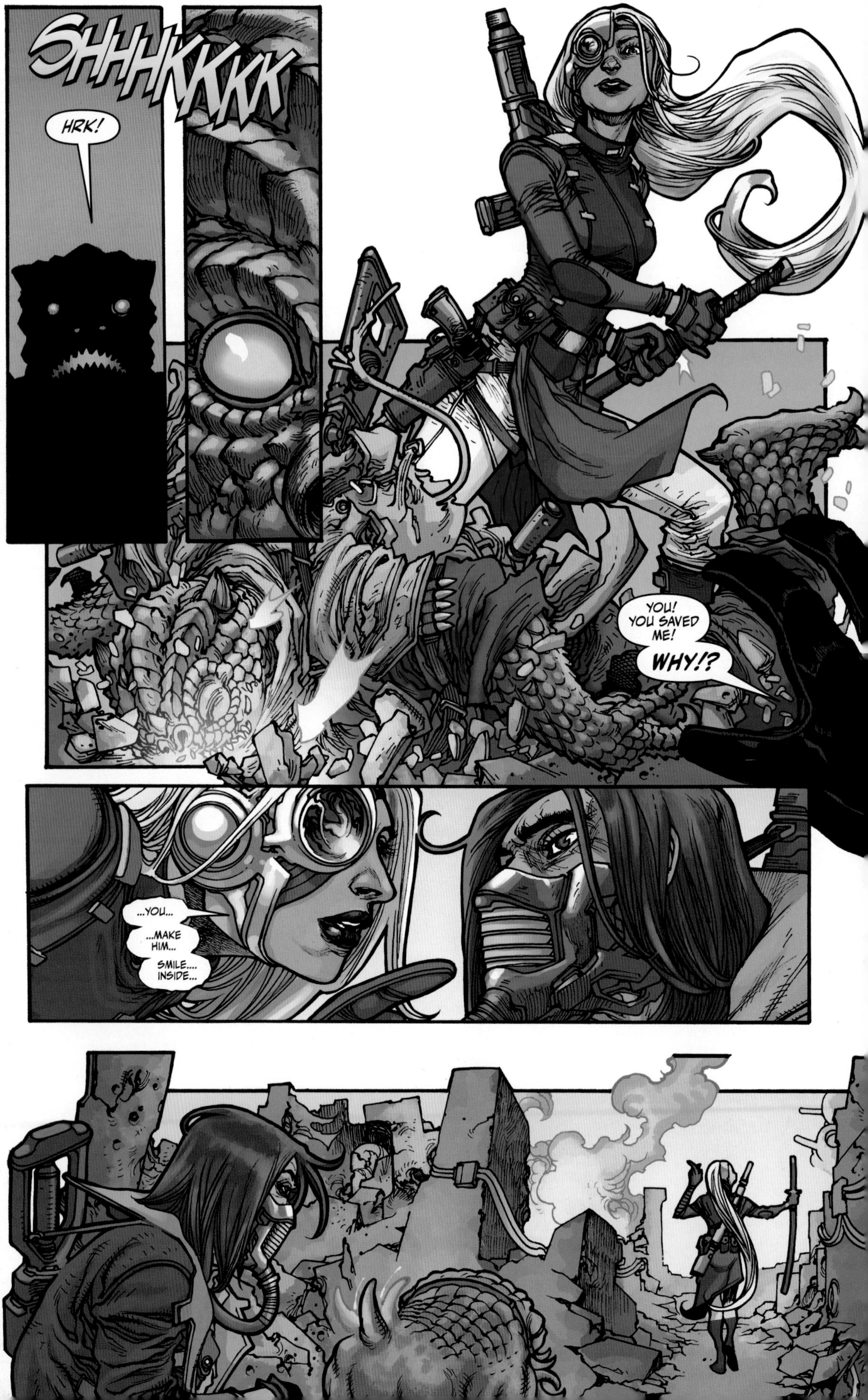
SHHHKKKK
HRK!
YOU! YOU SAVED ME! WHY!?
...YOU...
...MAKE HIM...
SMILE.... INSIDE...

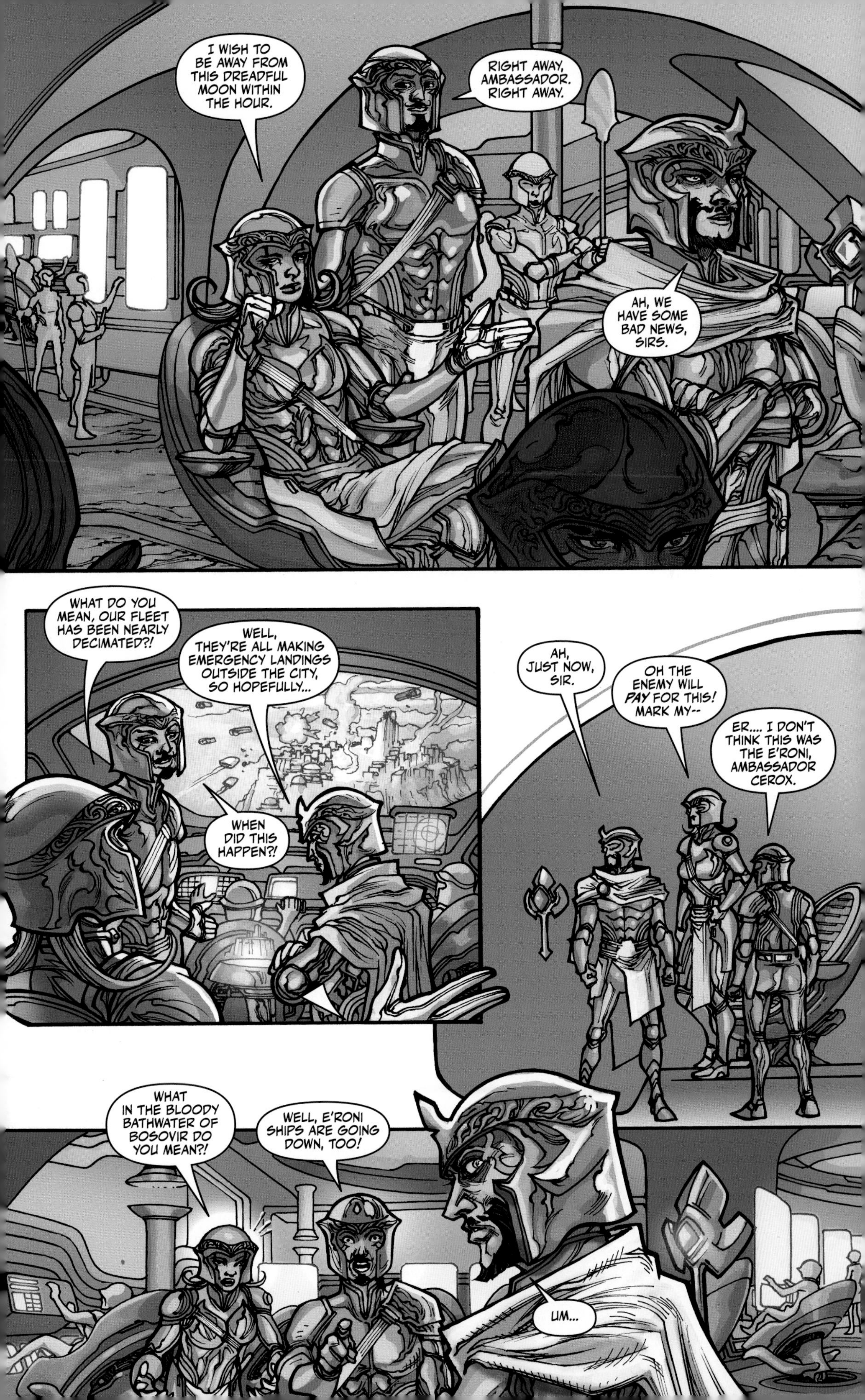
I WISH TO BE AWAY FROM THIS DREADFUL MOON WITHIN THE HOUR.
RIGHT AWAY, AMBASSADOR. RIGHT AWAY.
AH, WE HAVE SOME BAD NEWS, SIRS.
WHAT DO YOU MEAN, OUR FLEET HAS BEEN NEARLY DECIMATED?!
WELL, THEY'RE ALL MAKING EMERGENCY LANDINGS OUTSIDE THE CITY, SO HOPEFULLY...
WHEN DID THIS HAPPEN?!
AH, JUST NOW, SIR.
OH THE ENEMY WILL *PAY* FOR THIS! MARK MY--
ER.... I DON'T THINK THIS WAS THE E'RONI, AMBASSADOR CEROX.
WHAT IN THE BLOODY BATHWATER OF BOSOVIR DO YOU MEAN?!
WELL, E'RONI SHIPS ARE GOING DOWN, TOO!
UM...

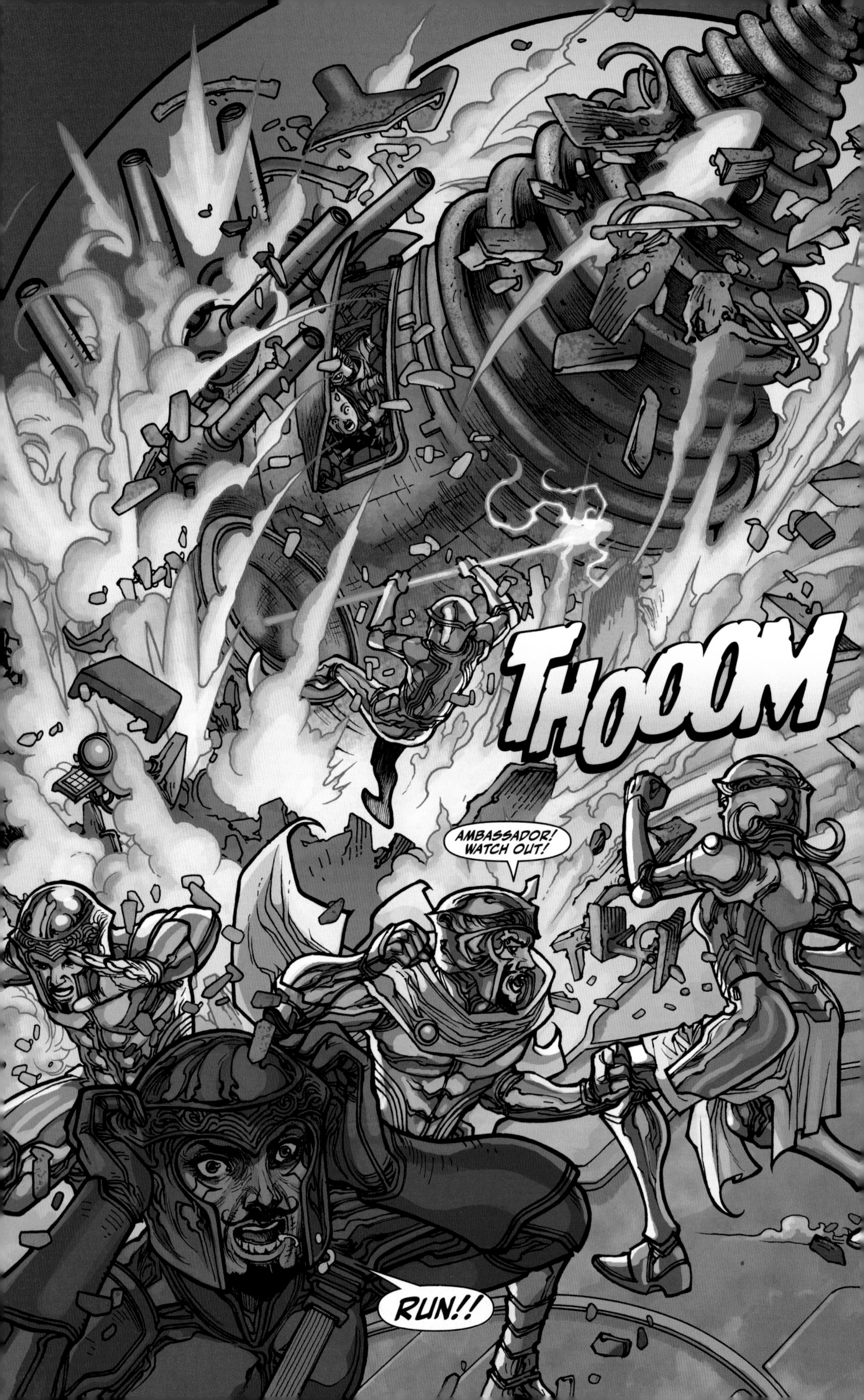
THOOOM
AMBASSADOR! WATCH OUT!
RUN!!

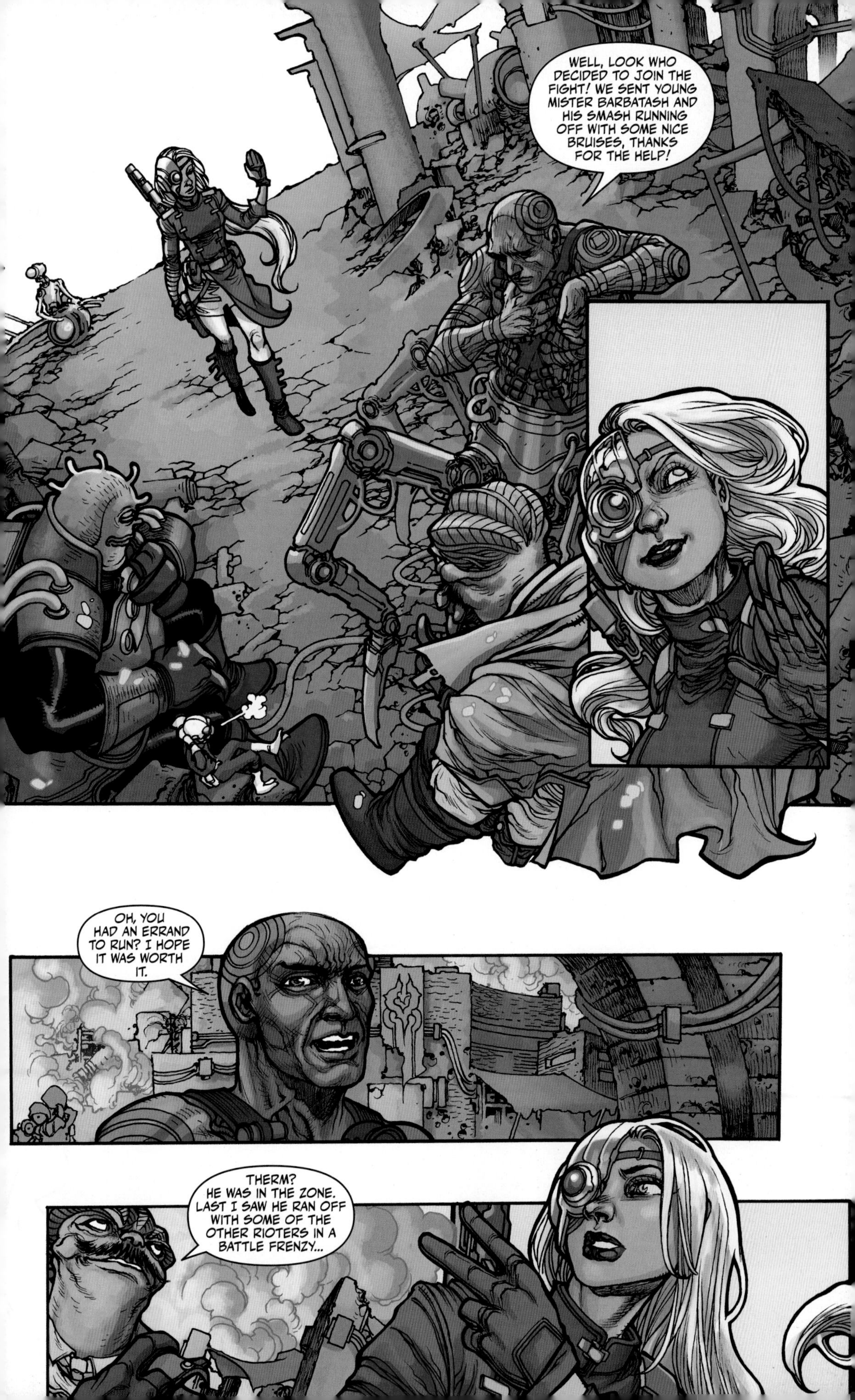
WELL, LOOK WHO DECIDED TO JOIN THE FIGHT! WE SENT YOUNG MISTER BARBATASH AND HIS SMASH RUNNING OFF WITH SOME NICE BRUISES, THANKS FOR THE HELP!
OH, YOU HAD AN ERRAND TO RUN? I HOPE IT WAS WORTH IT.
THERM? HE WAS IN THE ZONE. LAST I SAW HE RAN OFF WITH SOME OF THE OTHER RIOTERS IN A BATTLE FRENZY...

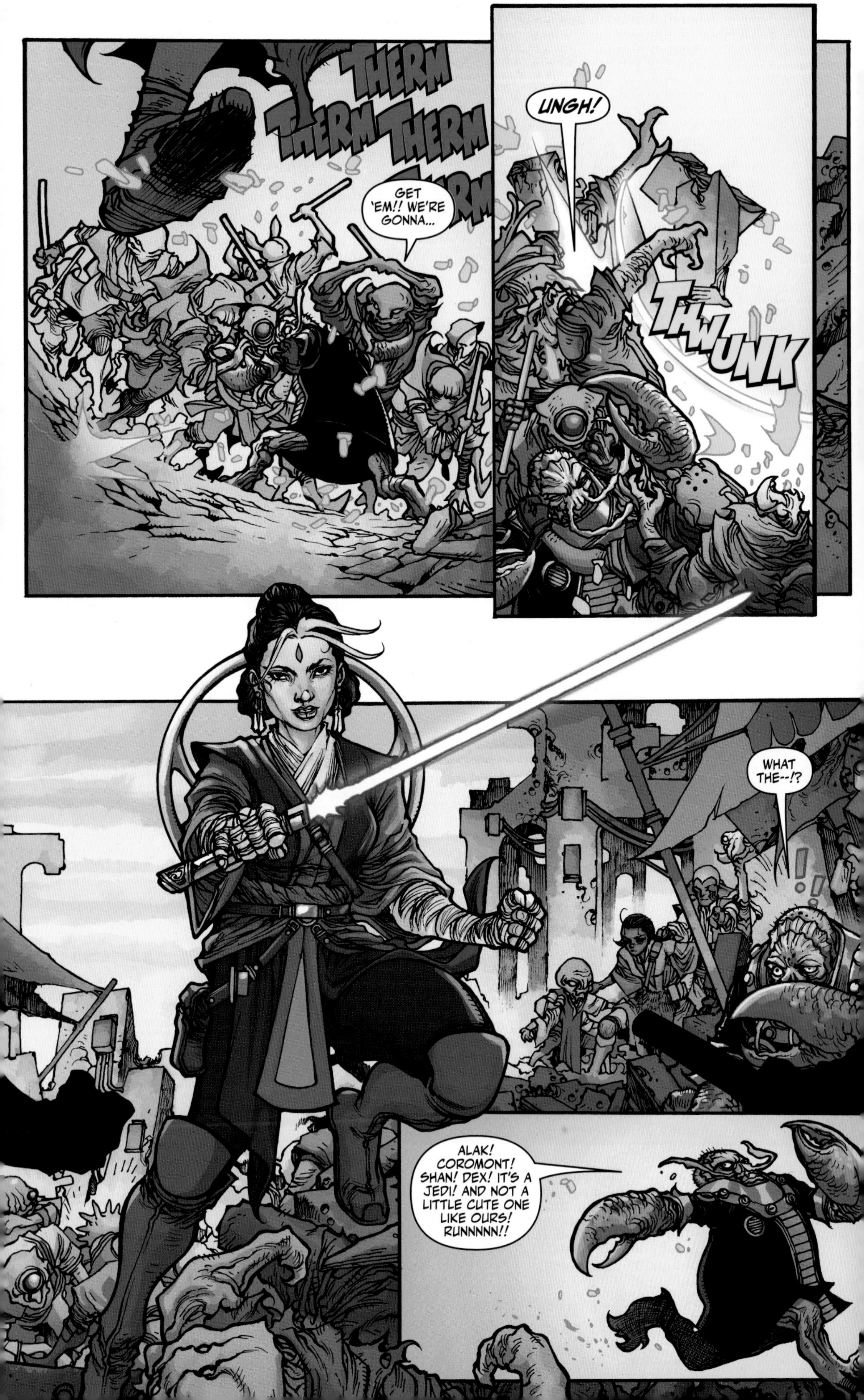
THERM THERM THERM THERM
GET 'EM!! WE'RE GONNA...
UNGH!
THWUNK
WHAT THE--!?
!
ALAK! COROMONT! SHAN! DEX! IT'S A JEDI! AND NOT A LITTLE CUTE ONE LIKE OURS! RUNNNNN!!

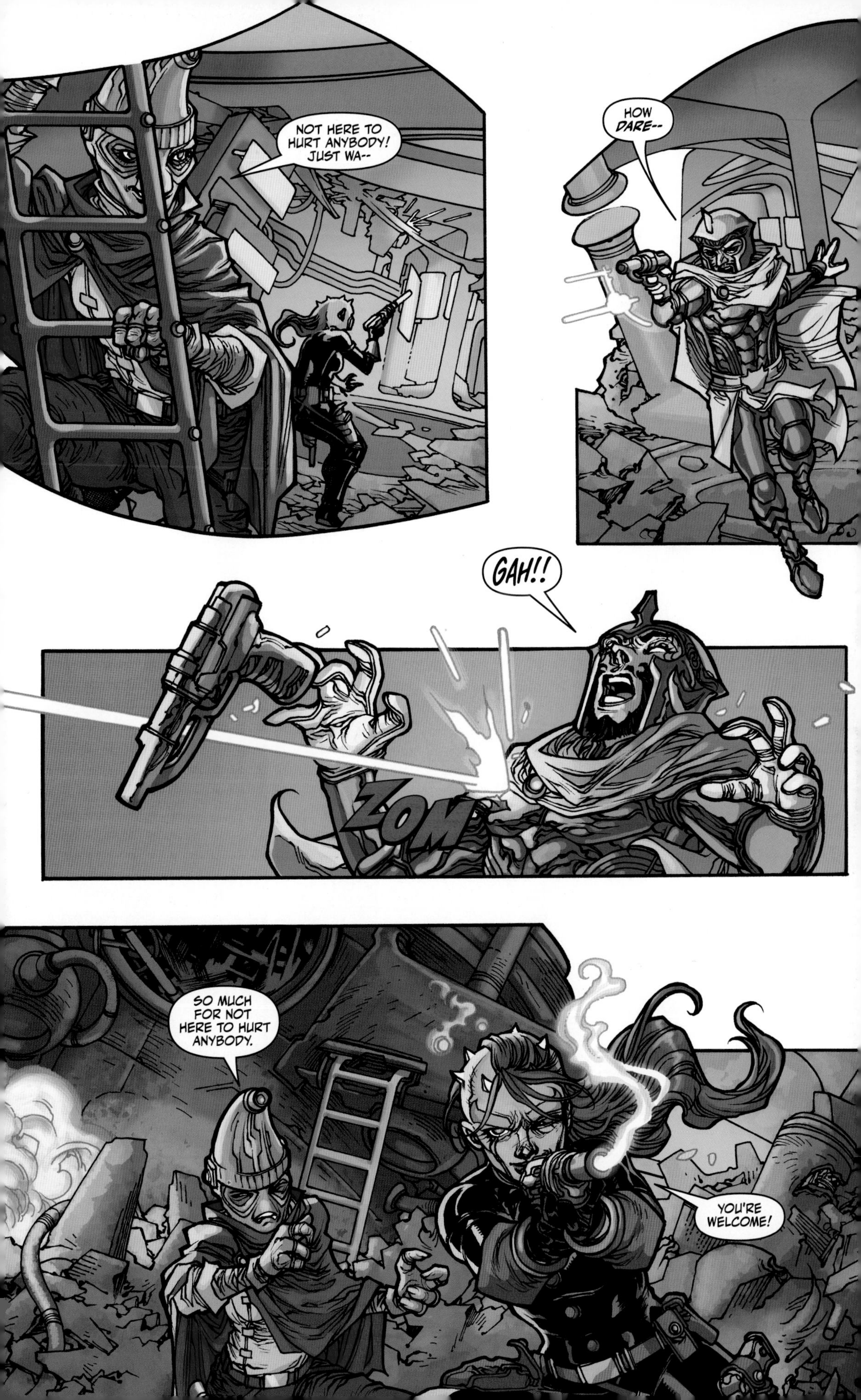
NOT HERE TO HURT ANYBODY! JUST WA--
HOW DARE--
GAH!!
ZOM
SO MUCH FOR NOT HERE TO HURT ANYBODY.
YOU'RE WELCOME!

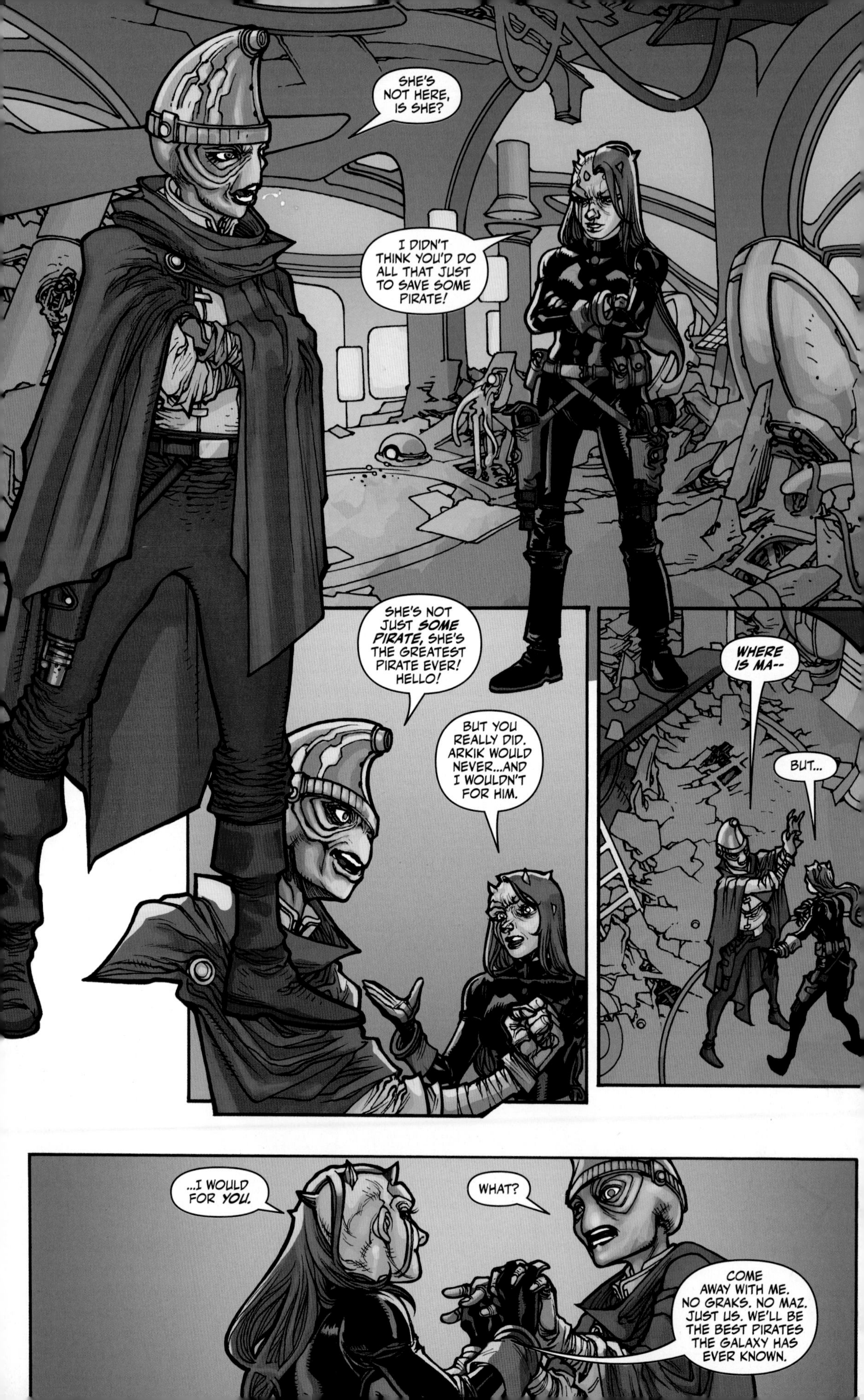
SHE'S NOT HERE, IS SHE?
I DIDN'T THINK YOU'D DO ALL THAT JUST TO SAVE SOME PIRATE!
SHE'S NOT JUST SOME PIRATE, SHE'S THE GREATEST PIRATE EVER! HELLO!
BUT YOU REALLY DID. ARKIK WOULD NEVER...AND I WOULDN'T FOR HIM.
WHERE IS MA--
BUT...
...I WOULD FOR YOU.
WHAT?
COME AWAY WITH ME. NO GRAKS. NO MAZ. JUST US. WE'LL BE THE BEST PIRATES THE GALAXY HAS EVER KNOWN.

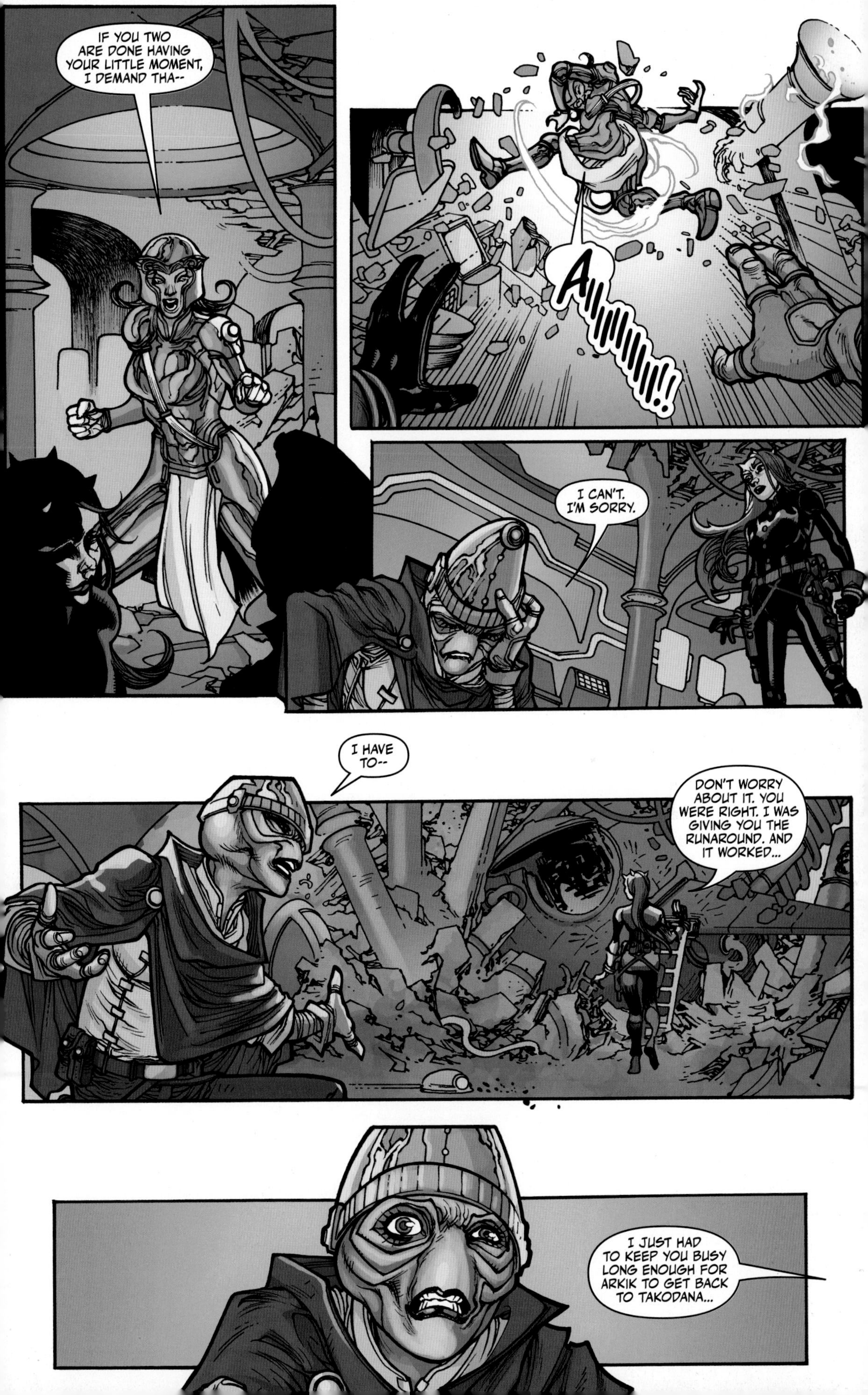
IF YOU TWO ARE DONE HAVING YOUR LITTLE MOMENT, I DEMAND THA--
AIIIIIIIII!!
I CAN'T. I'M SORRY.
I HAVE TO--
DON'T WORRY ABOUT IT. YOU WERE RIGHT. I WAS GIVING YOU THE RUNAROUND. AND IT WORKED...
I JUST HAD TO KEEP YOU BUSY LONG ENOUGH FOR ARKIK TO GET BACK TO TAKODANA...

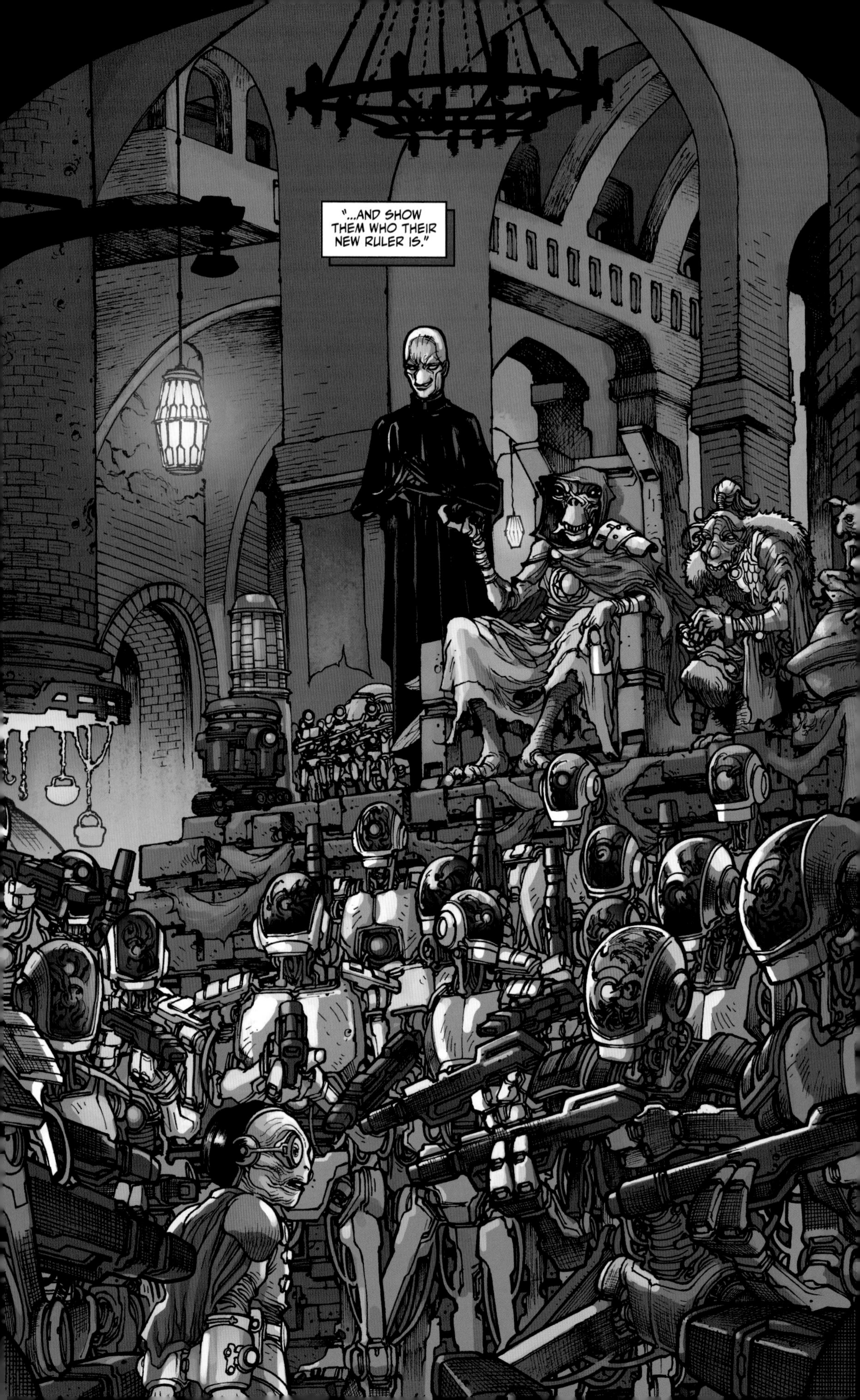
"...AND SHOW THEM WHO THEIR NEW RULER IS."

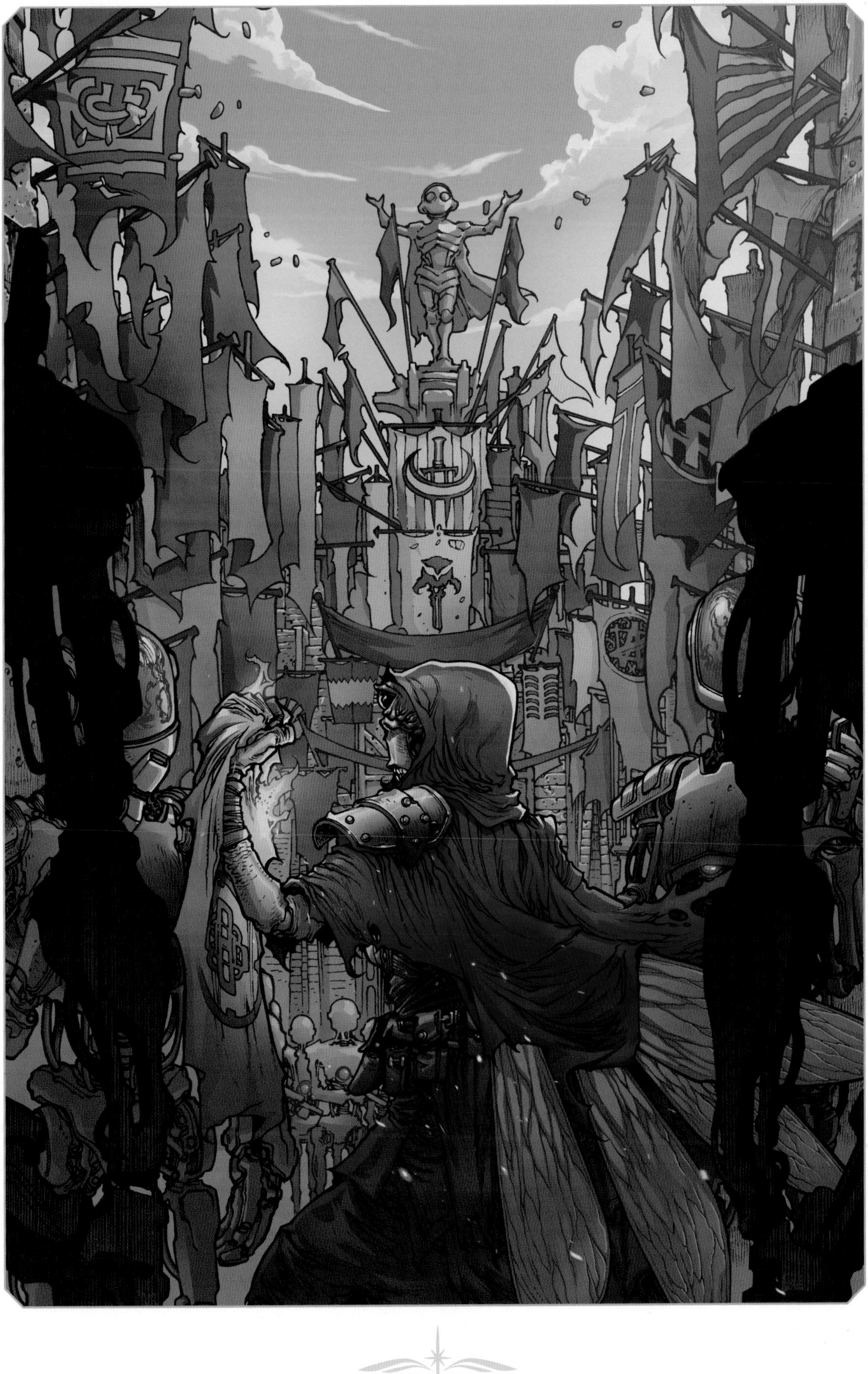

PART 3: THE BATTLE FOR TAKODANA, PART 1
COVER ART BY HARVEY TOLIBAO WITH KEVIN TOLIBAO

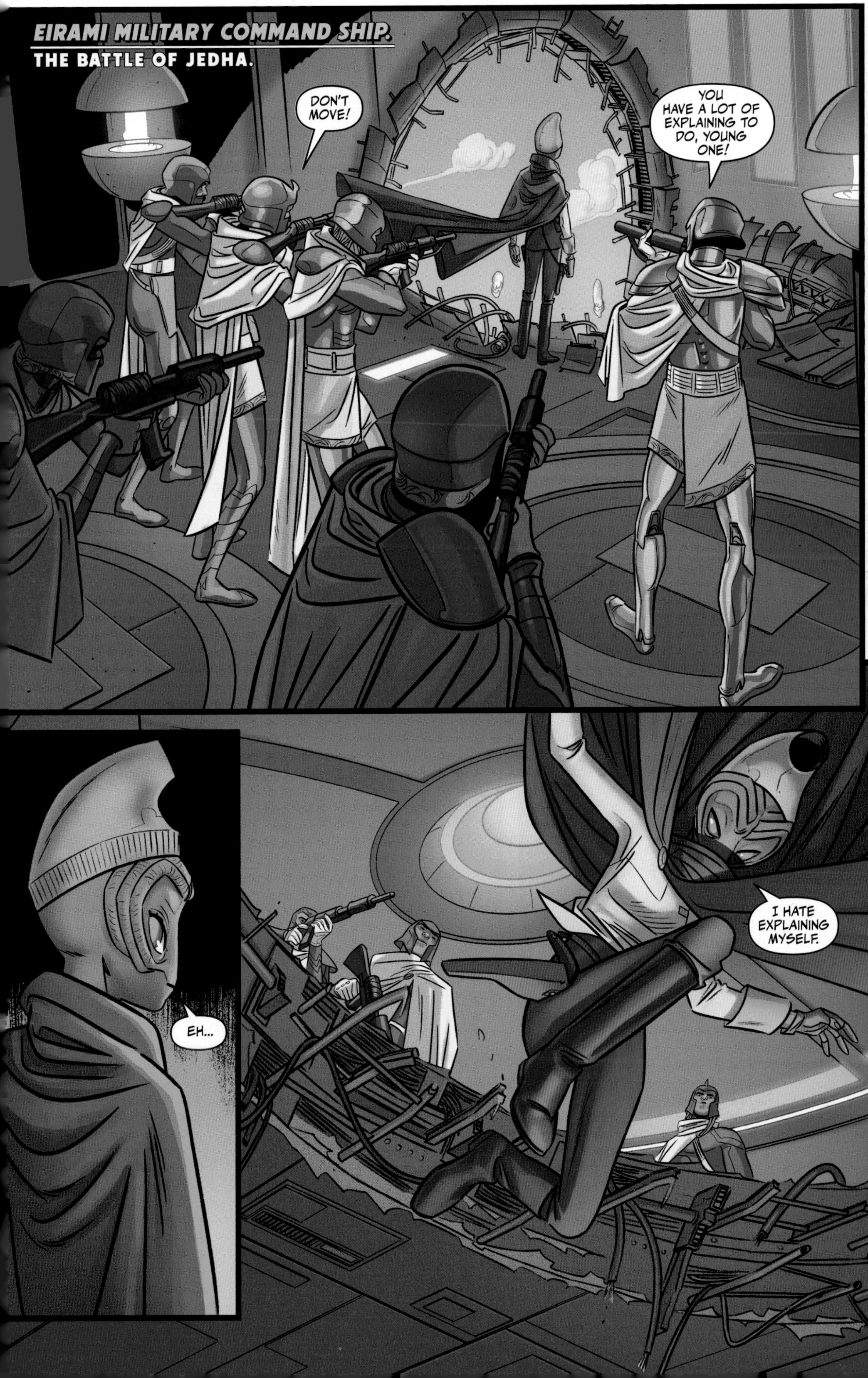
EIRAMI MILITARY COMMAND SHIP.
THE BATTLE OF JEDHA.
DON'T MOVE!
YOU HAVE A LOT OF EXPLAINING TO DO, YOUNG ONE!
EH...
I HATE EXPLAINING MYSELF.

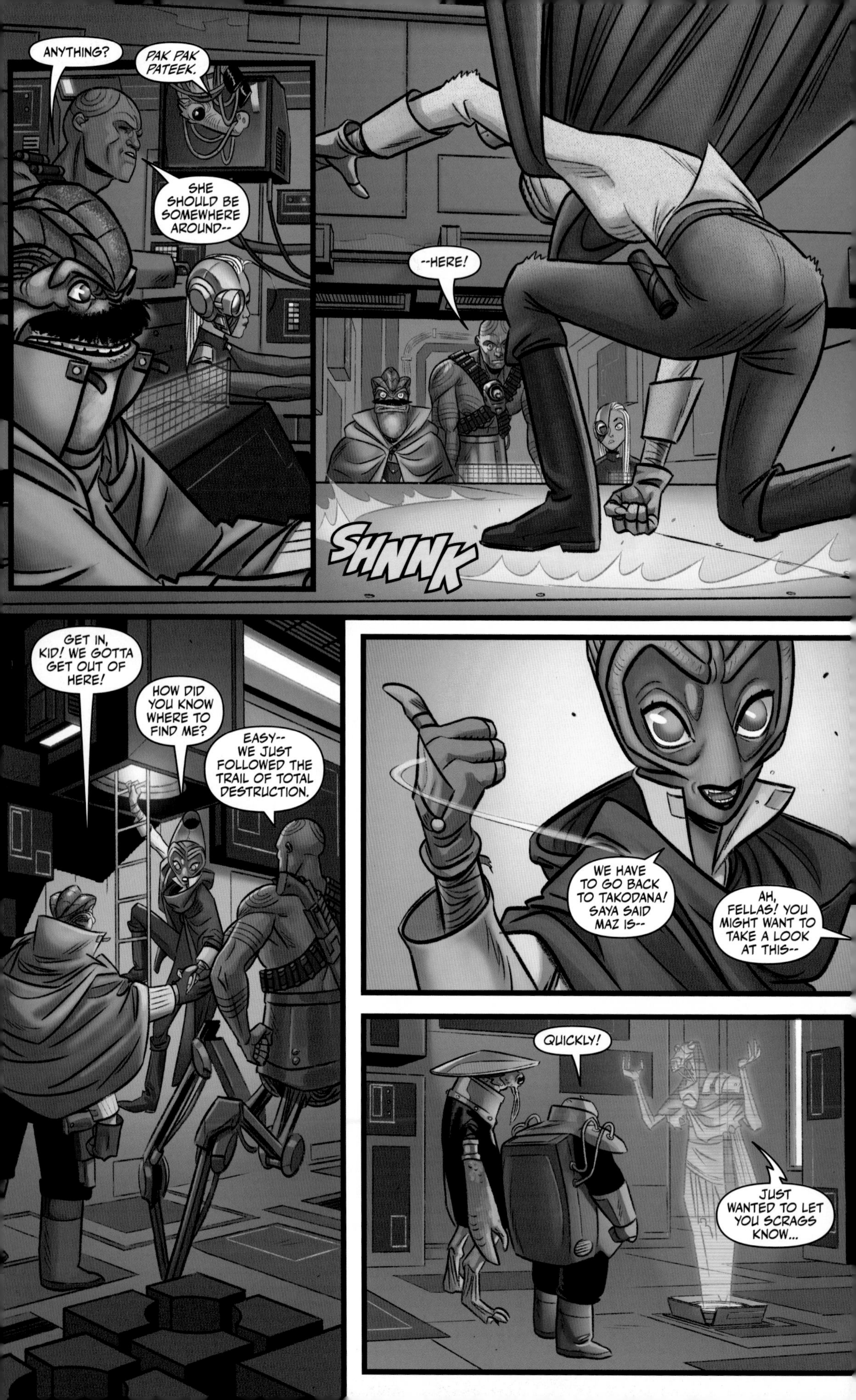

ANYTHING?
PAK PAK PATEEK.
SHE SHOULD BE SOMEWHERE AROUND--
--HERE!
SHNNK
GET IN, KID! WE GOTTA GET OUT OF HERE!
HOW DID YOU KNOW WHERE TO FIND ME?
EASY-- WE JUST FOLLOWED THE TRAIL OF TOTAL DESTRUCTION.
WE HAVE TO GO BACK TO TAKODANA! SAYA SAID MAZ IS--
AH, FELLAS! YOU MIGHT WANT TO TAKE A LOOK AT THIS--
QUICKLY!
JUST WANTED TO LET YOU SCRAGS KNOW...

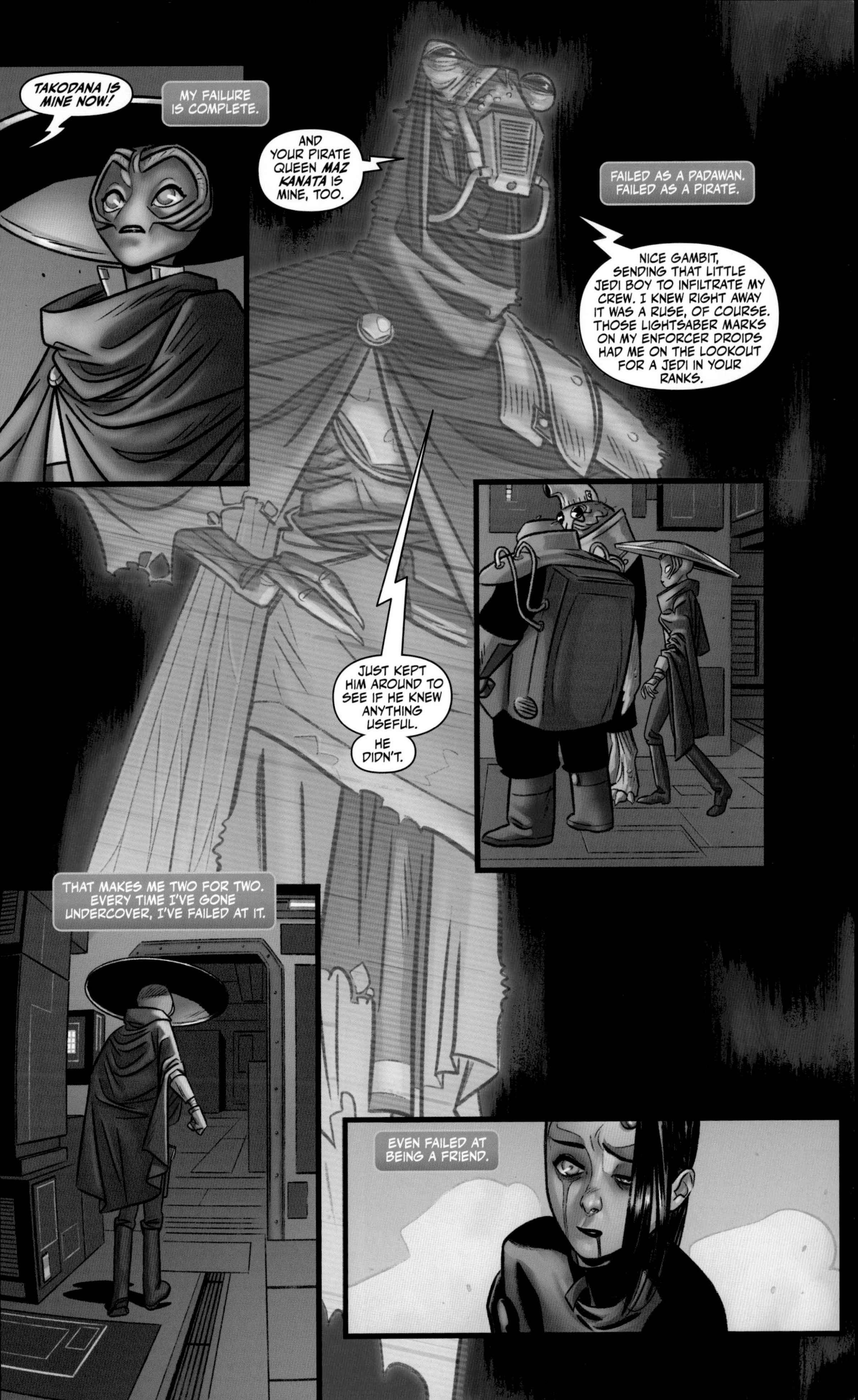
TAKODANA IS MINE NOW!
MY FAILURE IS COMPLETE.
AND YOUR PIRATE QUEEN MAZ KANATA IS MINE, TOO.
FAILED AS A PADAWAN. FAILED AS A PIRATE.
NICE GAMBIT, SENDING THAT LITTLE JEDI BOY TO INFILTRATE MY CREW. I KNEW RIGHT AWAY IT WAS A RUSE, OF COURSE. THOSE LIGHTSABER MARKS ON MY ENFORCER DROIDS HAD ME ON THE LOOKOUT FOR A JEDI IN YOUR RANKS.
JUST KEPT HIM AROUND TO SEE IF HE KNEW ANYTHING USEFUL.
HE DIDN'T.
THAT MAKES ME TWO FOR TWO. EVERY TIME I'VE GONE UNDERCOVER, I'VE FAILED AT IT.
EVEN FAILED AT BEING A FRIEND.

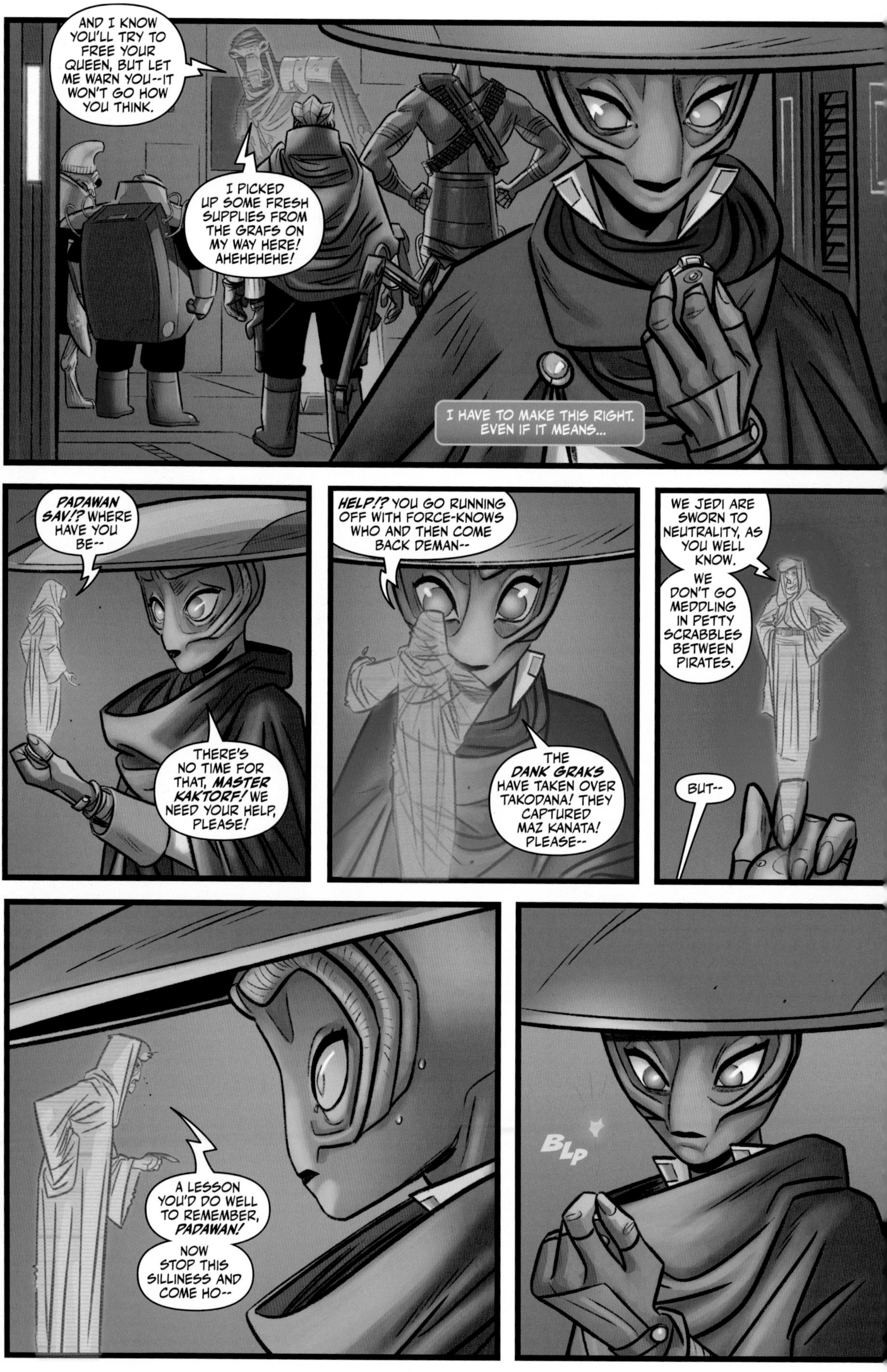

AND I KNOW YOU'LL TRY TO FREE YOUR QUEEN, BUT LET ME WARN YOU--IT WON'T GO HOW YOU THINK.
I PICKED UP SOME FRESH SUPPLIES FROM THE GRAFS ON MY WAY HERE! AHEHEHEHE!
I HAVE TO MAKE THIS RIGHT. EVEN IF IT MEANS...
PADAWAN SAV!? WHERE HAVE YOU BE--
THERE'S NO TIME FOR THAT, MASTER KAKTORF! WE NEED YOUR HELP, PLEASE!
HELP!? YOU GO RUNNING OFF WITH FORCE-KNOWS WHO AND THEN COME BACK DEMAN--
THE DANK GRAKS HAVE TAKEN OVER TAKODANA! THEY CAPTURED MAZ KANATA! PLEASE--
WE JEDI ARE SWORN TO NEUTRALITY, AS YOU WELL KNOW.
WE DON'T GO MEDDLING IN PETTY SCRABBLES BETWEEN PIRATES.
BUT--
A LESSON YOU'D DO WELL TO REMEMBER, PADAWAN!
NOW STOP THIS SILLINESS AND COME HO--
BLP

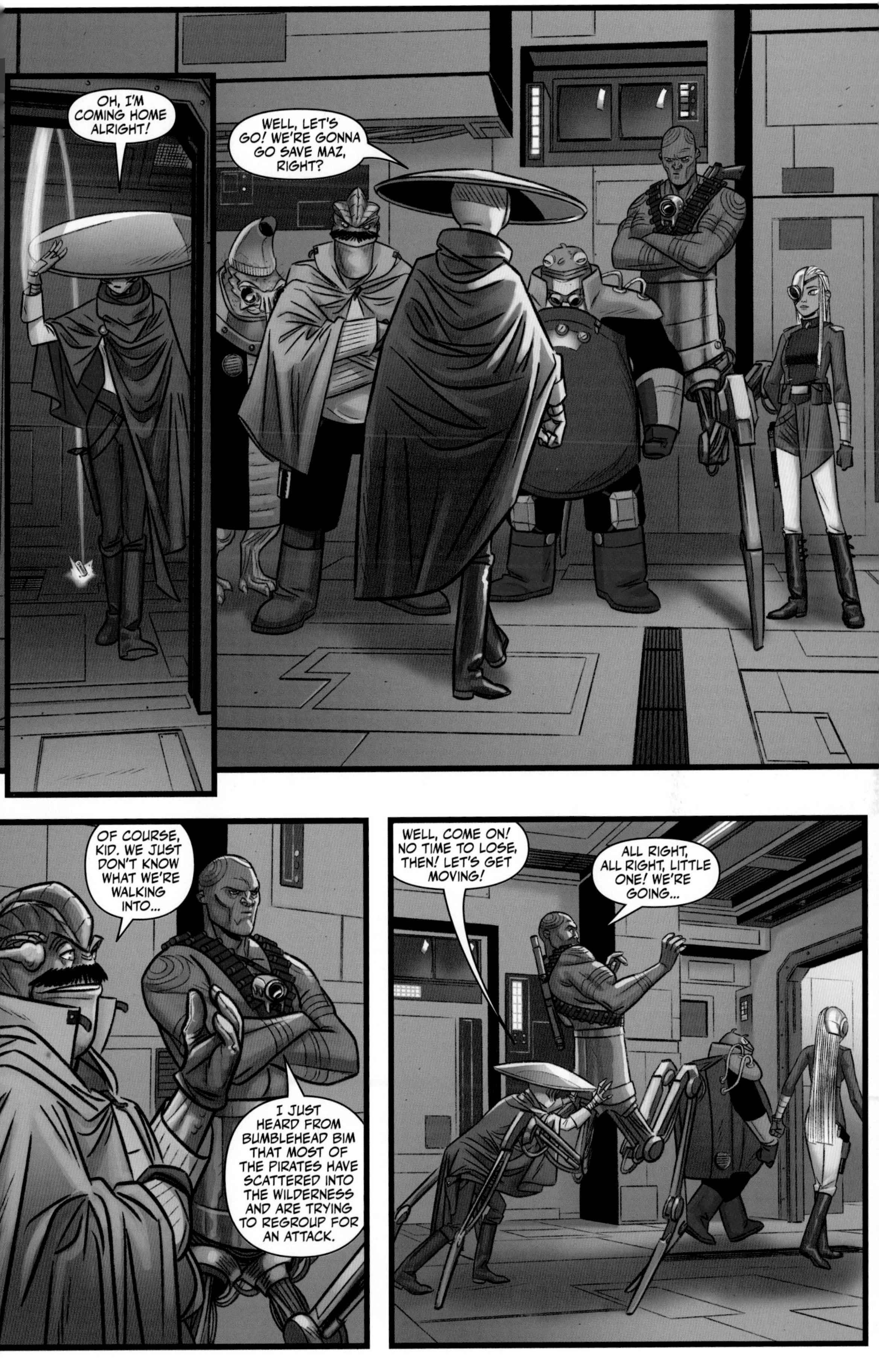
OH, I'M COMING HOME ALRIGHT!
WELL, LET'S GO! WE'RE GONNA GO SAVE MAZ, RIGHT?
OF COURSE, KID. WE JUST DON'T KNOW WHAT WE'RE WALKING INTO...
I JUST HEARD FROM BUMBLEHEAD BIM THAT MOST OF THE PIRATES HAVE SCATTERED INTO THE WILDERNESS AND ARE TRYING TO REGROUP FOR AN ATTACK.
WELL, COME ON! NO TIME TO LOSE, THEN! LET'S GET MOVING!
ALL RIGHT, ALL RIGHT, LITTLE ONE! WE'RE GOING...

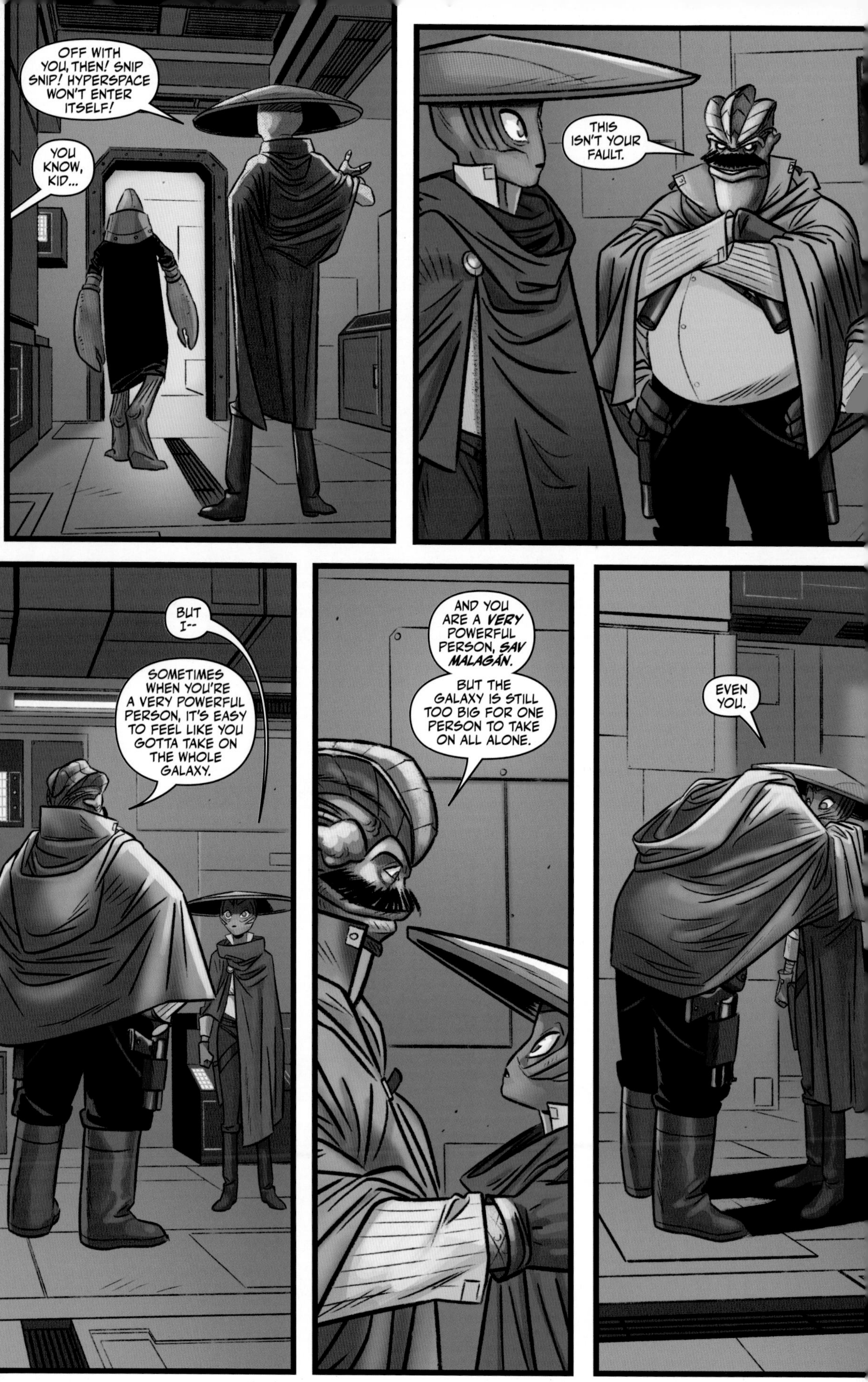
OFF WITH YOU, THEN! SNIP SNIP! HYPERSPACE WON'T ENTER ITSELF!
YOU KNOW, KID...
THIS ISN'T YOUR FAULT.
BUT I--
SOMETIMES WHEN YOU'RE A VERY POWERFUL PERSON, IT'S EASY TO FEEL LIKE YOU GOTTA TAKE ON THE WHOLE GALAXY.
AND YOU ARE A *VERY* POWERFUL PERSON, ***SAV MALAGÁN***.
BUT THE GALAXY IS STILL TOO BIG FOR ONE PERSON TO TAKE ON ALL ALONE.
EVEN YOU.

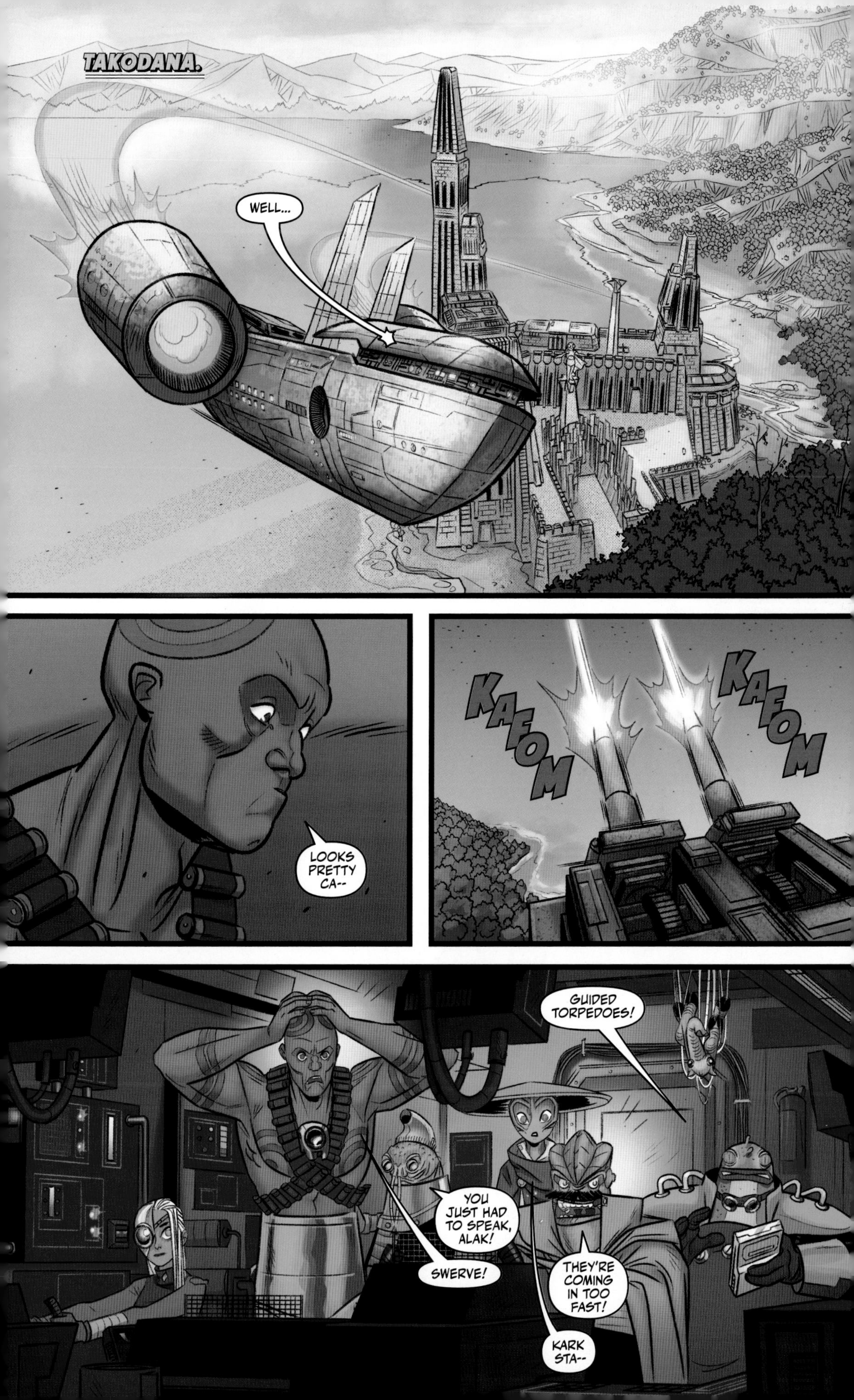
TAKODANA.
WELL...
LOOKS PRETTY CA--
KAFOM
KAFOM
GUIDED TORPEDOES!
YOU JUST HAD TO SPEAK, ALAK!
SWERVE!
THEY'RE COMING IN TOO FAST!
KARK STA--

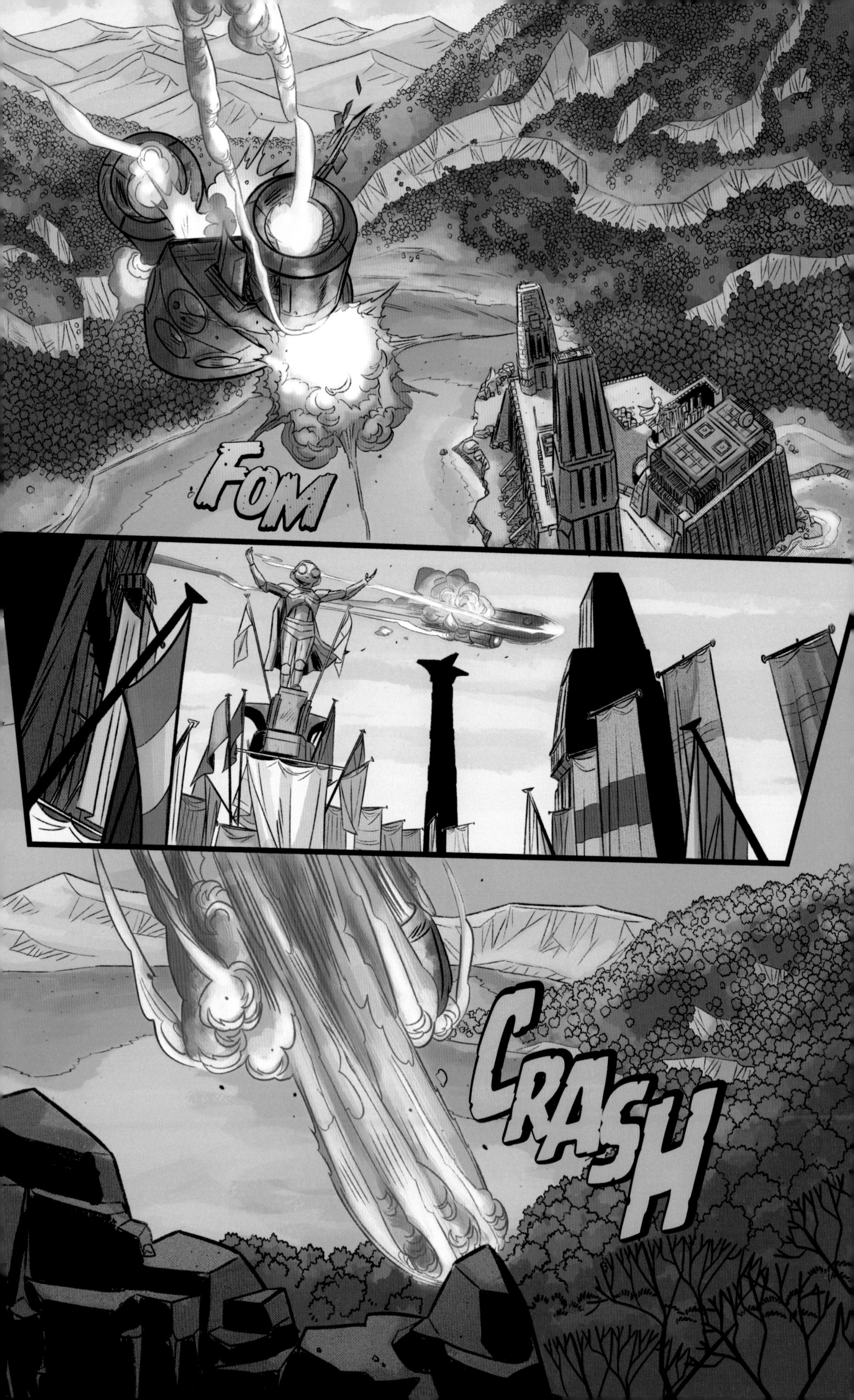
FOM
CRASH

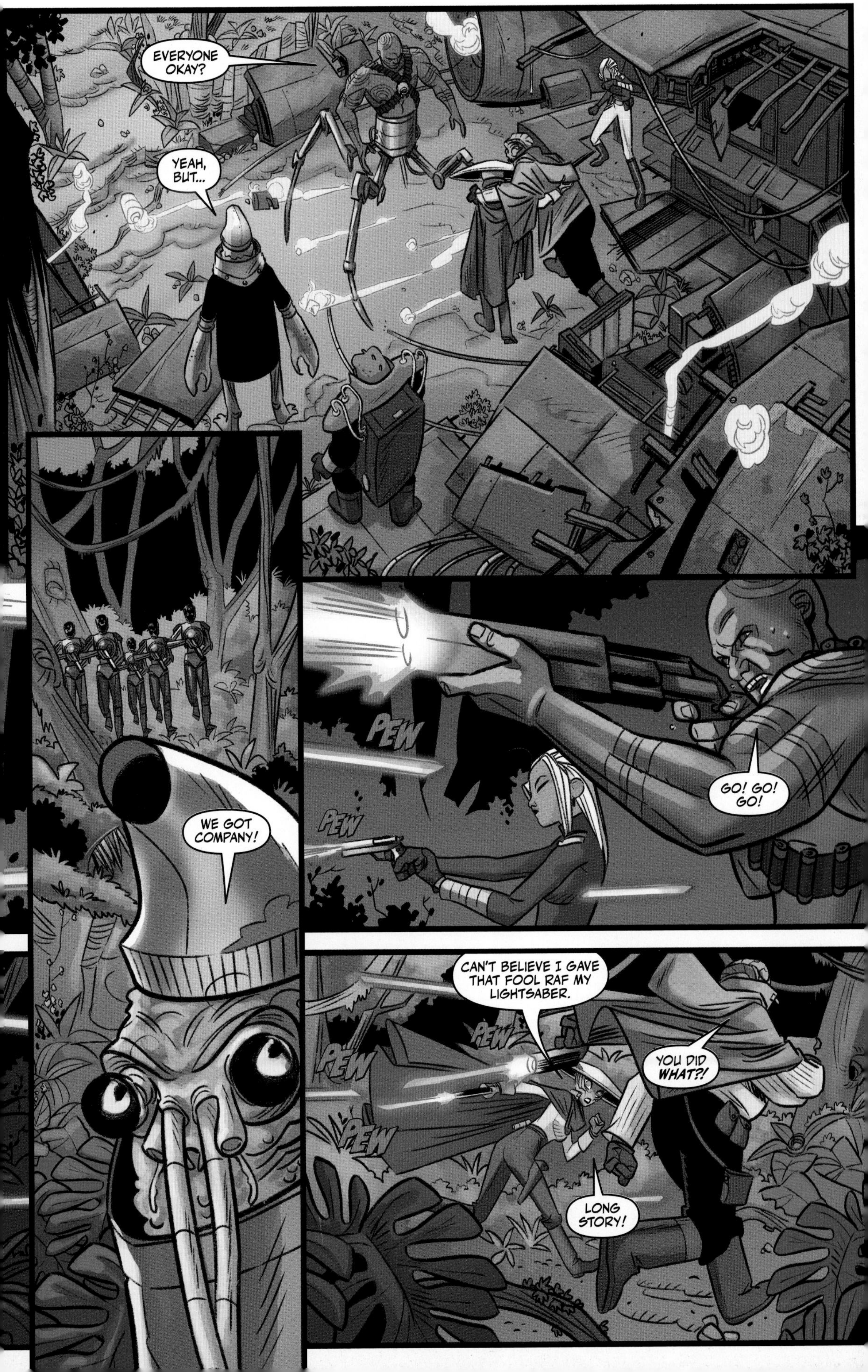
EVERYONE OKAY?
YEAH, BUT...
WE GOT COMPANY!
PEW
PEW
GO! GO! GO!
CAN'T BELIEVE I GAVE THAT FOOL RAF MY LIGHTSABER.
YOU DID WHAT?!
PEW
PEW
PEW
LONG STORY!

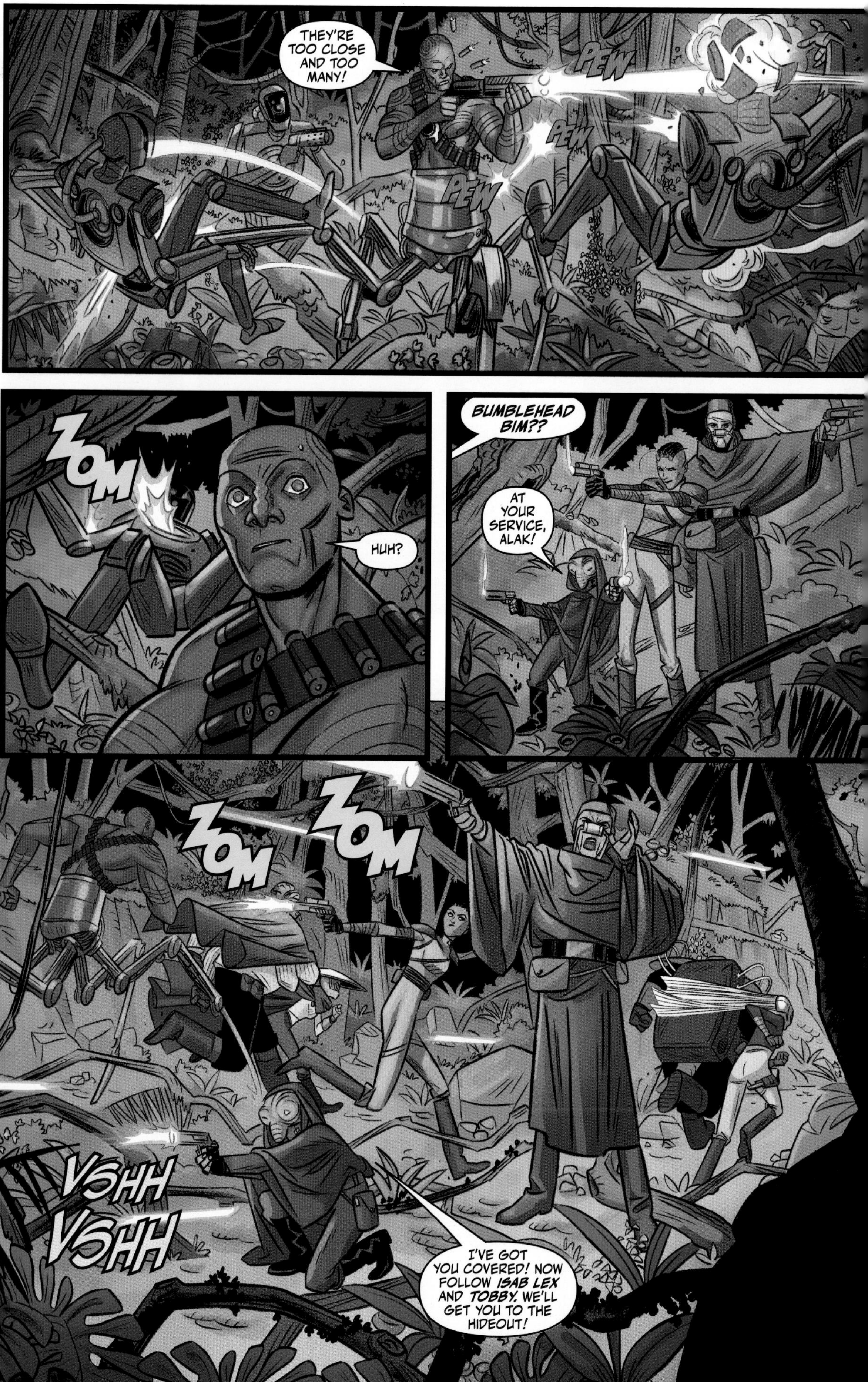
THEY'RE TOO CLOSE AND TOO MANY!
PEW
PEW
PEW
ZOM
HUH?
BUMBLEHEAD BIM??
AT YOUR SERVICE, ALAK!
ZOM
ZOM
VSHH
VSHH
I'VE GOT YOU COVERED! NOW FOLLOW ISAB LEX AND TOBBY. WE'LL GET YOU TO THE HIDEOUT!

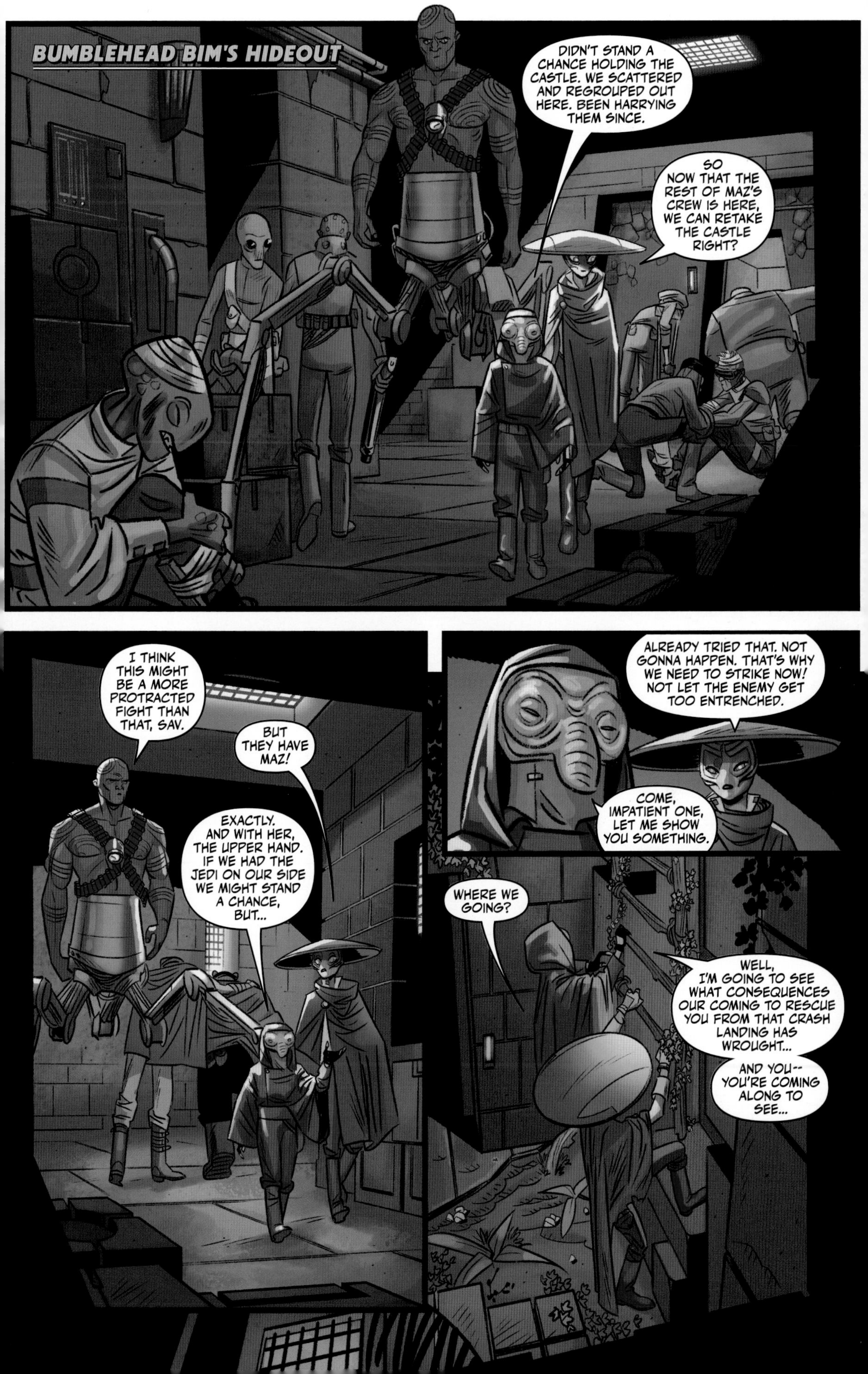
BUMBLEHEAD BIM'S HIDEOUT
DIDN'T STAND A CHANCE HOLDING THE CASTLE. WE SCATTERED AND REGROUPED OUT HERE. BEEN HARRYING THEM SINCE.
SO NOW THAT THE REST OF MAZ'S CREW IS HERE, WE CAN RETAKE THE CASTLE RIGHT?
I THINK THIS MIGHT BE A MORE PROTRACTED FIGHT THAN THAT, SAV.
BUT THEY HAVE MAZ!
EXACTLY. AND WITH HER, THE UPPER HAND. IF WE HAD THE JEDI ON OUR SIDE WE MIGHT STAND A CHANCE, BUT...
ALREADY TRIED THAT. NOT GONNA HAPPEN. THAT'S WHY WE NEED TO STRIKE NOW! NOT LET THE ENEMY GET TOO ENTRENCHED.
COME, IMPATIENT ONE, LET ME SHOW YOU SOMETHING.
WHERE WE GOING?
WELL, I'M GOING TO SEE WHAT CONSEQUENCES OUR COMING TO RESCUE YOU FROM THAT CRASH LANDING HAS WROUGHT...
AND YOU-- YOU'RE COMING ALONG TO SEE...

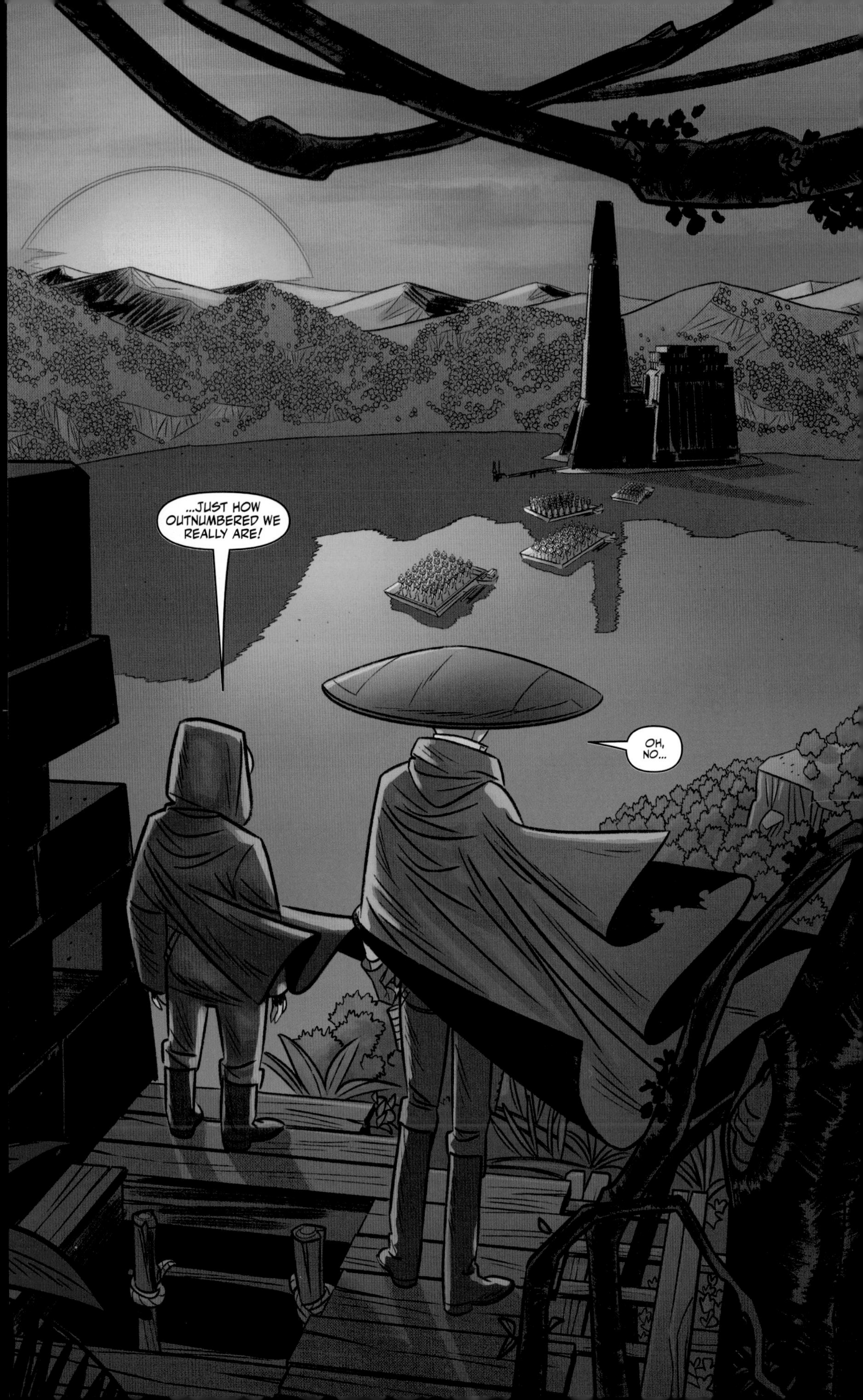
...JUST HOW OUTNUMBERED WE REALLY ARE!
OH, NO...

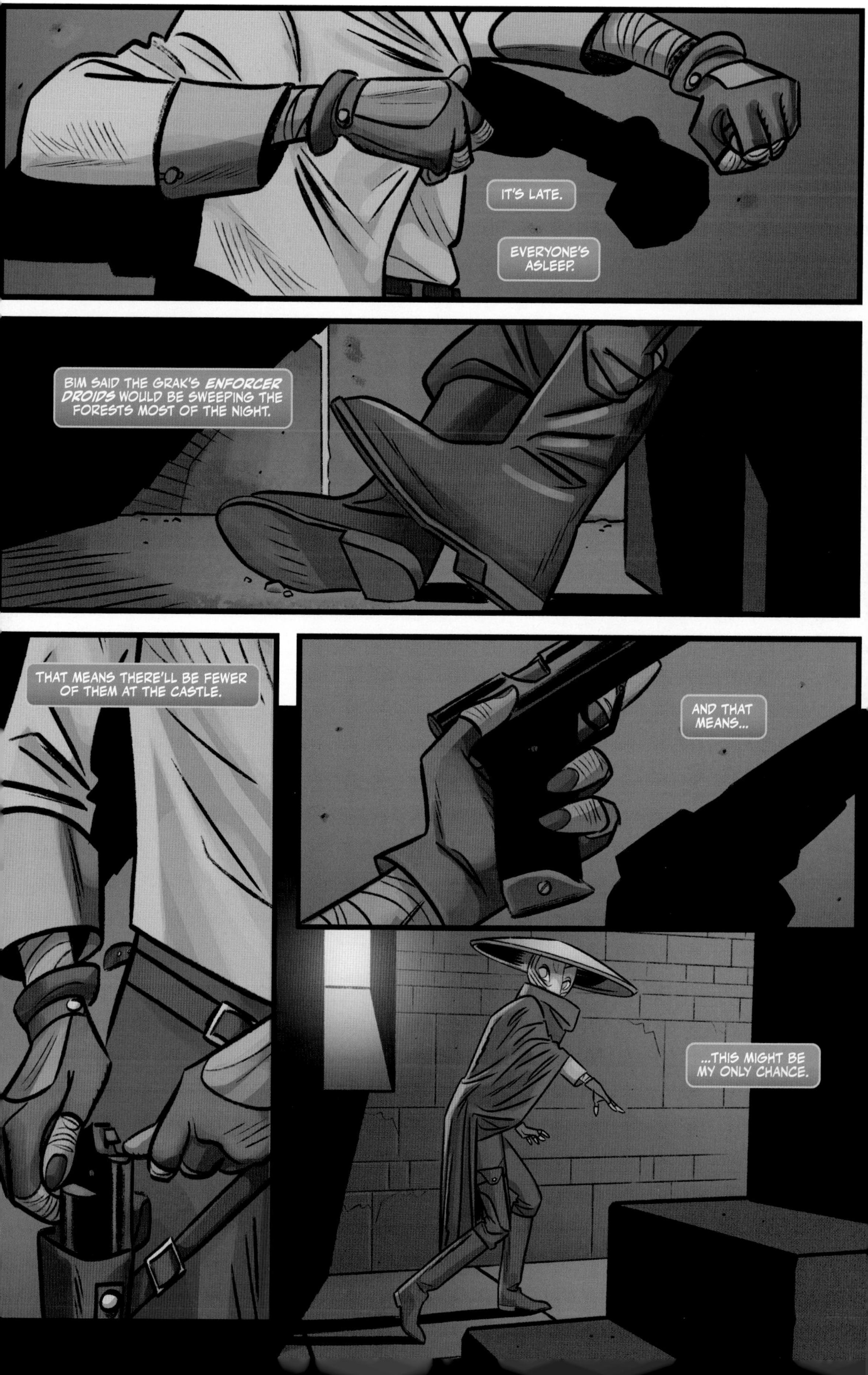
IT'S LATE.
EVERYONE'S ASLEEP.
BIM SAID THE GRAK'S *ENFORCER DROIDS* WOULD BE SWEEPING THE FORESTS MOST OF THE NIGHT.
THAT MEANS THERE'LL BE FEWER OF THEM AT THE CASTLE.
AND THAT MEANS...
...THIS MIGHT BE MY ONLY CHANCE.

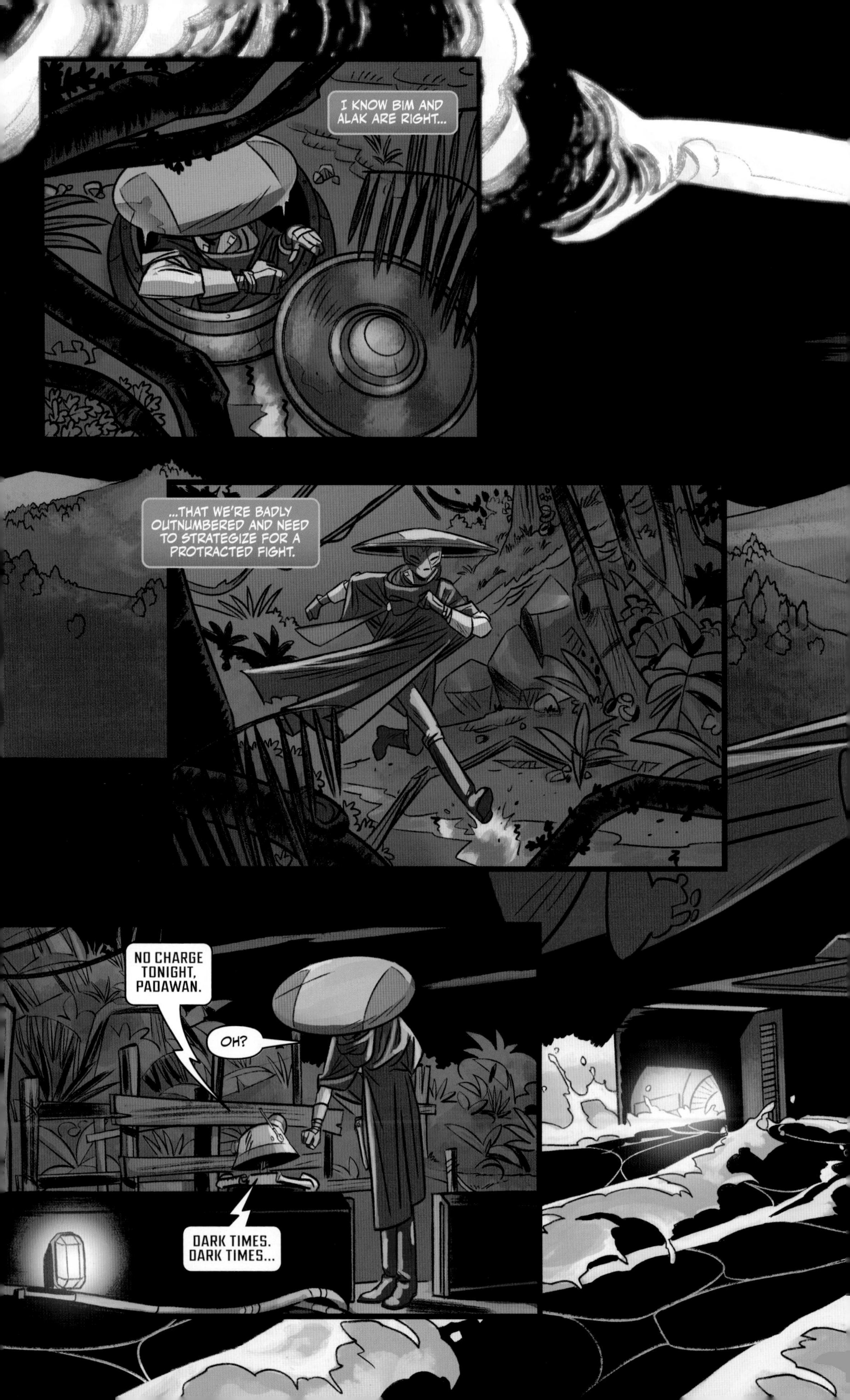
I KNOW BIM AND ALAK ARE RIGHT...
...THAT WE'RE BADLY OUTNUMBERED AND NEED TO STRATEGIZE FOR A PROTRACTED FIGHT.
NO CHARGE TONIGHT, PADAWAN.
OH?
DARK TIMES. DARK TIMES...

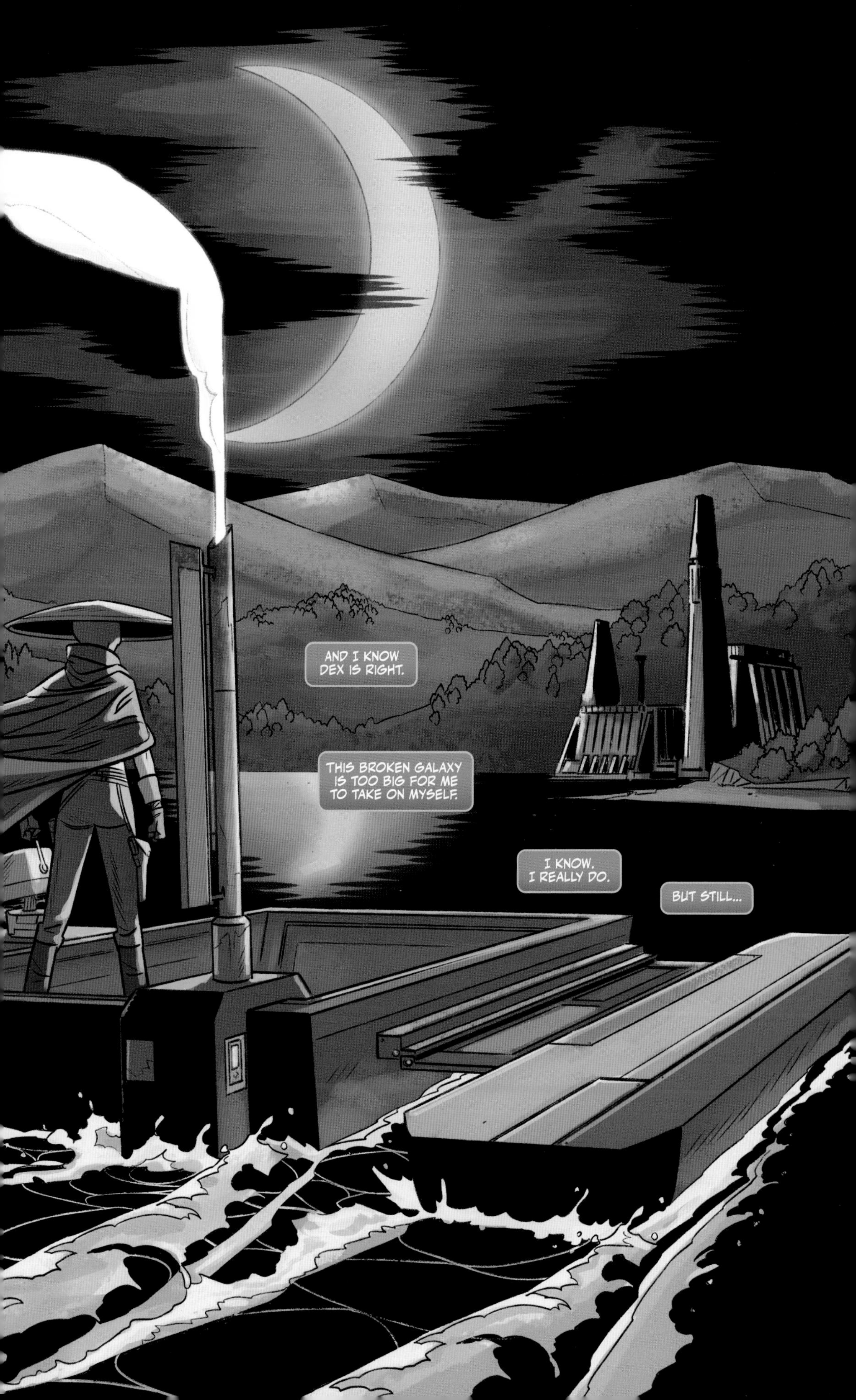
AND I KNOW
DEX IS RIGHT.
THIS BROKEN GALAXY
IS TOO BIG FOR ME
TO TAKE ON MYSELF.
I KNOW.
I REALLY DO.
BUT STILL...

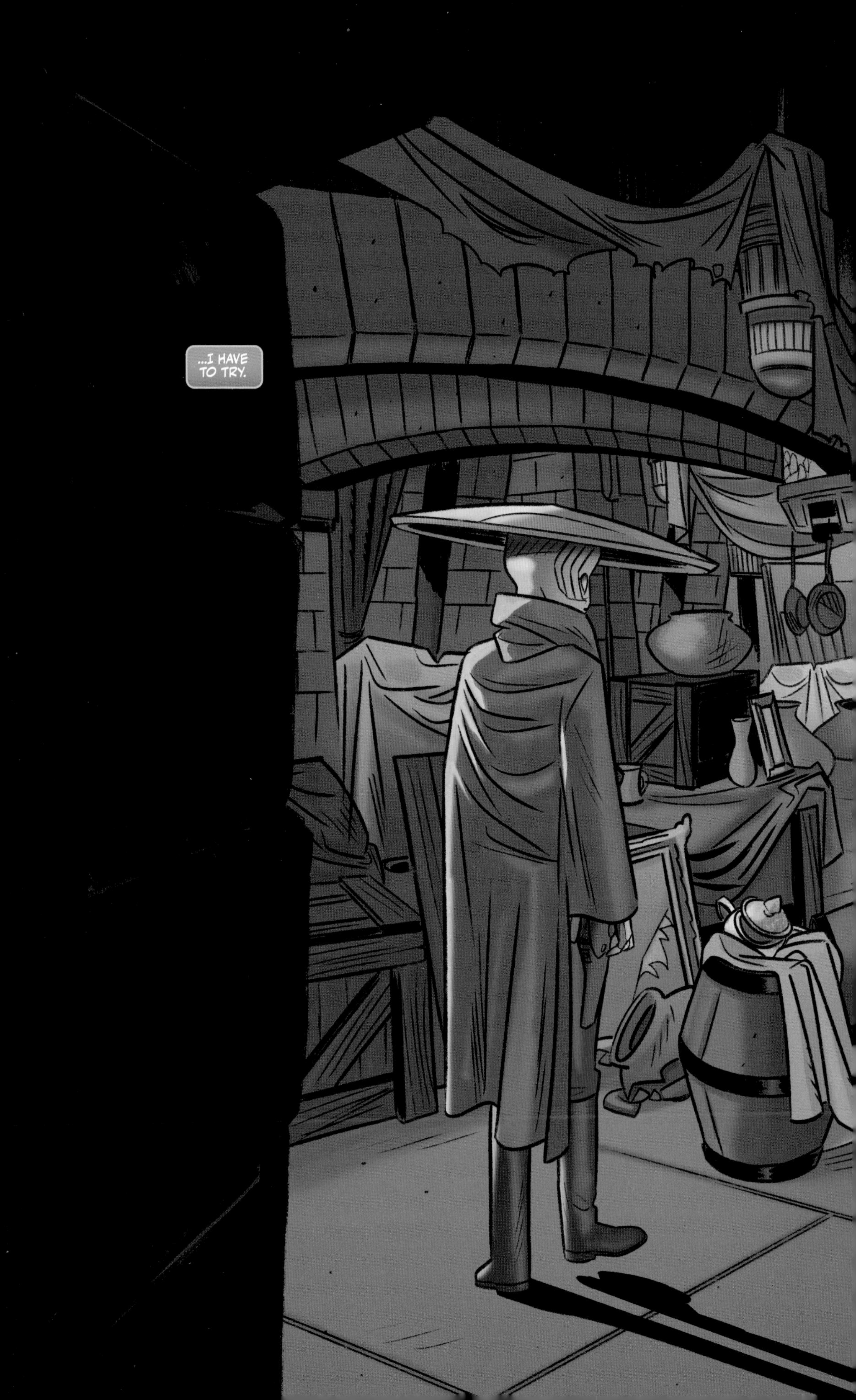
...I HAVE TO TRY.

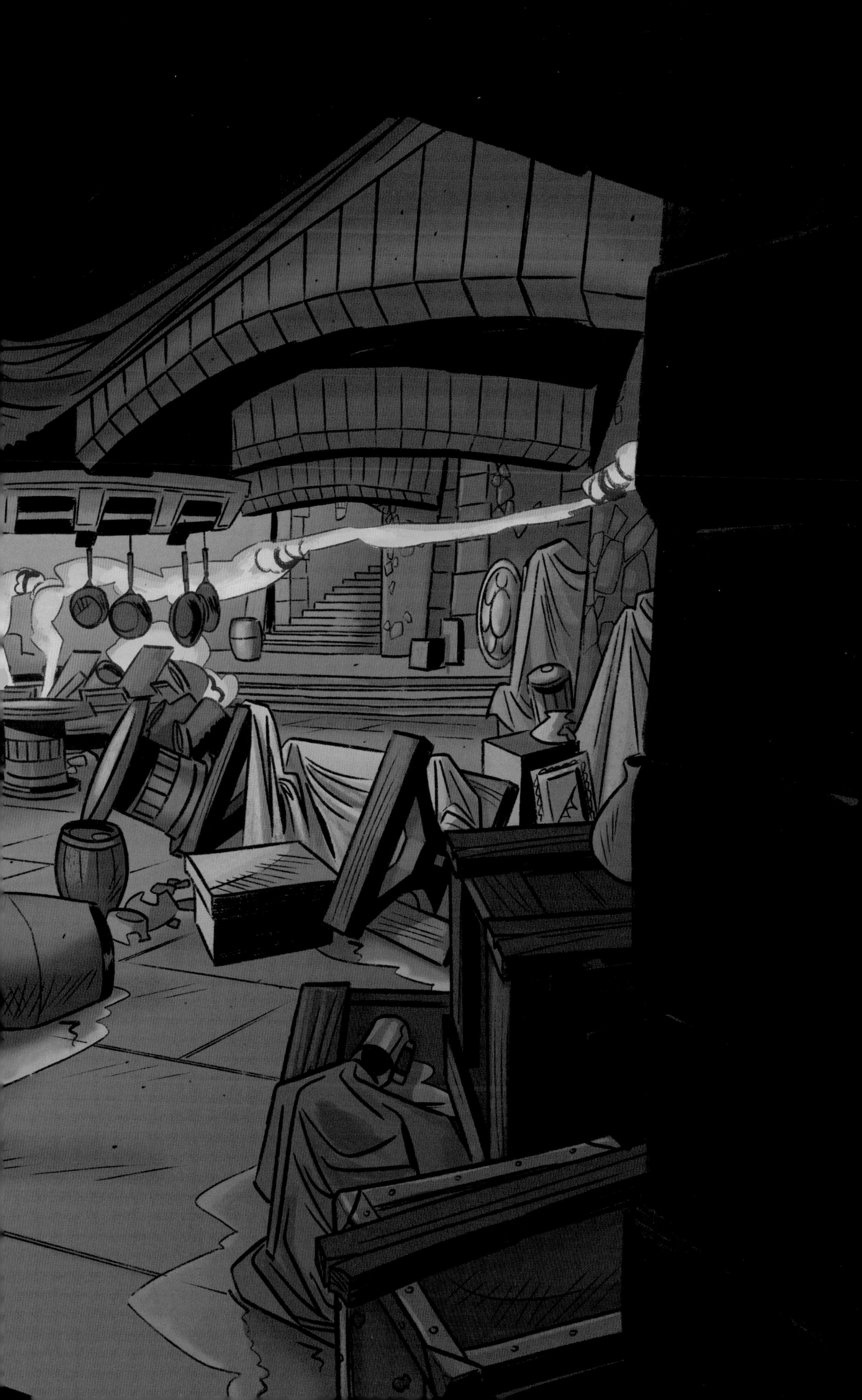

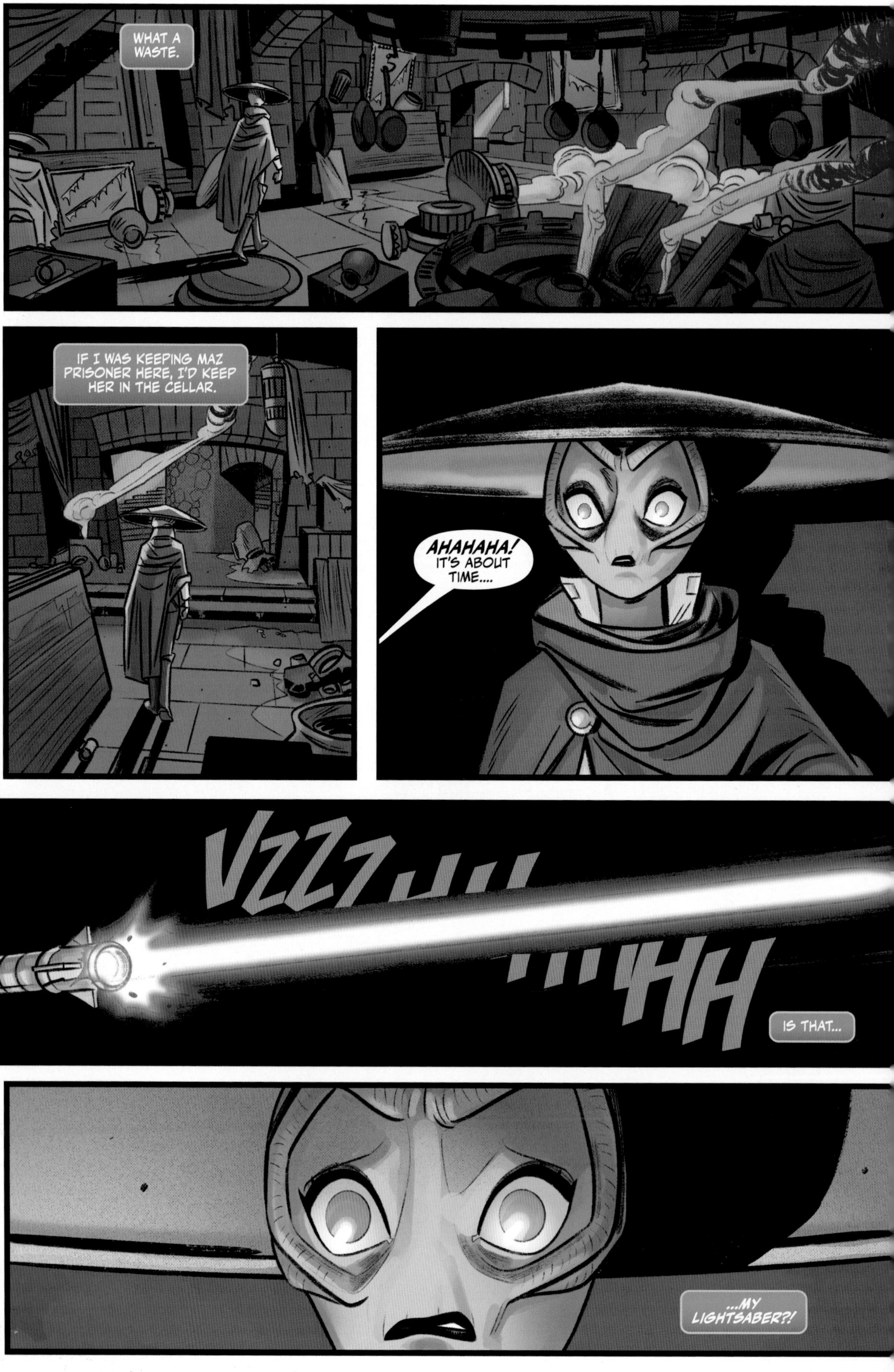
WHAT A WASTE.
IF I WAS KEEPING MAZ PRISONER HERE, I'D KEEP HER IN THE CELLAR.
AHAHAHA! IT'S ABOUT TIME....
VZZZHHHHHH
IS THAT...
...MY LIGHTSABER?!

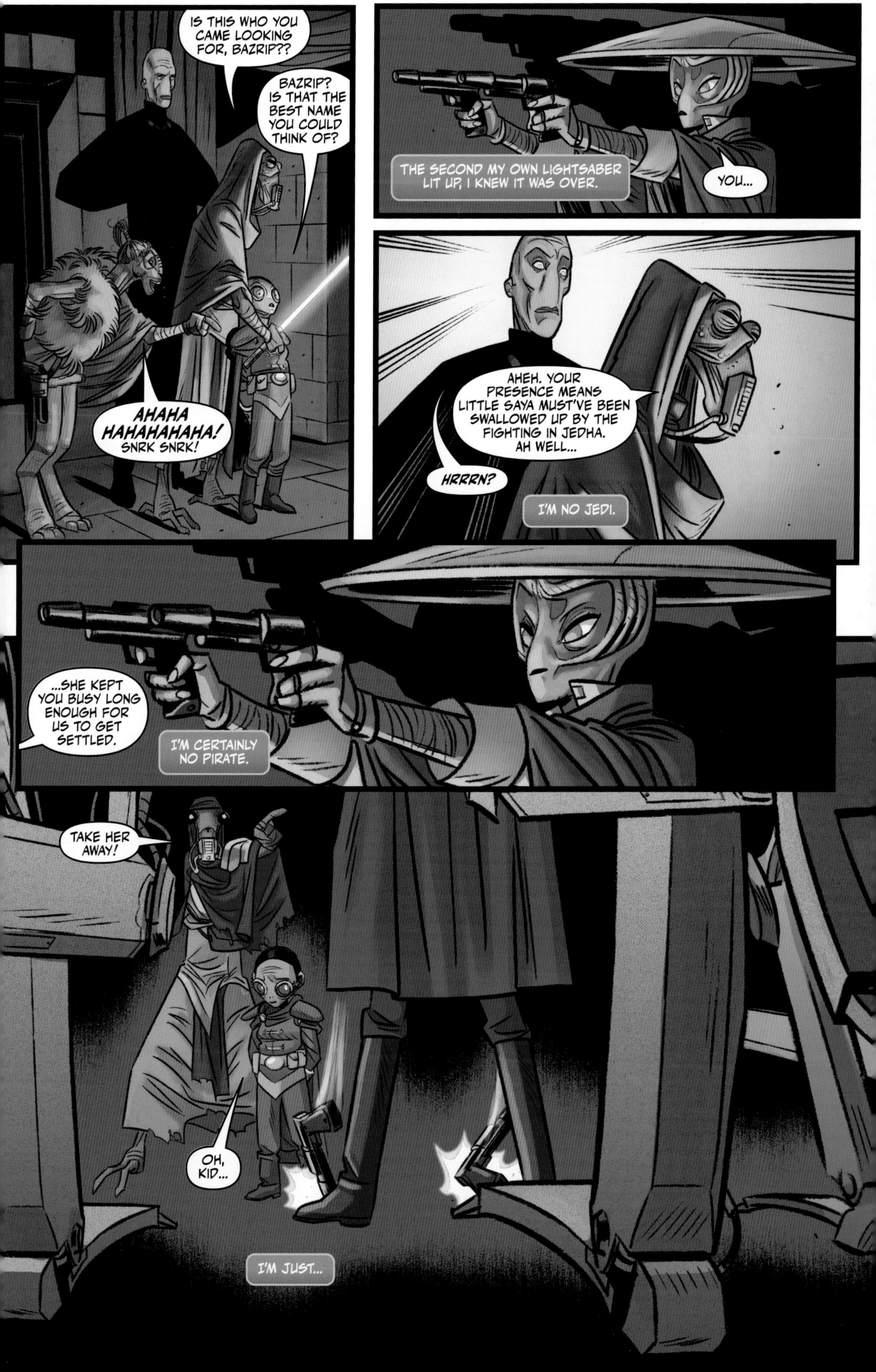
IS THIS WHO YOU CAME LOOKING FOR, BAZRIP??
BAZRIP? IS THAT THE BEST NAME YOU COULD THINK OF?
AHAHA HAHAHAHAHA! SNRK SNRK!
THE SECOND MY OWN LIGHTSABER LIT UP, I KNEW IT WAS OVER.
YOU...
AHEH. YOUR PRESENCE MEANS LITTLE SAYA MUST'VE BEEN SWALLOWED UP BY THE FIGHTING IN JEDHA. AH WELL...
HRRRN?
I'M NO JEDI.
...SHE KEPT YOU BUSY LONG ENOUGH FOR US TO GET SETTLED.
I'M CERTAINLY NO PIRATE.
TAKE HER AWAY!
OH, KID...
I'M JUST...

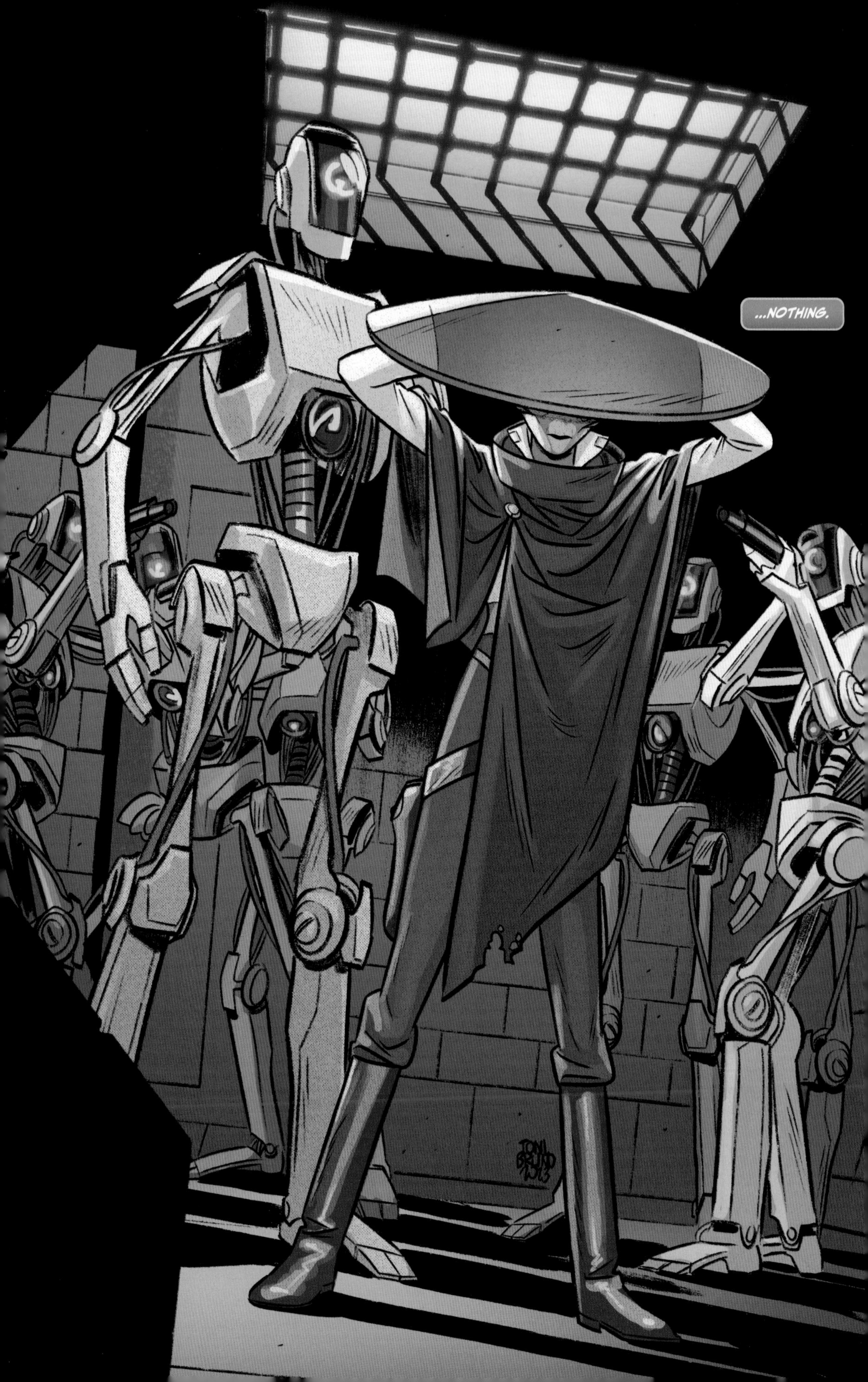
...NOTHING.

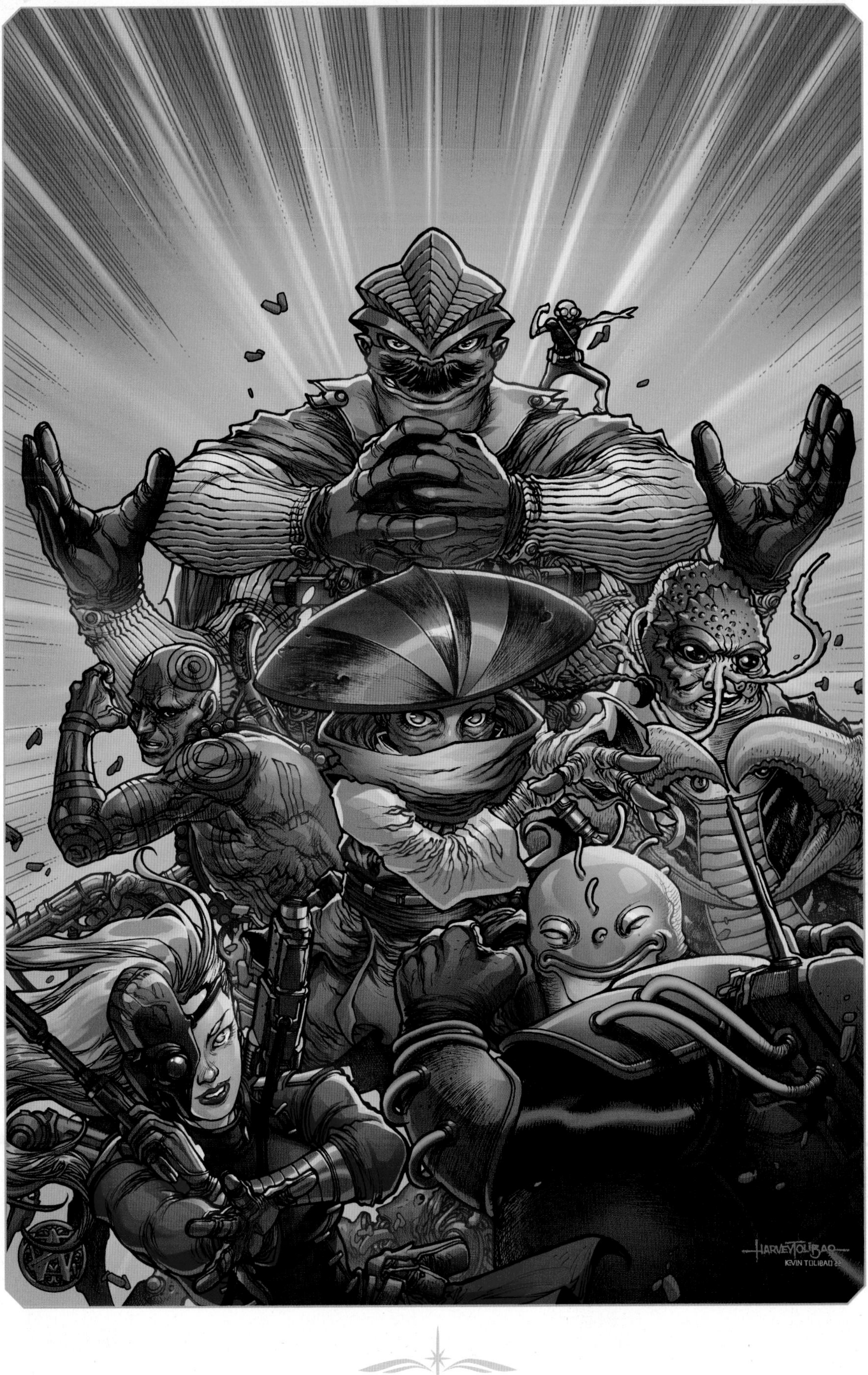

HARVEY TOLIBAO
KEVIN TOLIBAO 22

PART 4: THE BATTLE FOR TAKODANA, PART 2

COVER ART BY HARVEY TOLIBAO WITH KEVIN TOLIBAO

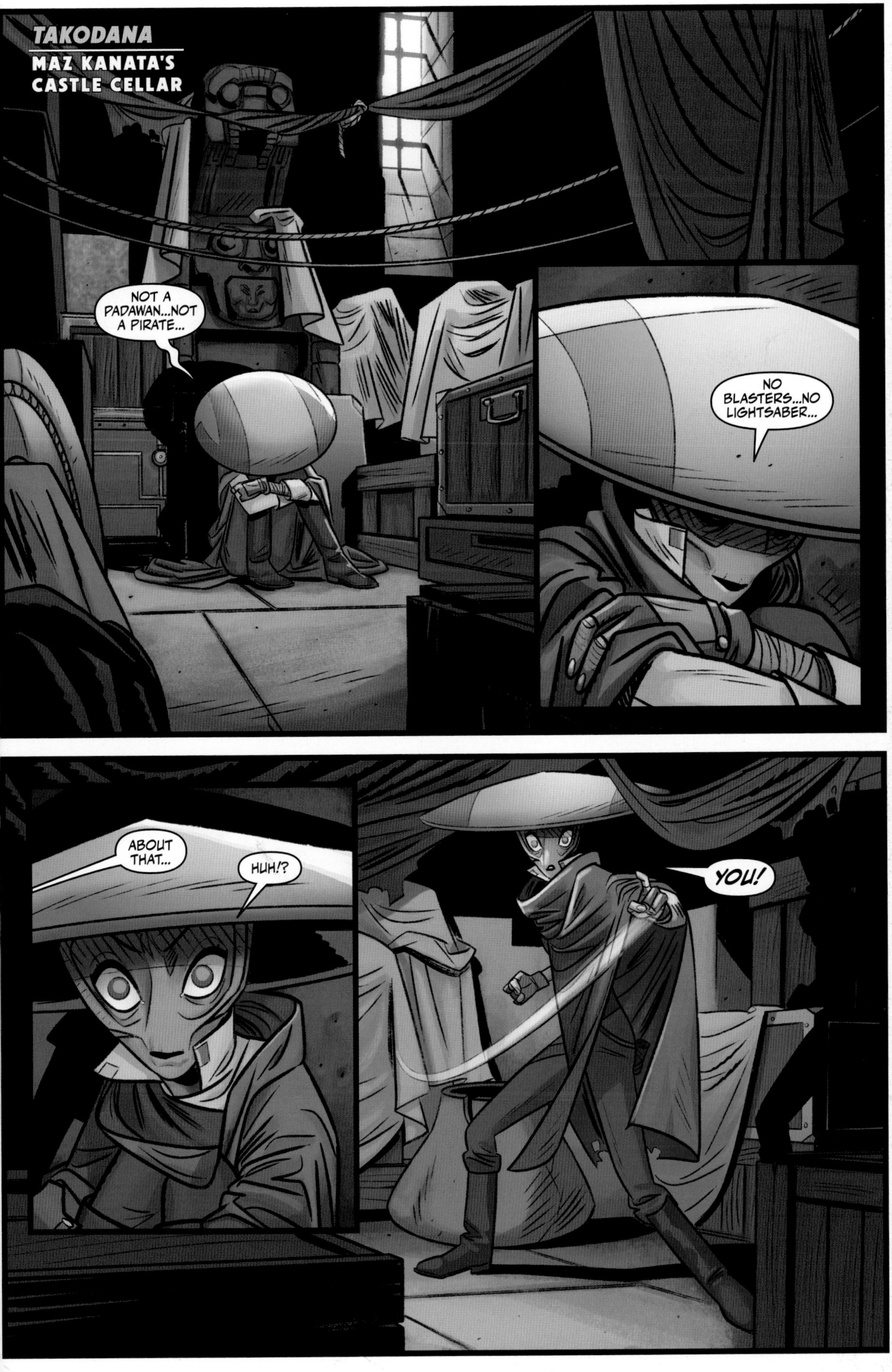
TAKODANA
MAZ KANATA'S CASTLE CELLAR
NOT A PADAWAN...NOT A PIRATE...
NO BLASTERS...NO LIGHTSABER...
ABOUT THAT...
HUH!?
YOU!

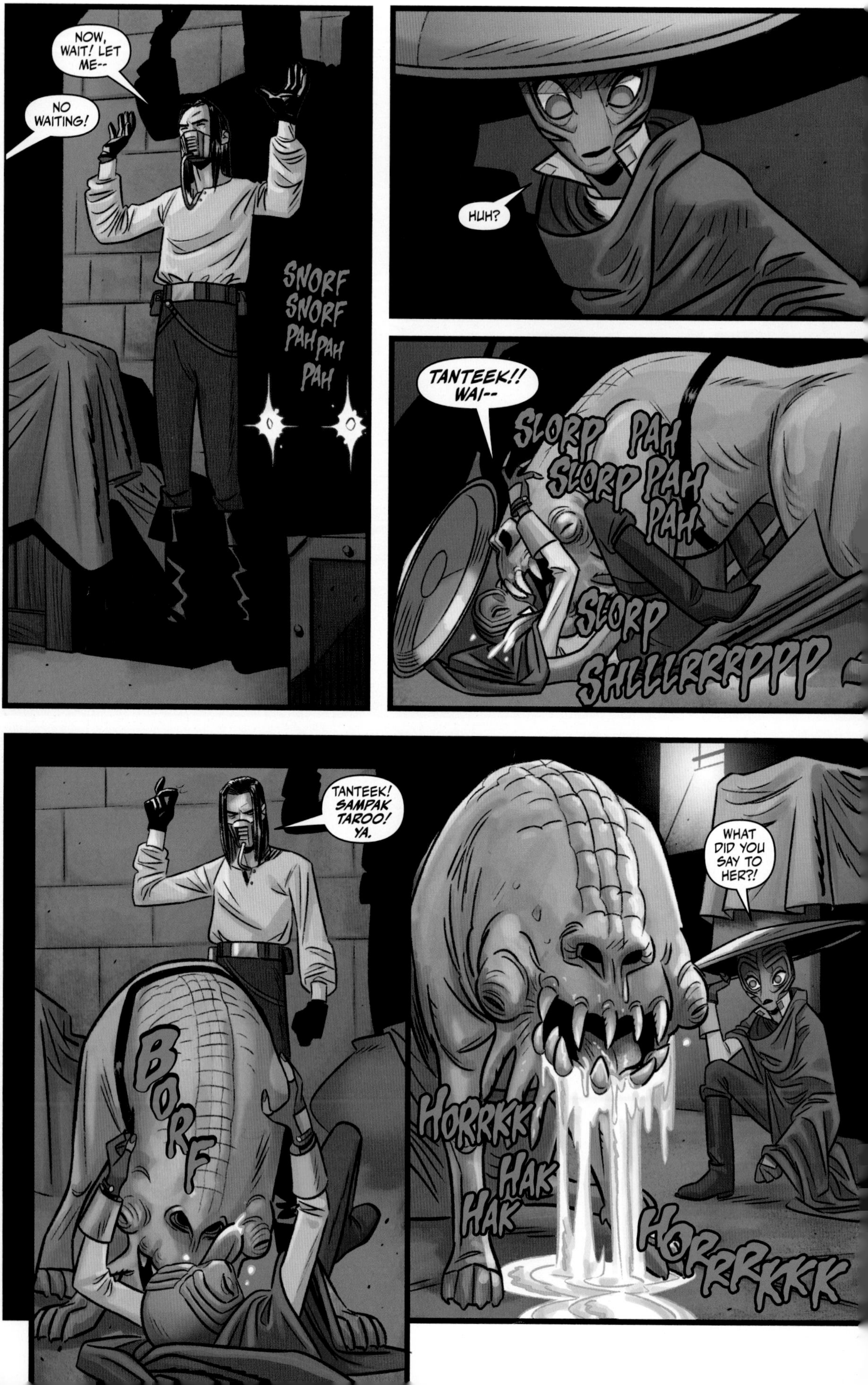

NOW, WAIT! LET ME--
NO WAITING!
SNORF SNORF PAH PAH PAH
HUH?
TANTEEK!! WAI--
SLORP PAH SLORP PAH PAH
SLORP
SHLLLRRRPPP
TANTEEK! SAMPAK TAROO! YA.
BORF
WHAT DID YOU SAY TO HER?!
HORRKK HAK HAK
HORRRKKK

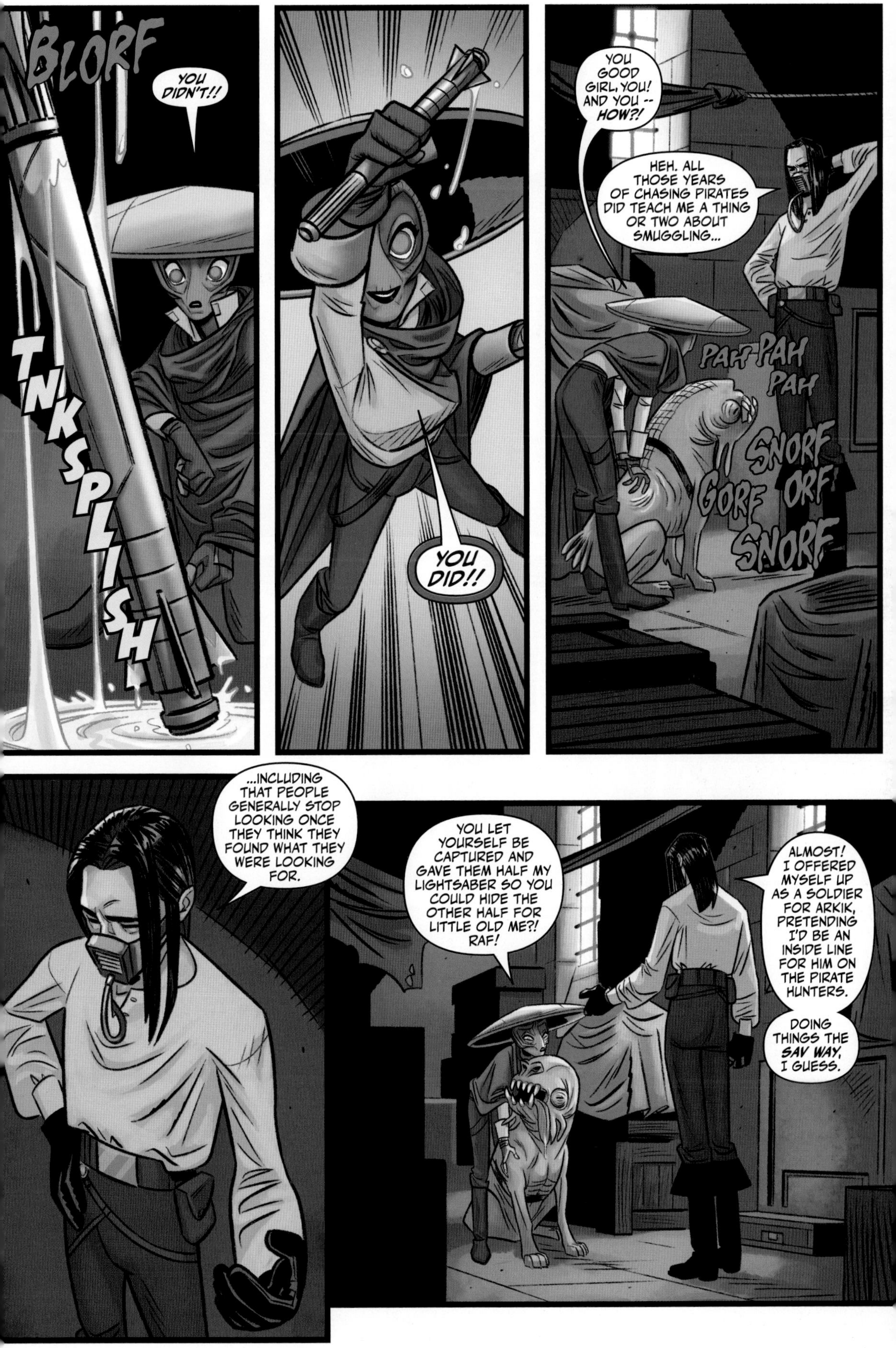
BLORF
YOU DIDN'T!!
TNKSPLISH
YOU DID!!
YOU GOOD GIRL, YOU! AND YOU -- HOW?!
HEH. ALL THOSE YEARS OF CHASING PIRATES DID TEACH ME A THING OR TWO ABOUT SMUGGLING...
PAH PAH PAH
SNORF GORF ORF SNORF
...INCLUDING THAT PEOPLE GENERALLY STOP LOOKING ONCE THEY THINK THEY FOUND WHAT THEY WERE LOOKING FOR.
YOU LET YOURSELF BE CAPTURED AND GAVE THEM HALF MY LIGHTSABER SO YOU COULD HIDE THE OTHER HALF FOR LITTLE OLD ME?! RAF!
ALMOST! I OFFERED MYSELF UP AS A SOLDIER FOR ARKIK, PRETENDING I'D BE AN INSIDE LINE FOR HIM ON THE PIRATE HUNTERS.
DOING THINGS THE SAV WAY, I GUESS.

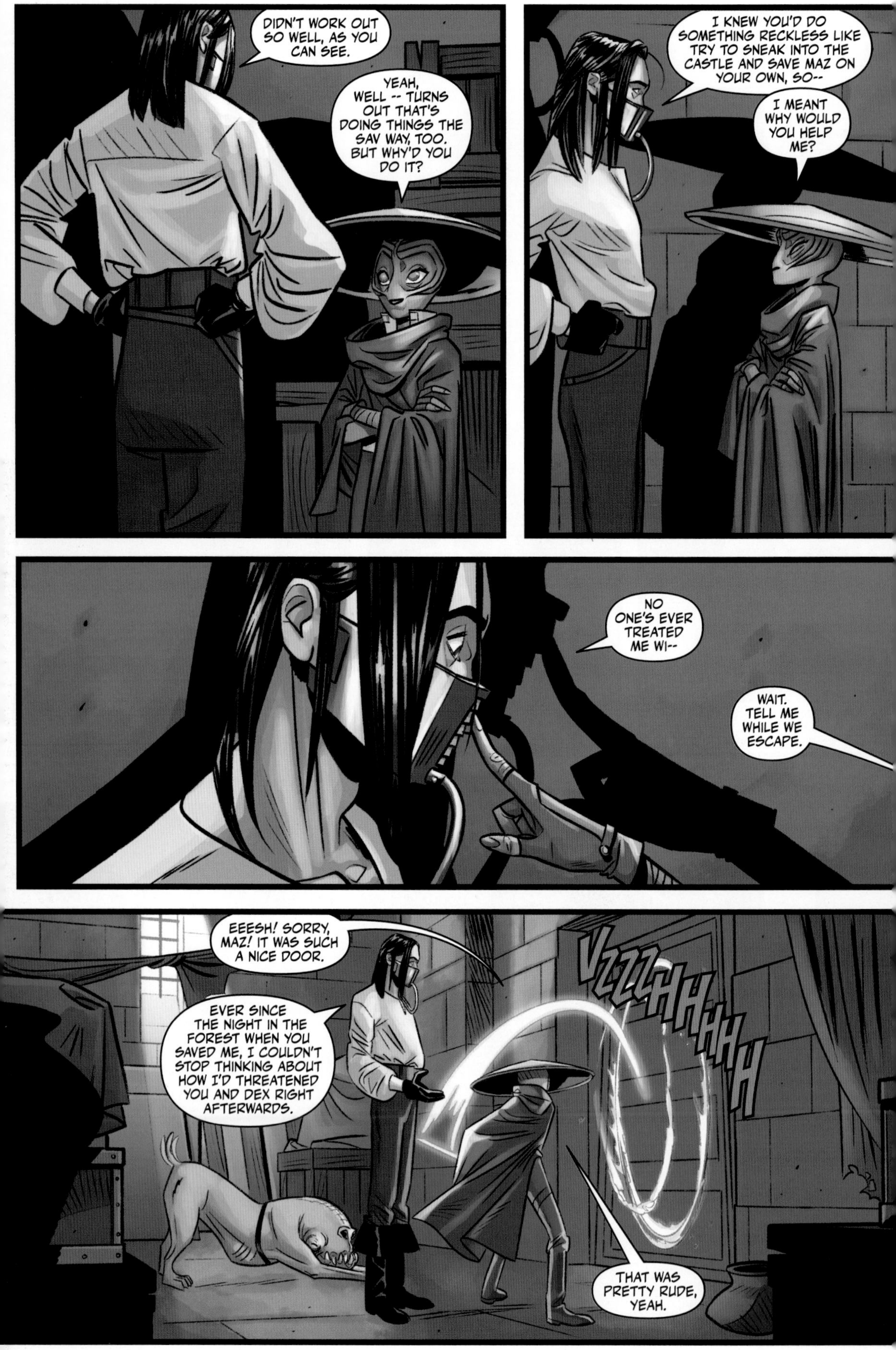
DIDN'T WORK OUT SO WELL, AS YOU CAN SEE.
YEAH, WELL -- TURNS OUT THAT'S DOING THINGS THE SAV WAY, TOO. BUT WHY'D YOU DO IT?
I KNEW YOU'D DO SOMETHING RECKLESS LIKE TRY TO SNEAK INTO THE CASTLE AND SAVE MAZ ON YOUR OWN, SO--
I MEANT WHY WOULD YOU HELP ME?
NO ONE'S EVER TREATED ME WI--
WAIT. TELL ME WHILE WE ESCAPE.
EEESH! SORRY, MAZ! IT WAS SUCH A NICE DOOR.
VZZZHHHHHH
EVER SINCE THE NIGHT IN THE FOREST WHEN YOU SAVED ME, I COULDN'T STOP THINKING ABOUT HOW I'D THREATENED YOU AND DEX RIGHT AFTERWARDS.
THAT WAS PRETTY RUDE, YEAH.

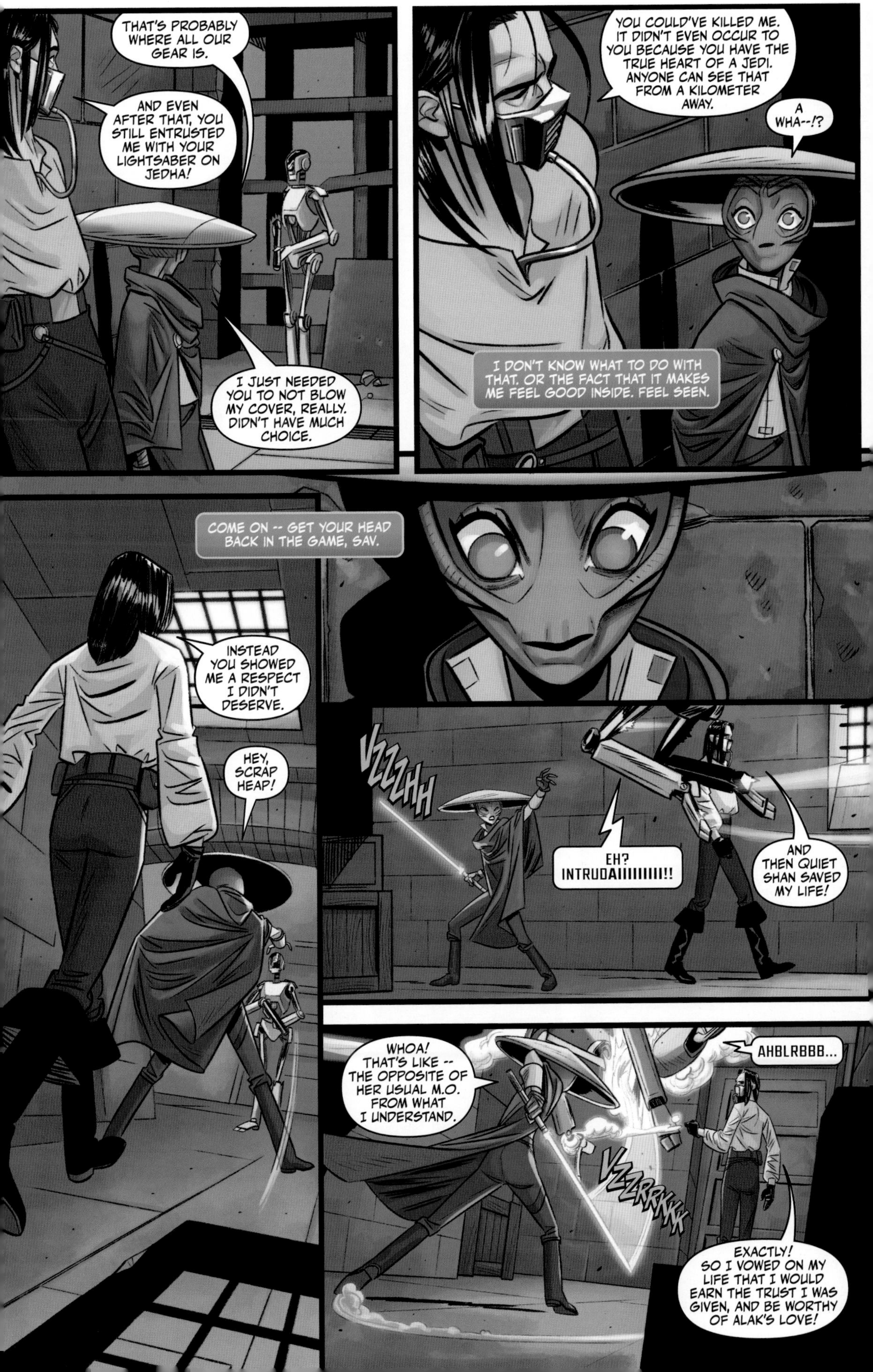
THAT'S PROBABLY WHERE ALL OUR GEAR IS.
AND EVEN AFTER THAT, YOU STILL ENTRUSTED ME WITH YOUR LIGHTSABER ON JEDHA!
I JUST NEEDED YOU TO NOT BLOW MY COVER, REALLY. DIDN'T HAVE MUCH CHOICE.
YOU COULD'VE KILLED ME. IT DIDN'T EVEN OCCUR TO YOU BECAUSE YOU HAVE THE TRUE HEART OF A JEDI. ANYONE CAN SEE THAT FROM A KILOMETER AWAY.
A WHA--!?
I DON'T KNOW WHAT TO DO WITH THAT. OR THE FACT THAT IT MAKES ME FEEL GOOD INSIDE. FEEL SEEN.
COME ON -- GET YOUR HEAD BACK IN THE GAME, SAV.
INSTEAD YOU SHOWED ME A RESPECT I DIDN'T DESERVE.
HEY, SCRAP HEAP!
VZZZHH
EH? INTRUDAIIIIIIIIII!!
AND THEN QUIET SHAN SAVED MY LIFE!
WHOA! THAT'S LIKE -- THE OPPOSITE OF HER USUAL M.O. FROM WHAT I UNDERSTAND.
AHBLRBBB...
VZZRRKKK
EXACTLY! SO I VOWED ON MY LIFE THAT I WOULD EARN THE TRUST I WAS GIVEN, AND BE WORTHY OF ALAK'S LOVE!

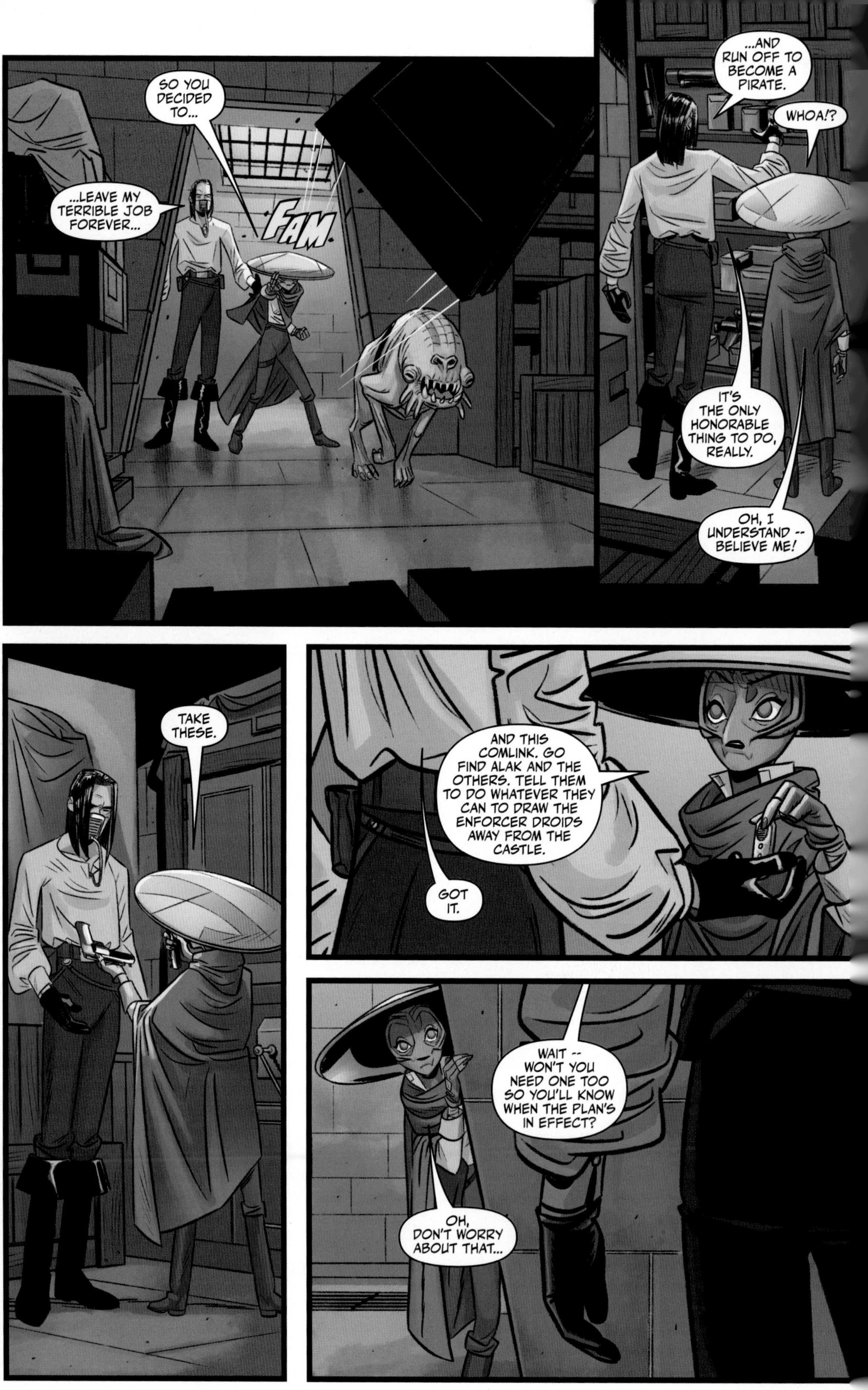

SO YOU DECIDED TO...
...LEAVE MY TERRIBLE JOB FOREVER...
FAM
...AND RUN OFF TO BECOME A PIRATE.
WHOA!?
IT'S THE ONLY HONORABLE THING TO DO, REALLY.
OH, I UNDERSTAND -- BELIEVE ME!
TAKE THESE.
AND THIS COMLINK. GO FIND ALAK AND THE OTHERS. TELL THEM TO DO WHATEVER THEY CAN TO DRAW THE ENFORCER DROIDS AWAY FROM THE CASTLE.
GOT IT.
WAIT -- WON'T YOU NEED ONE TOO SO YOU'LL KNOW WHEN THE PLAN'S IN EFFECT?
OH, DON'T WORRY ABOUT THAT...

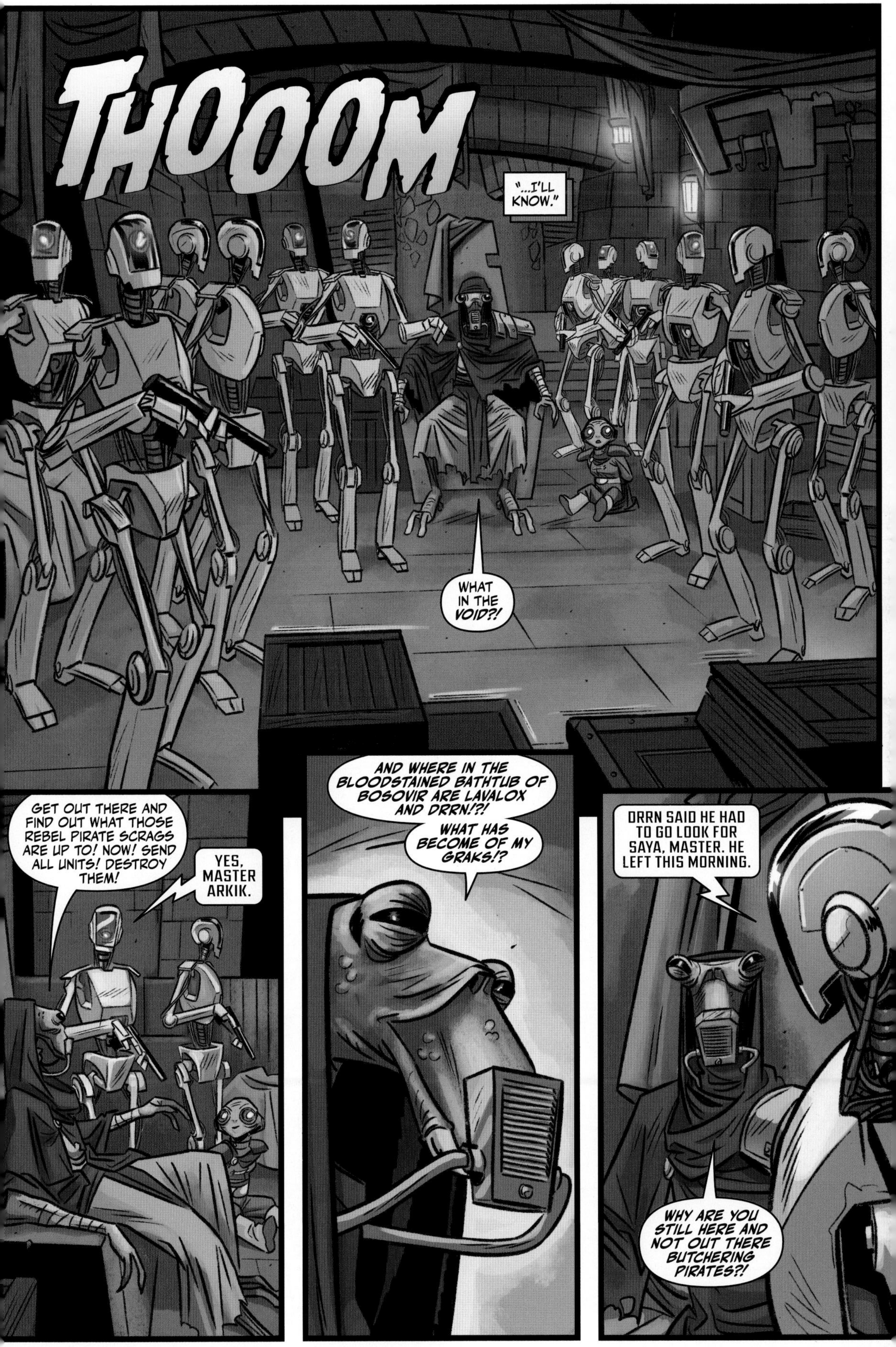
THOOOM
"...I'LL KNOW."
WHAT IN THE VOID?!
GET OUT THERE AND FIND OUT WHAT THOSE REBEL PIRATE SCRAGS ARE UP TO! NOW! SEND ALL UNITS! DESTROY THEM!
YES, MASTER ARKIK.
AND WHERE IN THE BLOODSTAINED BATHTUB OF BOSOVIR ARE LAVALOX AND DRRN!?!
WHAT HAS BECOME OF MY GRAKS!?
DRRN SAID HE HAD TO GO LOOK FOR SAYA, MASTER. HE LEFT THIS MORNING.
WHY ARE YOU STILL HERE AND NOT OUT THERE BUTCHERING PIRATES?!

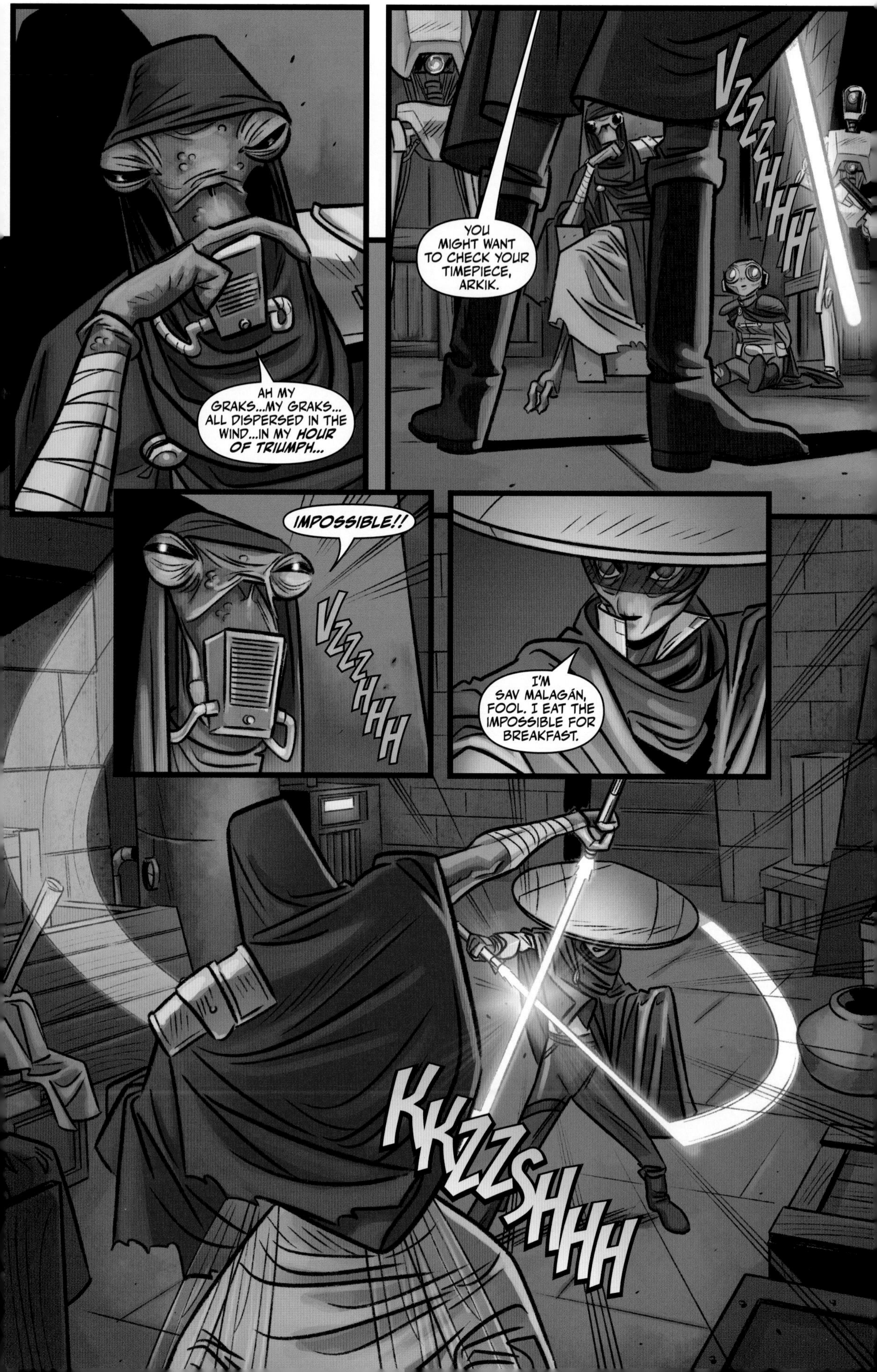
AH MY GRAKS...MY GRAKS... ALL DISPERSED IN THE WIND...IN MY *HOUR OF TRIUMPH...*
YOU MIGHT WANT TO CHECK YOUR TIMEPIECE, ARKIK.
VZZZHHHH
IMPOSSIBLE!!
VZZZHHHH
I'M SAV MALAGÁN, FOOL. I EAT THE IMPOSSIBLE FOR BREAKFAST.
KKZZSHHHH

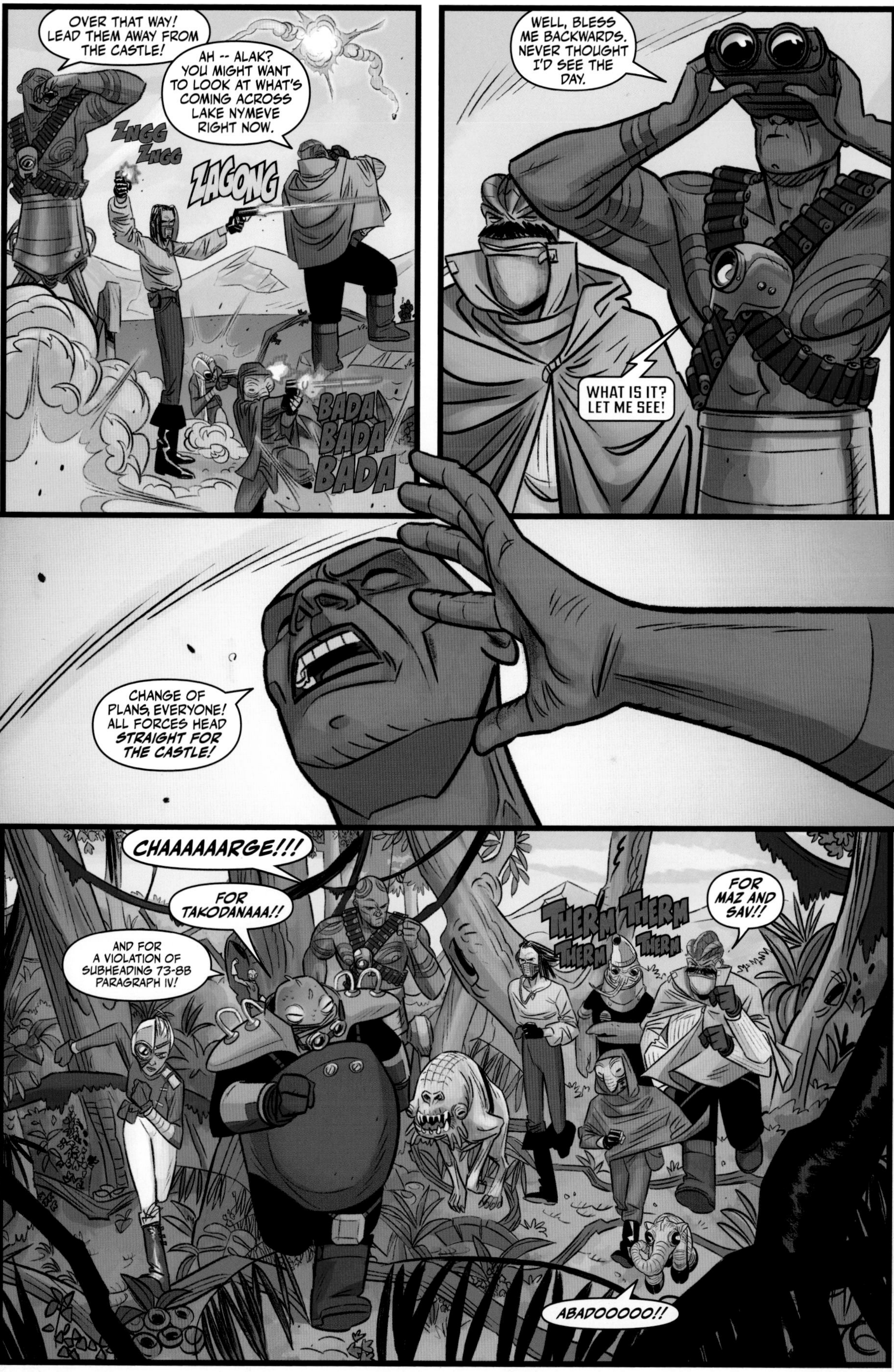
OVER THAT WAY! LEAD THEM AWAY FROM THE CASTLE!
AH -- ALAK? YOU MIGHT WANT TO LOOK AT WHAT'S COMING ACROSS LAKE NYMEVE RIGHT NOW.
ZNGG ZNGG
ZAGONG
BADA BADA BADA
WELL, BLESS ME BACKWARDS. NEVER THOUGHT I'D SEE THE DAY.
WHAT IS IT? LET ME SEE!
CHANGE OF PLANS, EVERYONE! ALL FORCES HEAD STRAIGHT FOR THE CASTLE!
CHAAAAAARGE!!!
FOR TAKODANAAA!!
AND FOR A VIOLATION OF SUBHEADING 73-8B PARAGRAPH IV!
THERM THERM THERM THERM
FOR MAZ AND SAV!!
ABADOOOOO!!

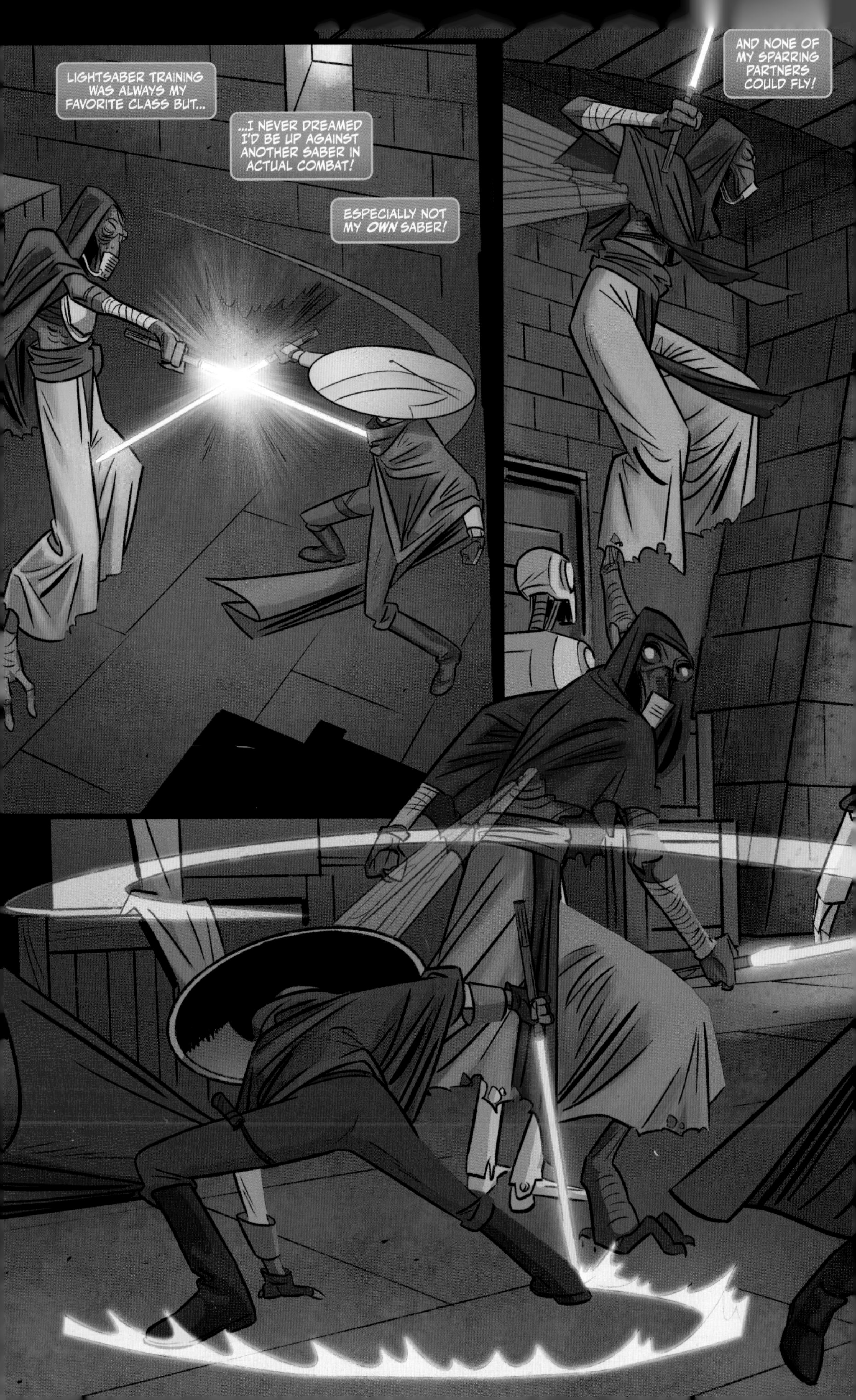
LIGHTSABER TRAINING WAS ALWAYS MY FAVORITE CLASS BUT...
...I NEVER DREAMED I'D BE UP AGAINST ANOTHER SABER IN ACTUAL COMBAT!
ESPECIALLY NOT MY *OWN* SABER!
AND NONE OF MY SPARRING PARTNERS COULD FLY!

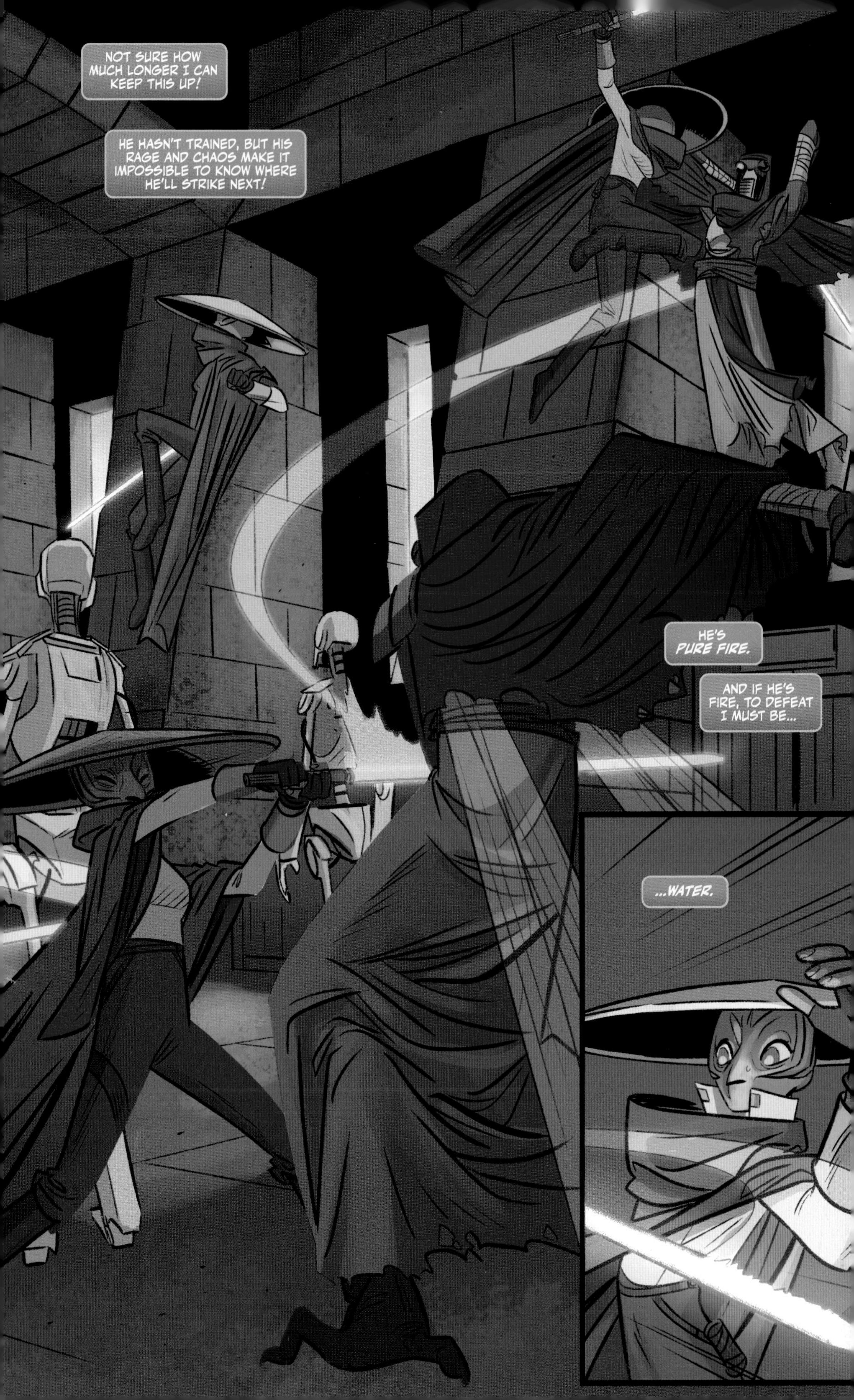
NOT SURE HOW MUCH LONGER I CAN KEEP THIS UP!
HE HASN'T TRAINED, BUT HIS RAGE AND CHAOS MAKE IT IMPOSSIBLE TO KNOW WHERE HE'LL STRIKE NEXT!
HE'S *PURE FIRE.*
AND IF HE'S FIRE, TO DEFEAT I MUST BE...
...WATER.

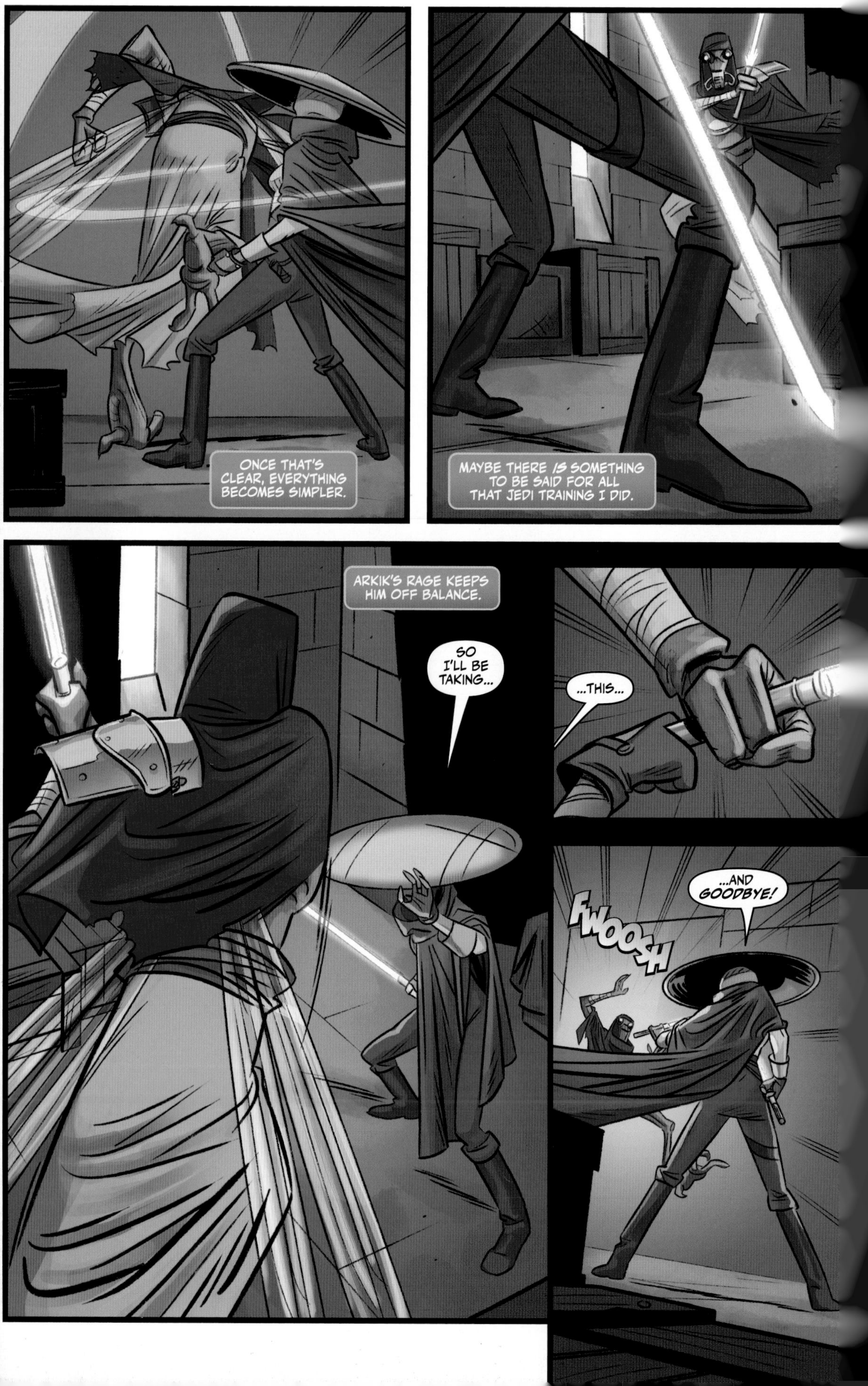
ONCE THAT'S CLEAR, EVERYTHING BECOMES SIMPLER.
MAYBE THERE IS SOMETHING TO BE SAID FOR ALL THAT JEDI TRAINING I DID.
ARKIK'S RAGE KEEPS HIM OFF BALANCE.
SO I'LL BE TAKING...
...THIS...
FWOOSH
...AND GOODBYE!

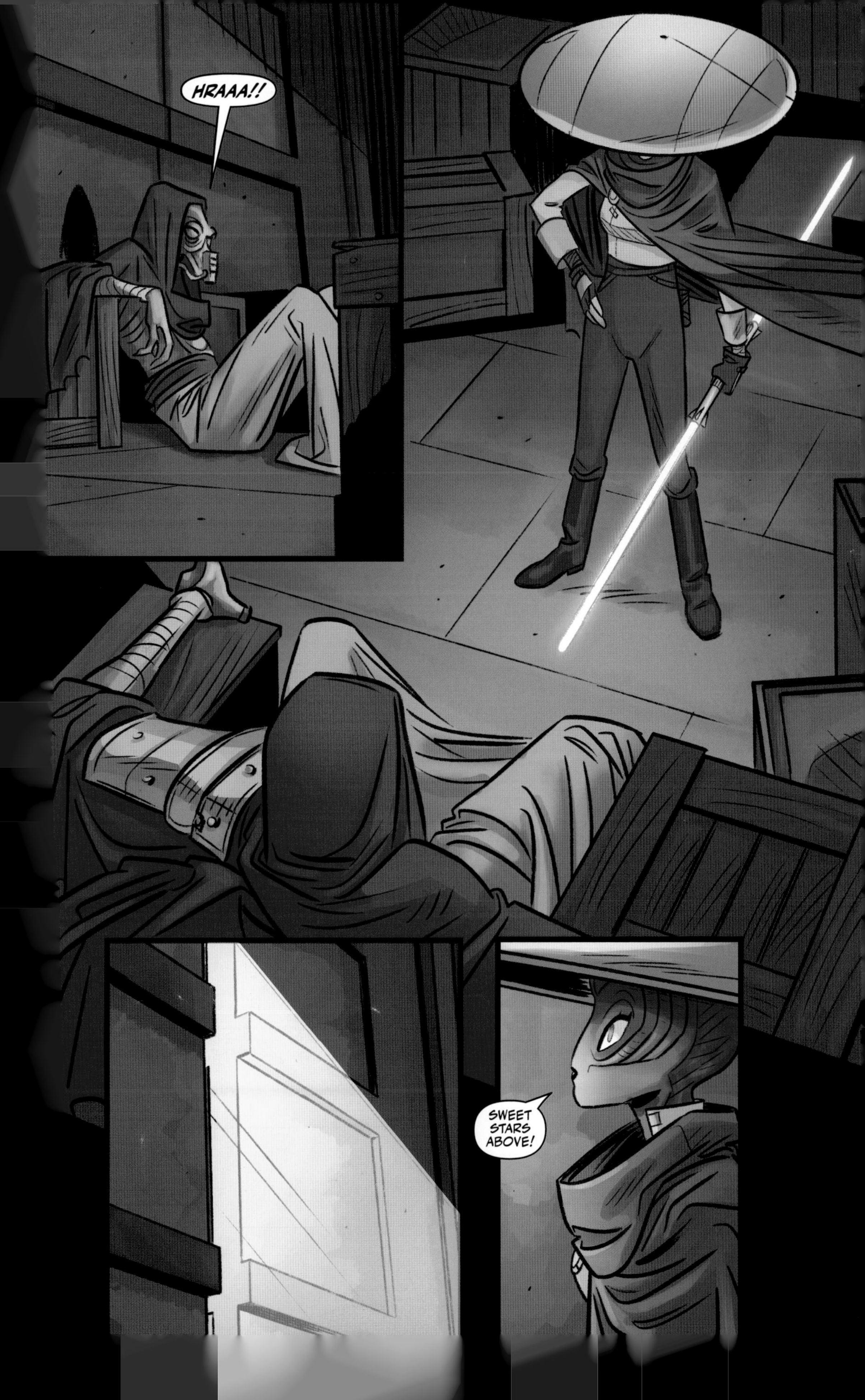
HRAAA!!
SWEET STARS ABOVE!

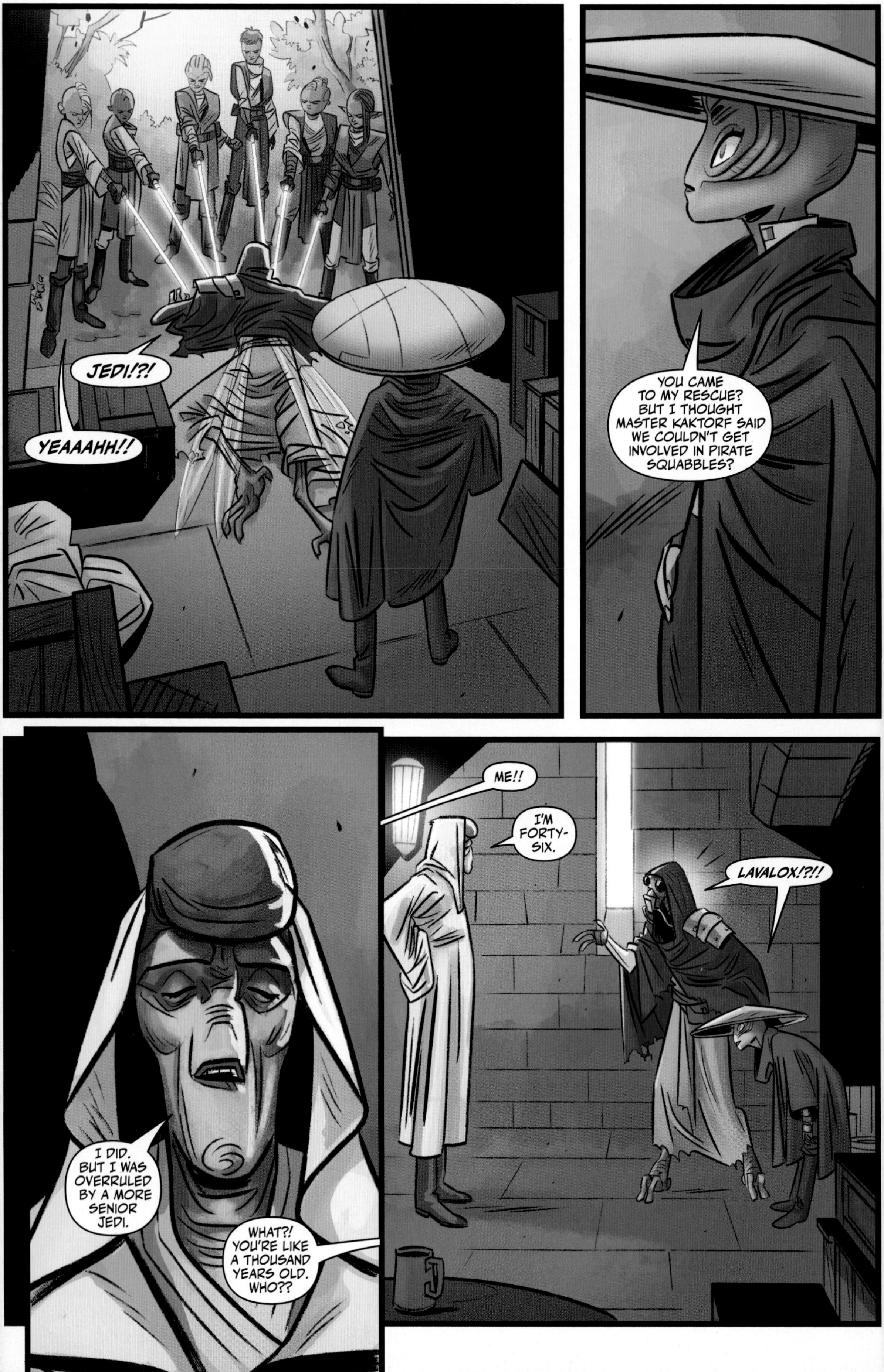

JEDI!?!
YEAAAHH!!
YOU CAME TO MY RESCUE? BUT I THOUGHT MASTER KAKTORF SAID WE COULDN'T GET INVOLVED IN PIRATE SQUABBLES?
I DID. BUT I WAS OVERRULED BY A MORE SENIOR JEDI.
WHAT?! YOU'RE LIKE A THOUSAND YEARS OLD. WHO??
ME!!
I'M FORTY-SIX.
LAVALOX!?!!

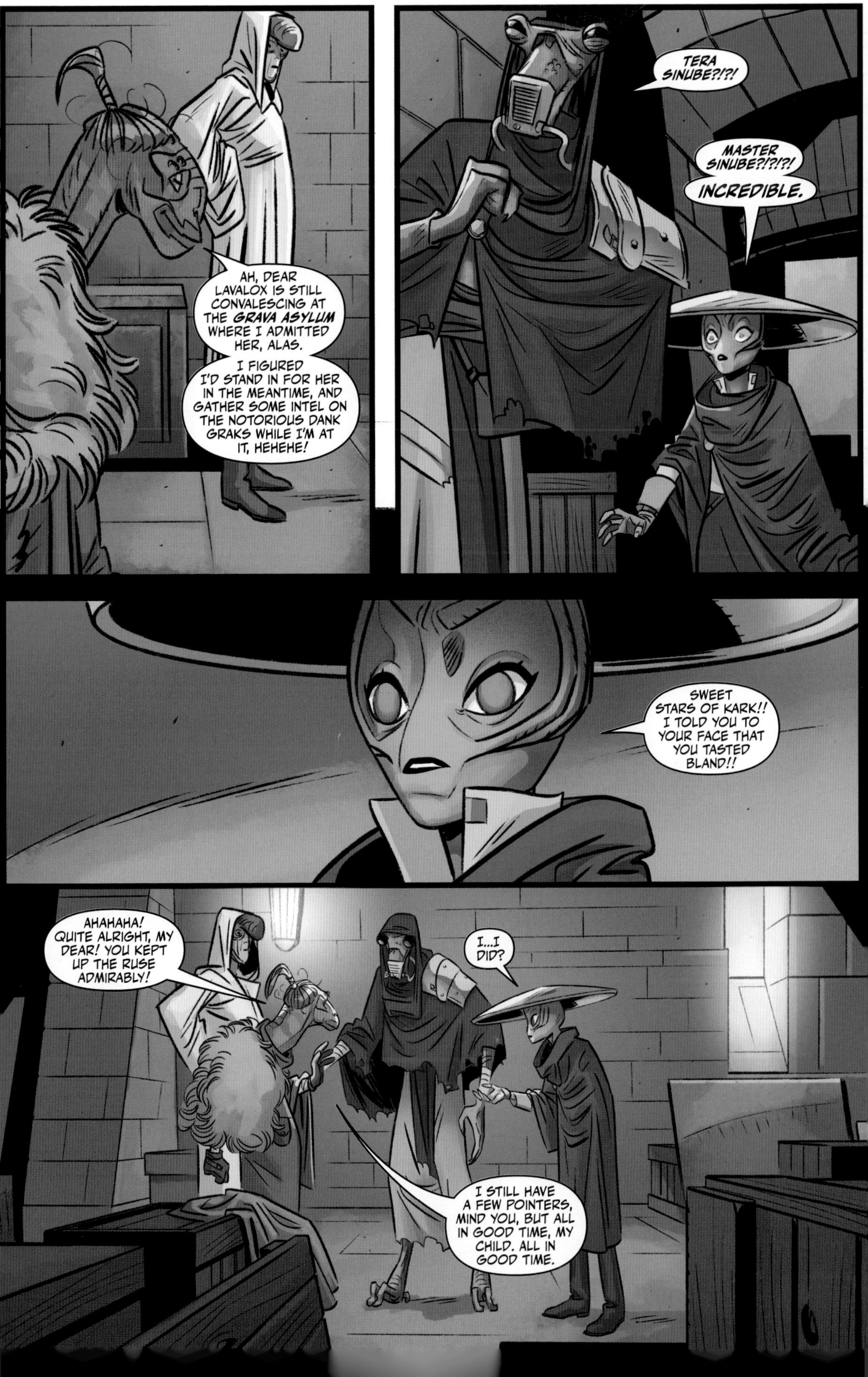
AH, DEAR LAVALOX IS STILL CONVALESCING AT THE GRAVA ASYLUM WHERE I ADMITTED HER, ALAS.
I FIGURED I'D STAND IN FOR HER IN THE MEANTIME, AND GATHER SOME INTEL ON THE NOTORIOUS DANK GRAKS WHILE I'M AT IT, HEHEHE!
TERA SINUBE?!?!
MASTER SINUBE?!?!?!
INCREDIBLE.
SWEET STARS OF KARK!! I TOLD YOU TO YOUR FACE THAT YOU TASTED BLAND!!
AHAHAHA! QUITE ALRIGHT, MY DEAR! YOU KEPT UP THE RUSE ADMIRABLY!
I...I DID?
I STILL HAVE A FEW POINTERS, MIND YOU, BUT ALL IN GOOD TIME, MY CHILD. ALL IN GOOD TIME.

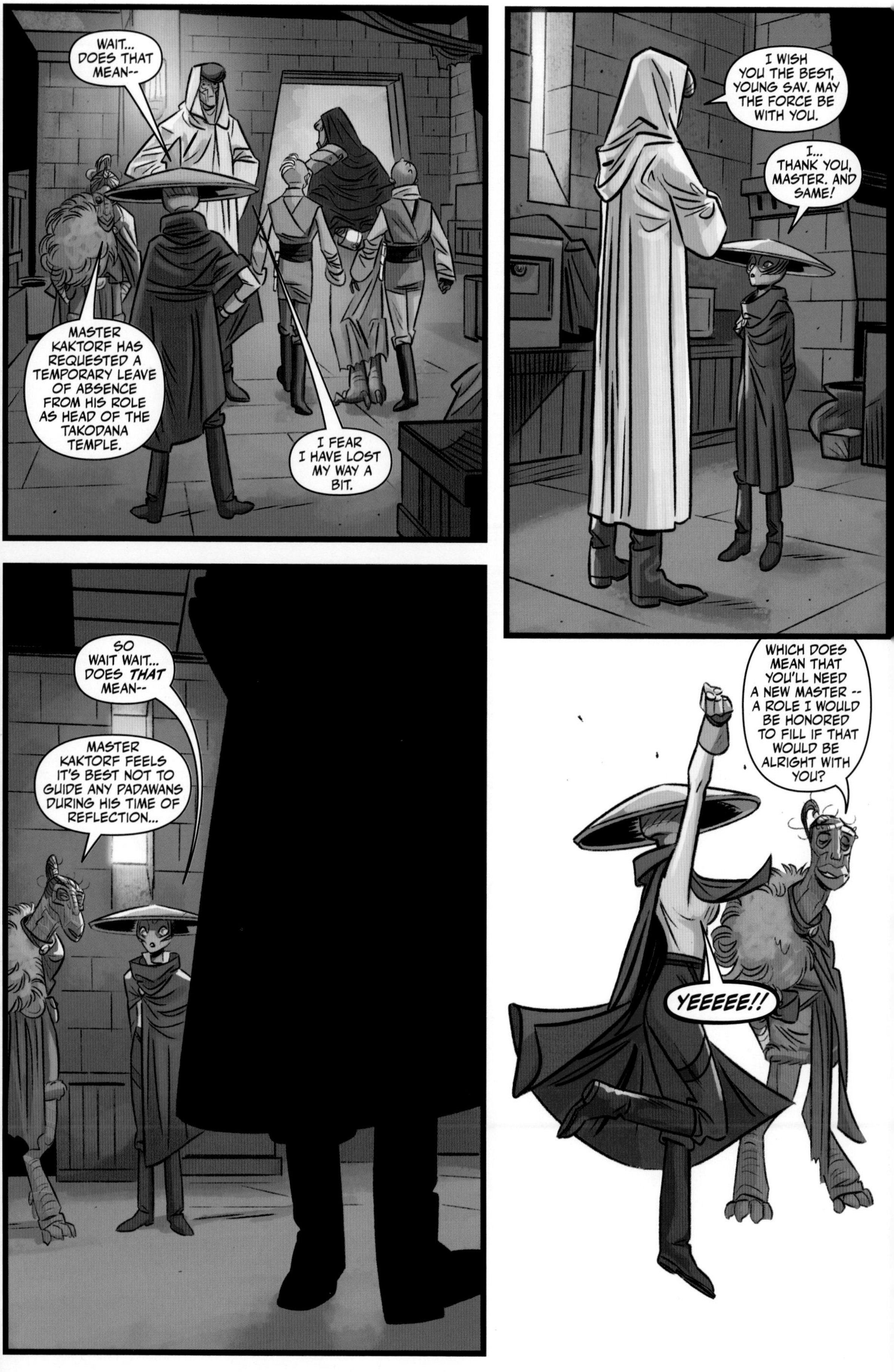
WAIT... DOES THAT MEAN--
MASTER KAKTORF HAS REQUESTED A TEMPORARY LEAVE OF ABSENCE FROM HIS ROLE AS HEAD OF THE TAKODANA TEMPLE.
I FEAR I HAVE LOST MY WAY A BIT.
I WISH YOU THE BEST, YOUNG SAV. MAY THE FORCE BE WITH YOU.
I... THANK YOU, MASTER. AND SAME!
SO WAIT WAIT... DOES *THAT* MEAN--
MASTER KAKTORF FEELS IT'S BEST NOT TO GUIDE ANY PADAWANS DURING HIS TIME OF REFLECTION...
WHICH DOES MEAN THAT YOU'LL NEED A NEW MASTER -- A ROLE I WOULD BE HONORED TO FILL IF THAT WOULD BE ALRIGHT WITH YOU?
YEEEEE!!

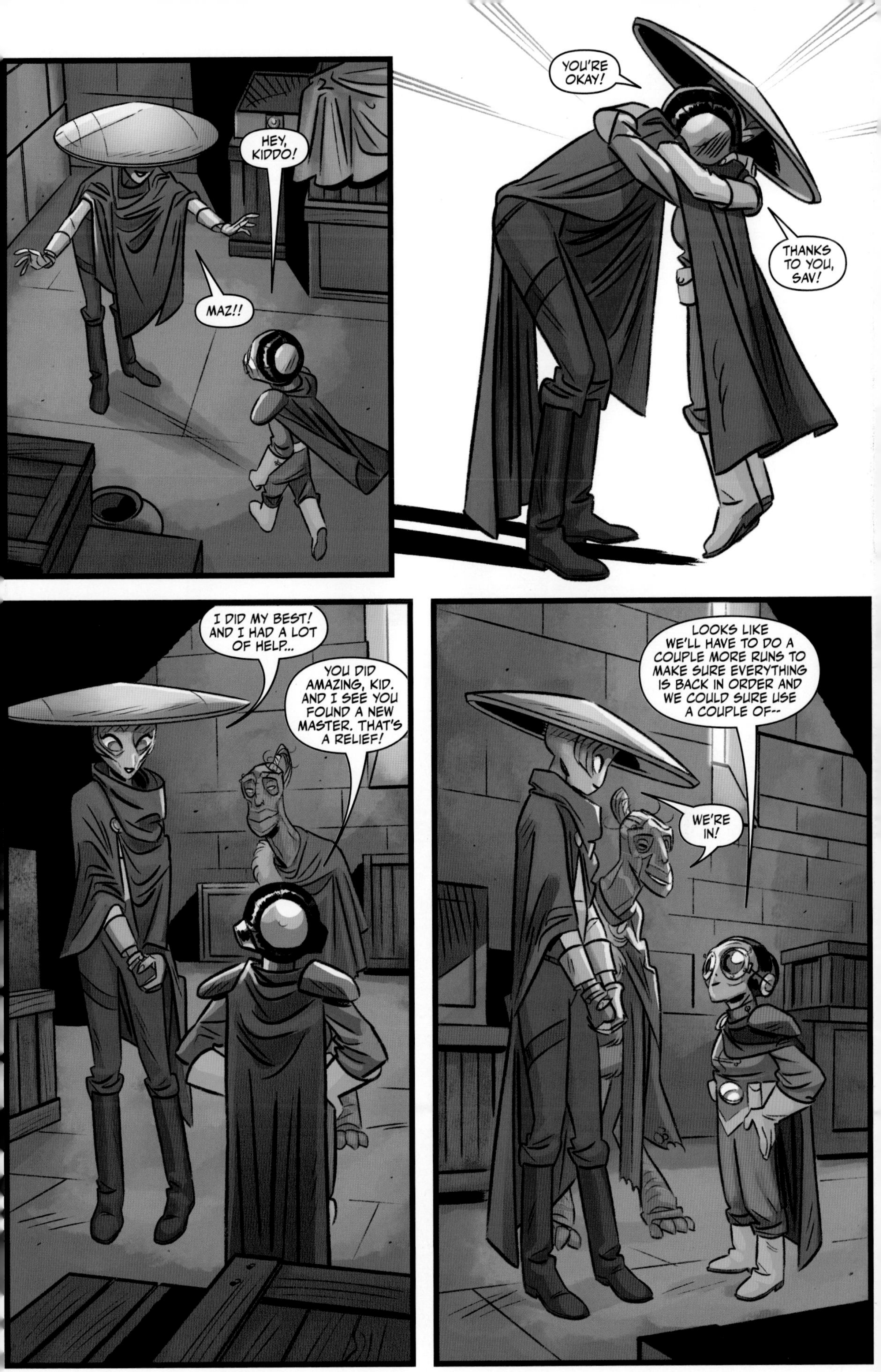
HEY, KIDDO!
MAZ!!
YOU'RE OKAY!
THANKS TO YOU, SAV!
I DID MY BEST! AND I HAD A LOT OF HELP...
YOU DID AMAZING, KID. AND I SEE YOU FOUND A NEW MASTER. THAT'S A RELIEF!
LOOKS LIKE WE'LL HAVE TO DO A COUPLE MORE RUNS TO MAKE SURE EVERYTHING IS BACK IN ORDER AND WE COULD SURE USE A COUPLE OF--
WE'RE IN!

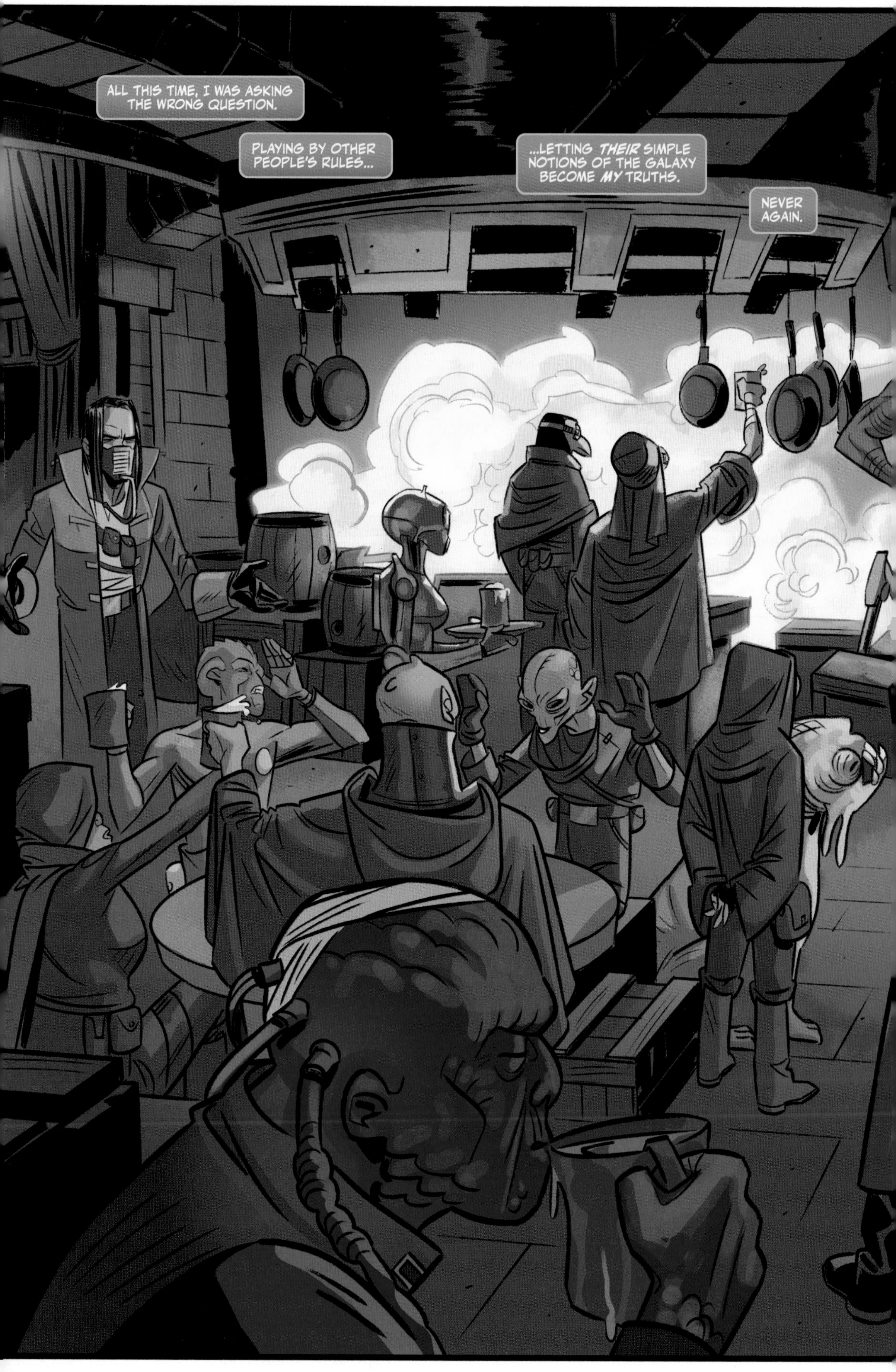
ALL THIS TIME, I WAS ASKING THE WRONG QUESTION.
PLAYING BY OTHER PEOPLE'S RULES...
...LETTING *THEIR* SIMPLE NOTIONS OF THE GALAXY BECOME *MY* TRUTHS.
NEVER AGAIN.

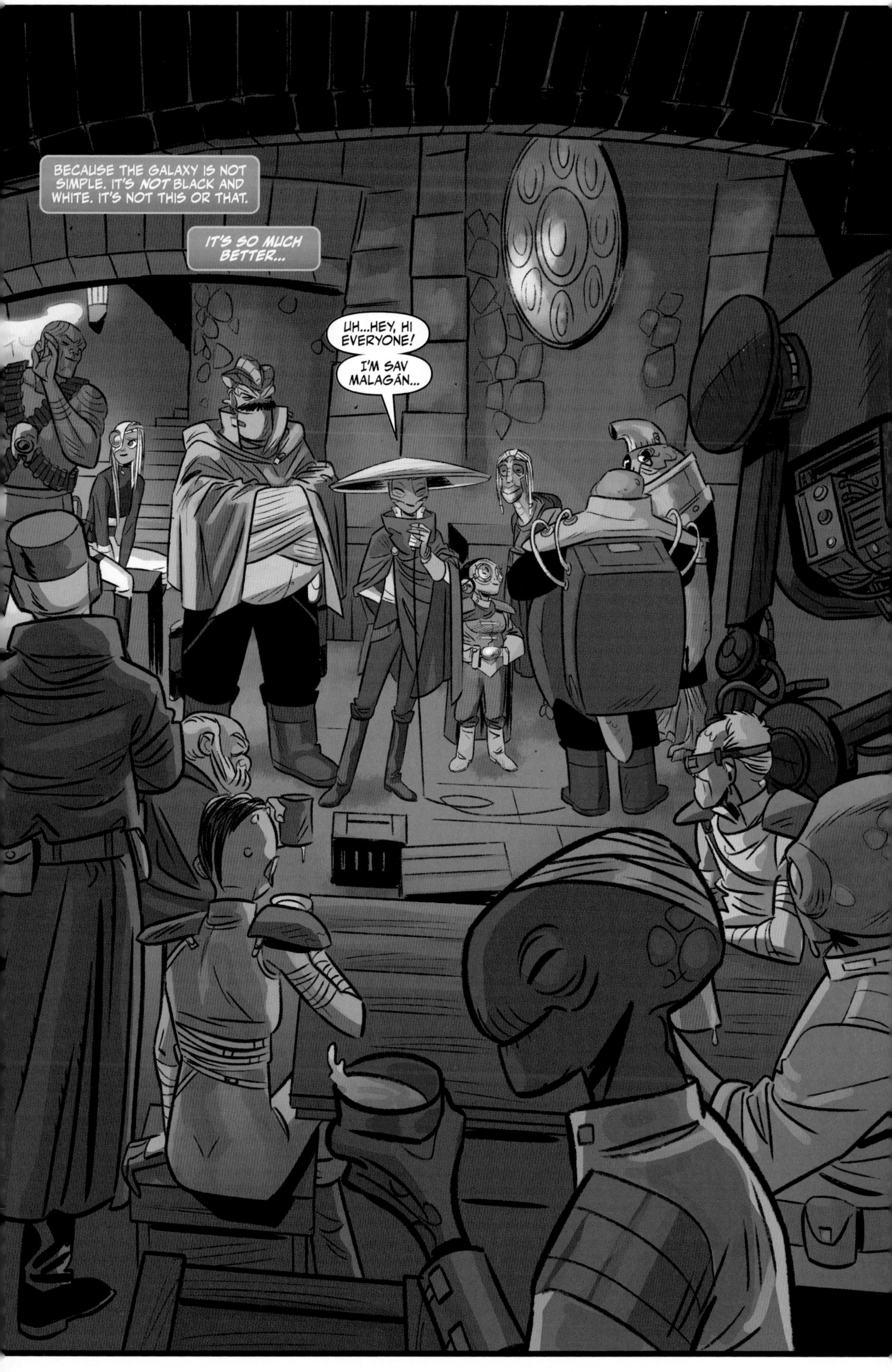

BECAUSE THE GALAXY IS NOT SIMPLE. IT'S *NOT* BLACK AND WHITE. IT'S NOT THIS OR THAT.
IT'S SO MUCH BETTER...
UH...HEY, HI EVERYONE!
I'M SAV MALAGÁN...

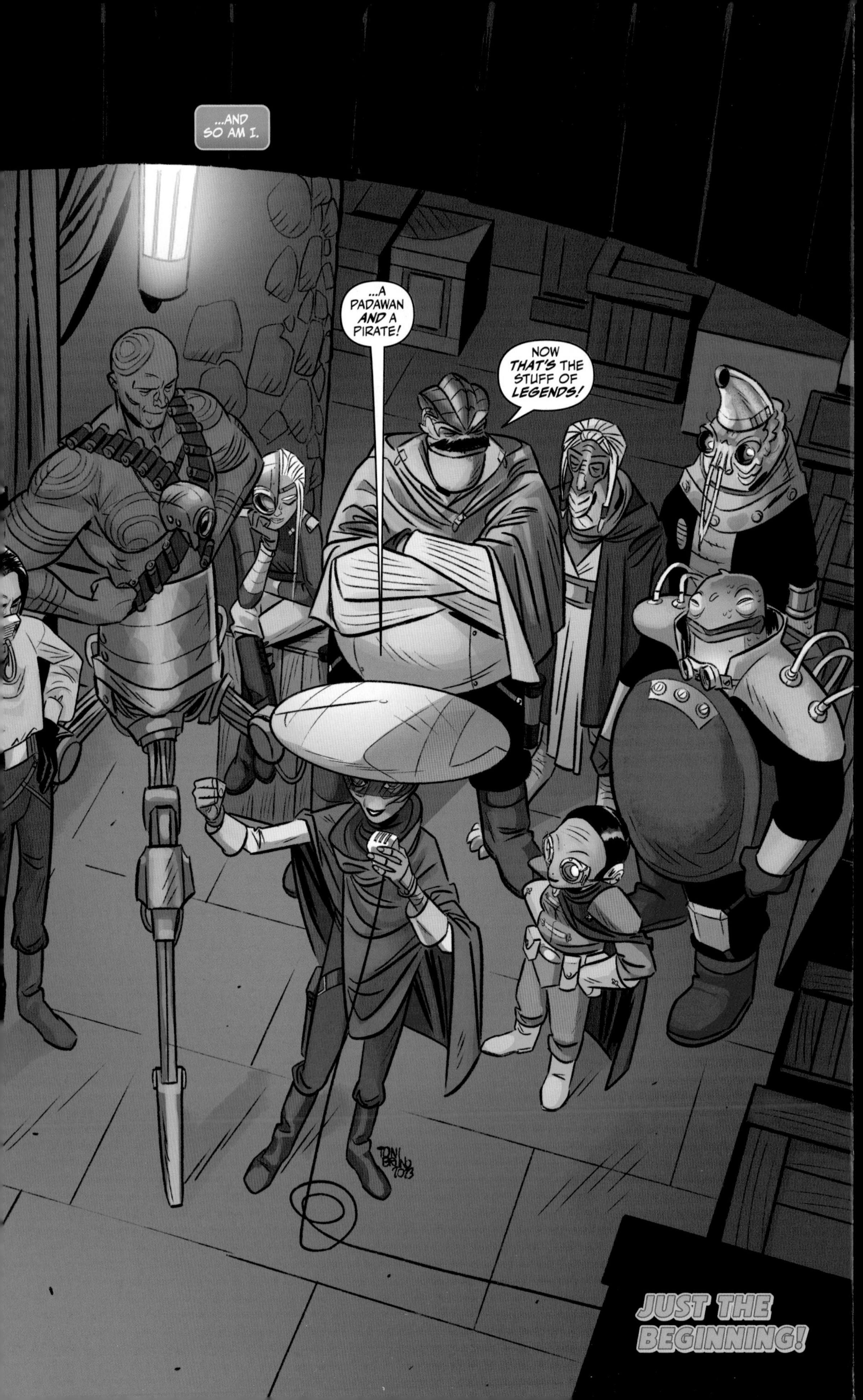
...AND SO AM I.
...A PADAWAN AND A PIRATE!
NOW THAT'S THE STUFF OF LEGENDS!
JUST THE BEGINNING!

"FOR LIGHT AND LIFE!"

Set hundreds of years before the Skywalker Saga, *The High Republic* chronicles a time of galactic renaissance, when the Jedi are at the height of their power and the Republic is experiencing unparalleled peace. Check out these epic tales from Phases I and II of *Star Wars: The High Republic Adventures* from Dark Horse Comics!

PHASE I

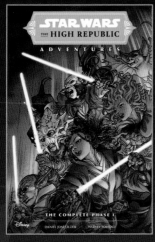

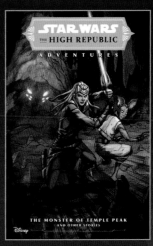

STAR WARS
THE HIGH REPUBLIC
ADVENTURES
THE COMPLETE PHASE I
DANIEL JOSÉ OLDER
HARVEY TOLIBAO

STAR WARS: THE HIGH REPUBLIC ADVENTURES — THE COMPLETE PHASE 1 TPB
ISBN 978-1-50673-780-5 • $29.99
AUGUST 2023

STAR WARS
THE HIGH REPUBLIC
ADVENTURES
THE MONSTER OF TEMPLE PEAK
AND OTHER STORIES

STAR WARS: THE HIGH REPUBLIC ADVENTURES — THE MONSTER OF TEMPLE PEAK AND OTHER STORIES TPB
ISBN 978-1-50673-779-9 • $19.99
OCTOBER 2023

PHASE II

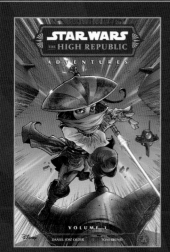

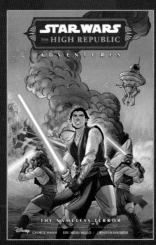

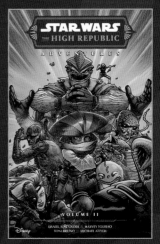

STAR WARS
THE HIGH REPUBLIC
ADVENTURES
VOLUME 1
DANIEL JOSÉ OLDER
TONI BRUNO

STAR WARS: THE HIGH REPUBLIC ADVENTURES VOLUME 1 TPB
ISBN 978-1-50673-292-3 • $19.99
SEPTEMBER 2023

STAR WARS
THE HIGH REPUBLIC
ADVENTURES
THE NAMELESS TERROR
GEORGE MANN
EDUARDO MELLO
ORNELLA SAVARESE

STAR WARS: THE HIGH REPUBLIC ADVENTURES — THE NAMELESS TERROR TPB
ISBN 978-1-50673-567-2 • $19.99
AUGUST 2023

STAR WARS
THE HIGH REPUBLIC
ADVENTURES
VOLUME II
DANIEL JOSÉ OLDER
HARVEY TOLIBAO
TONI BRUNO
MICHAEL ATIYEH

STAR WARS: THE HIGH REPUBLIC ADVENTURES VOLUME 2 TPB
ISBN 978-1-50673-293-0 • $19.99
FEBRUARY 2024

Disney · Lucasfilm

DARK HORSE BOOKS

AVAILABLE AT YOUR LOCAL COMICS SHOP OR BOOKSTORE

TO FIND A COMICS SHOP NEAR YOU, VISIT COMICSHOPLOCATOR.COM
FOR MORE INFORMATION OR TO ORDER DIRECT, VISIT DARKHORSE.COM
*Prices and availability subject to change without notice.

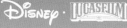

STAR WARS™

ALSO AVAILABLE

THE ART OF STAR WARS: VISIONS
978-1-50672-851-3 | $49.99

THE ART OF STAR WARS: REBELS
978-1-50671-091-4 | $39.99

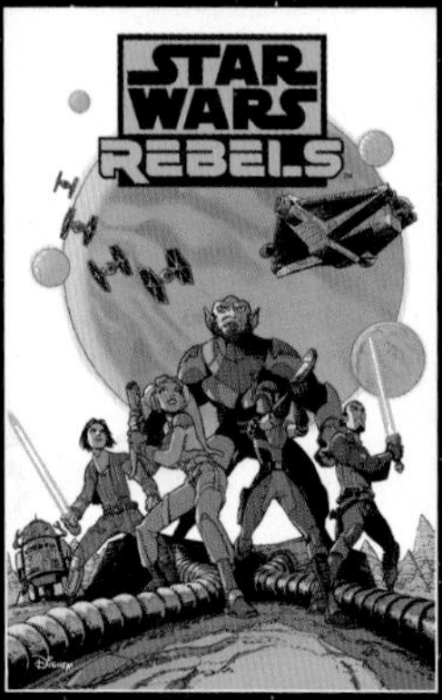

STAR WARS REBELS

STAR WARS: REBELS
978-1-50673-301-2 | $29.99

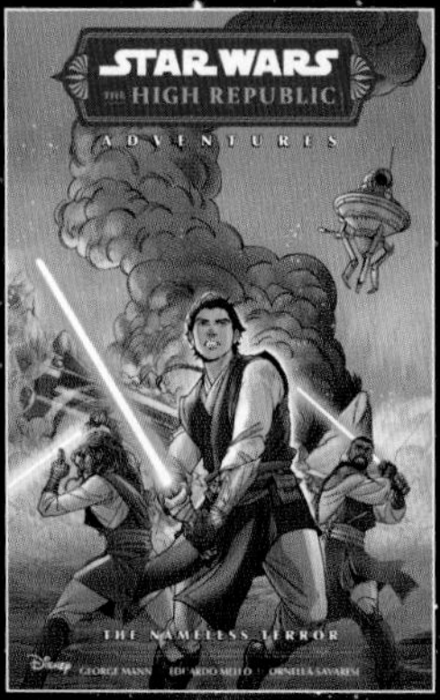

STAR WARS
THE HIGH REPUBLIC
ADVENTURES
THE NAMELESS TERROR

STAR WARS: HIGH REPUBLIC ADVENTURES—THE NAMELESS TERROR
978-1-50673-567-2 | $19.99

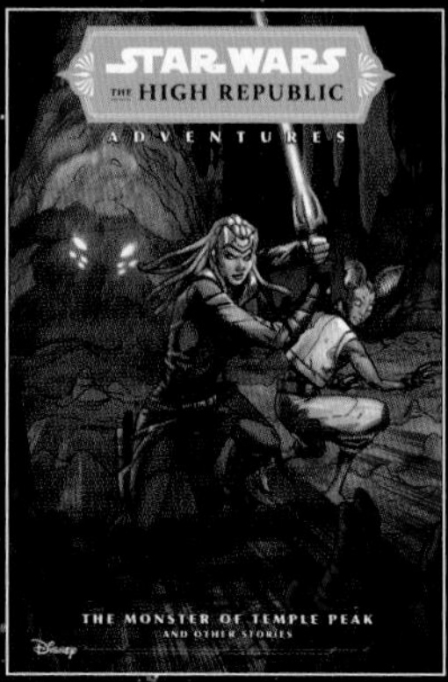

STAR WARS
THE HIGH REPUBLIC
ADVENTURES
THE MONSTER OF TEMPLE PEAK

STAR WARS: HIGH REPUBLIC ADVENTURES—THE MONSTER OF TEMPLE PEAK AND OTHER STORIES
978-1-50673-779-9 | $19.99

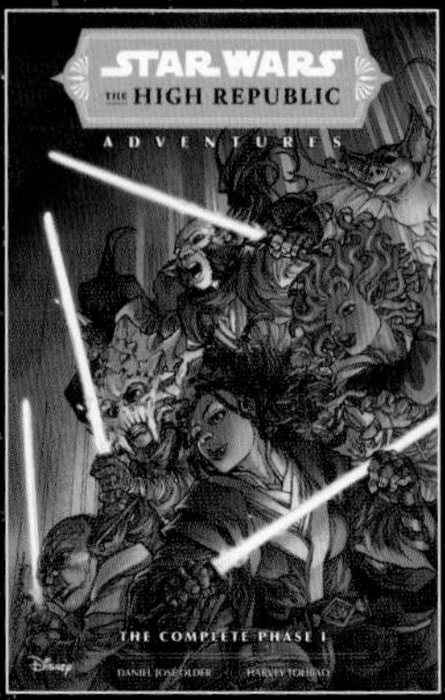

STAR WARS
THE HIGH REPUBLIC
ADVENTURES
THE COMPLETE PHASE I

STAR WARS: THE HIGH REPUBLIC ADVENTURES—THE COMPLETE PHASE 1
978-1-50673-780-5 | $29.99

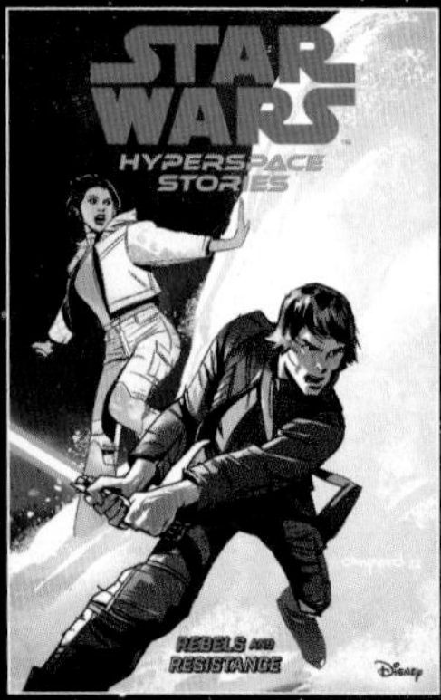

STAR WARS
HYPERSPACE STORIES
REBELS AND RESISTANCE

STAR WARS: HYPERSPACE STORIES VOLUME 1—REBELS AND RESISTANCE
978-1-50673-286-2 | $19.99

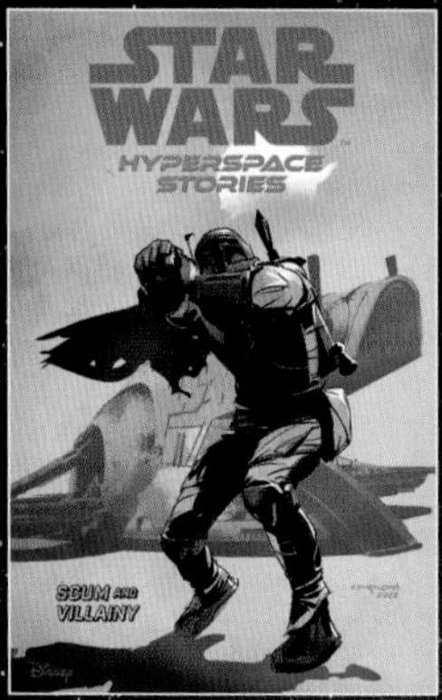

STAR WARS
HYPERSPACE STORIES
SCUM AND VILLAINY

STAR WARS HYPERSPACE STORIES VOLUME 2—SCUM AND VILLAINY
978-1-50673-287-9 | $19.99

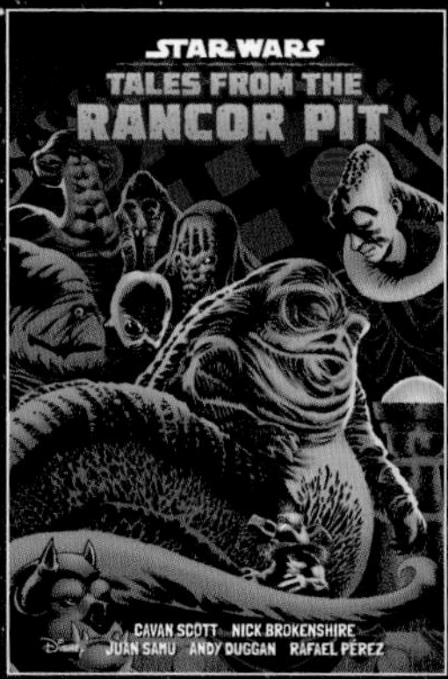

STAR WARS
TALES FROM THE RANCOR PIT
CAVAN SCOTT NICK BROKENSHIRE
JUAN SAMU ANDY DUGGAN RAFAEL PEREZ

STAR WARS: TALES FROM THE RANCOR PIT
978-1-50673-284-8 | $19.99

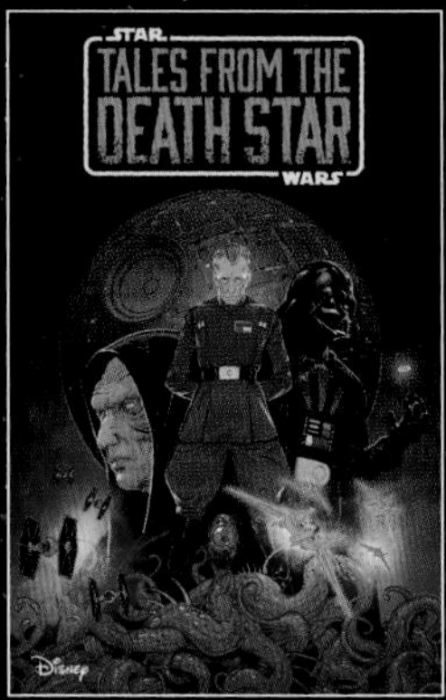

STAR WARS
TALES FROM THE DEATH STAR

STAR WARS: TALES FROM THE DEATH STAR
978-1-50673-829-1 | $24.99

And check out our two monthly comics series!

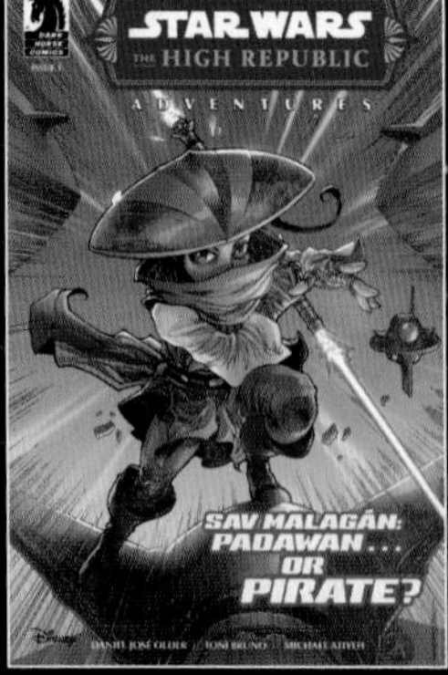

STAR WARS
THE HIGH REPUBLIC
ADVENTURES
SAV MALAGÁN: PADAWAN... OR PIRATE?

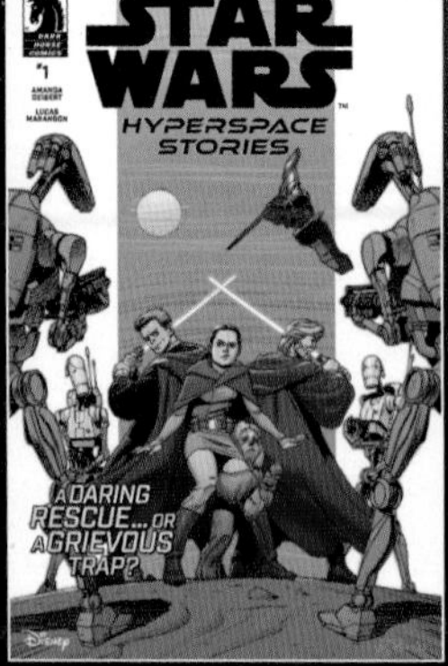

STAR WARS
HYPERSPACE STORIES
A DARING RESCUE... OR A GRIEVOUS TRAP?